3/00 me
03/08

# LENOIR

# LENOIR

A NOVEL

*Ken Greenhall*

ZOLAND BOOKS

*Cambridge, Massachusetts*

First edition published in 1998 by
Zoland Books, Inc.
384 Huron Avenue
Cambridge, Massachusetts 02138

PUBLISHER'S NOTE
This book is a work of fiction. Names, characters, places,
and incidents are either the product of the author's
imagination or are used fictitiously.

The cover illustration is Peter Paul Rubens's
*Four Heads of a Negro*, Museés royaux
des Beaux-Arts de Belgique, Bruxelles —
Koninklíjke Musea voor Schone
Kunsten van België, Brussel.

FIRST EDITION

Book design by Boskydell Studio
Printed in the United States of America

05 04 03 02 01 00 99 98   8 7 6 5 4 3 2 1

This book is printed on acid-free paper, and its binding
materials have been chosen for strength and durability.

Library of Congress Cataloging-in-Publication Data
Greenhall, Ken.
Lenoir : a novel / by Ken Greenhall. — 1st ed.
p.   cm.
ISBN 0-944072-93-3
1. Africans — Europe — History — 17th century — Fiction.   2. Blacks —
Europe — History — 17th century — Fiction.   I. Title.
PS3557.R3947L4   1998
813'.54—dc21                                                    98-22278
                                                                      CIP

*To Susan Llewellyn and Jérôme Boivin*

In Rubens's *Four Heads of a Negro* there is something compelling about the psychological variety of expression depicted in what clearly was the same individual (one wonders what he may have been in life).

Julius S. Held, *Rubens and His Circle*

.

# PART I

# I

**T**HEY ARE DERANGED.

    They are pale, their country is flat and wet, and they have no souls. I believe they are being punished for having only one god.

Their lives are busy and complicated, yet they do not understand the simplest of facts about human existence. For example, it is not clear to them that when one makes an image of a person, one disturbs that person's soul. They are obsessed with making images, rubbing paint on pieces of cloth or wood — even on plaster walls. They cleverly and tirelessly make images — pictures of one another, of their man-god nailed to a post, even of flowers and food.

They buy and sell many things — including African people like me.

They do not believe they will die.

Their languages are ridiculous, although as you will see, I know most of the words in the language spoken by the Walloons (a language originated by a people called the French, who — according to Mr. Twee — have pulled in their horns and are ruled by a cardinal, whatever that means). I can also speak, with more difficulty, the language called Dutch (which Mr. Twee says is best suited to telling jokes about sex and chamber pots). Both of these languages have complicated ways of talking about the past and the future, which is something that does not interest me. Yet the languages have all the words necessary for the thoughts that I have, and I am proud that I have learned them so easily.

I have no hope that I will ever return to my homeland. But I hope someday to live in the land to the south, a land in which there are hills and in which the people have a king.

My captors call me Lenoir, which any sensible person will agree is much less melodious than Mbatgha, my name in my homeland.

I am a practical person; therefore I seldom think of the shameful events that separated me from my family and from the village in which I was born. I am simply thankful for the great beauty that is mine, a beauty so astounding that the many picture makers of this land — this Holland, or Netherland, as some call it — are bidding for the privilege of recording my beauty and further disarranging my soul.

But although I have adopted their ways of speaking and am content now to say "fingers" rather than "children of the hand," I will never adopt their degrading beliefs.

At the moment I am in a tavern, drinking beer with Mr. Rembrandt Harmenszoon van Rijn and my agent, Mr. Twee, as they speak of vast numbers of guilders. In my village, we had only nine numbers. And nine was also the number of wives a man was allowed to take at a given time. We had no need for more numbers, although some greedy men would occasionally have a need for more wives. But these flatlanders have numbers for everything, even for the years, this one being 1640.

"Rubens wants him," Mr. Twee says.

Mr. van Rijn shrugs, then finishes his beer with a toss of the head. I think he has tossed his head this way many times.

Mr. Twee says, "Rubens is a great man."

"So Rubens is a great man," Mr. van Rijn says. "I am only a great painter. And I am not wealthy."

"Oh, please, Rembrandt," Mr. Twee continues. "You've got a big house."

"A big house but a small income. And my wife is very ill."

I add, "You have my sympathy, Mr. van Rijn. In my homeland, it is a great tragedy to be without a healthy wife, for it is the wives who grow our crops and do our trading."

He has been sneaking glances at me, but now he stares at me directly. His sad eyes make me forget about his strange, big nose. He says to me, "I have costumes that would look good on you, Lenoir. A feathered sienna turban. An ocher silk cloak."

Mr. Twee announces, "You would have to work quickly. Rubens needs him soon . . . a big Adoration job."

Mr. Twee is lying. He has never had anything to do with the great man Rubens. "But," he continues, "I can tell you want to do Lenoir. He can pose for a flat fee . . . a modest one."

Mr. van Rijn replies, "I don't pay people to do their portraits. They pay me. I told you, I am not wealthy."

Mr. Twee, who does not seem to understand the strange European idea of truth any better than I do, says, "Rembrandt, am I supposed to be a rich man? How could I be rich? What you earn, I earn only ten percent of. Semi-indigent . . . that's what I am."

But I believe that Mr. Twee is actually semiwealthy. He is a go-between who finds portraitists for merchants and burghers here in Amsterdam and in other cities of this country. He paid a flatteringly large price for me. (How much would *you* fetch on the open market?) I have been called a chattel slave, but in truth I am many things. I am model, secretary, traveling companion, and medicine man.

At the moment, I am what Mr. Twee calls bait. He continues: "You don't understand, Rembrandt. Mr. Lenoir is a professional model. He is one of the great Magi."

Although I don't correct Mr. Twee, the truth is that I am the greatest Magus. I grace many Adoration scenes — often, in my opinion, becoming the main focus of attention, being a more interesting figure than either the child (these picture makers don't do infants well) or the dull-looking woman they call the Virgin. (Virginity is a concept that my people do not have; we have children and adults.) But because of someone named Calvin, there is less demand here for Adorations than in sunnier countries (where they follow the one named Pope) — which is another reason I dream of traveling south.

As Mr. Twee and Mr. van Rijn haggle, I look at the painter. He is a small man with a large nose. His curled hair is not yet gray, yet he has the sad expression one usually sees in old men. He is so well known that he signs his pictures with only his first name, yet he does not look as if he is pleased with his life.

I realize that I have been staring impolitely, so I look about the tavern, peering through the ever-present haze of tobacco smoke. In this country, when in small public rooms, one sees not people but smoke and garments — hats, ruffs, capes — garments so ridiculously large and heavy that many of the burghers suffer constantly from stiffness of the neck. I catch them looking enviously at my delicate red-and-gold cap and my colorful, simple robe.

Mr. van Rijn, who doesn't even seem to be wearing a shirt under his paint-stained smock, announces, "I need a big commission. That's what I need from you, Twee. A big commission. One of those group portraits — a big group, with a fee from each person in the group."

"I'm working on it," Mr. Twee says. "But in the meantime, what about Lenoir?"

Mr. van Rijn is looking at me again. "I could trade you a painting for Lenoir's posing time . . . a study, actually. A nude."

I can imagine the painting — the background of heavy shadows that the painters seem to think they must use. I have sat in many bright, colorful rooms only to see them shown later in a picture as gloomy and mud colored. These painters all misrepresent things. Sometimes I look over their shoulders as they make their paintings, and I see something much brighter than they see. For although the light in this country is not as yellow as in my homeland, there is a glow to the colors that I find pleasing. The painters start with darkness — placing pale faces and white collars against it. As I look about the café now, I notice that the collars are not as white and freshly starched as they are in the endless pictures made by this country's deceiving painters.

Mr. Twee is pretending not to be interested in getting a free nude painting, which he knows could bring a good price even if it is an unfinished study. "Well, I suppose I can glance at it," he says. Then Mr. Twee, who doesn't like to pay for drinks (or for anything else), leaps up. "I've got an errand. I'll meet you at your studio." He runs out of the tavern. As he passes the proprietor, he points back in our direction.

I rise and give the proprietor a dignified gesture, holding up the palm of my hand, which I hope will remind him that life is too brief to waste arguing about tiny sums of money. The proprietor says something loudly about *gelt*.

I reply with my favorite expression in the Dutch language: "*Nee verstaan*," and I lead Mr. van Rijn out to the street. He is moving unsteadily, as do many of the people in this city, where they find it necessary to convert gentle wine into harsh brandy.

Mr. van Rijn, staggering, says, "Twee is a scoundrel."

He is speaking the language of the Walloons, which I take as a favor to me. "Yes," I say. "One of the best, I think, Mr. van Rijn."

"Call me Rembrandt."

It is strangely quiet in Mr. Rembrandt's house. The only noise is the irritating tick of a large clock of the kind one hears in many houses here. I don't know why these people want to be reminded constantly of time.

The painter's studio is crowded with strange objects — broken pieces of stone people, metal helmets, feathers, and clothes. The only picture I can see is an unfinished one of Mr. Rembrandt himself. I wonder what strange thing happens to a person's soul when the person himself disturbs it.

Then I hear a familiar mumbling and see that Mr. Twee is sitting in a corner, his face hidden by a small painter's panel that I can see only from the back. He peers over the top of it and winks, which probably means he is looking at a nude man — something that is more to his taste than a nude woman. He lowers his head and disappears behind the picture again. When Mr. Twee looks at a picture, he wants to have either his greed or his lust stimulated. In some cases, as possibly with this one, both those things happen. I have no wish to see the picture. White bodies are repugnant to me, especially male bodies. They seem to be decomposing. I admit, however, that I am overcoming my dislike of the pale female body.

While Mr. Rembrandt and I wait, I ask him, politely in Dutch, "Why is there so much darkness in your paintings?"

"Darkness is easy to paint," he answers. I wonder if that is why he is eager to paint my portrait.

Eventually, Mr. Twee says from behind the canvas he has been studying, "Okay. Lenoir will pose. Two sessions, two hours each. I get this painting."

Mr. Rembrandt says, "*Three* sessions, *three* hours each."

"Three sessions, *two* hours each."

"Done."

I walk over to see the painting that Mr. Twee finds so valuable. It is, as I expected, a nude. But it surprises me twice. First, it is a woman.

Second, it is a black woman.

I ask Mr. Rembrandt if this woman lives in Amsterdam. He smiles a tiny smile.

*

At dusk, I sit by candlelight with Nghana, my parrot, on my shoulder. I play my drum and chant a song that I recall from my youth:

> Don't think I won't come.
> The path before me
> is a crooked line.
> But I hope it will lead me to a safe end.
> The loss of my people
> has confused the route for me.
> Wish me well with neither hatred nor jealousy.

I wonder whether my voice, as it drifts through the quiet, dark streets, is being heard by a young, full-breasted, dark-skinned woman whose body hair is tightly curled and utterly black.

# 2

M R. TWEE SAYS it is dangerous to do business with burghers before the sun is halfway up or with painters before it is halfway down. He does not speak in terms of the sun, of course, but in terms of the numbers called hours, which break the day and night up into small pieces that are convenient for the transaction of business. He listens for the sound of the church bells, which tell him where the sun is. It may be that the bells are needed because the sun is so often hidden by clouds.

As the bells sound and we wait for business time, we do pleasant things. First, Mr. Twee reads aloud a few adventures from *The Ingenious Gentleman Don Quixote of La Mancha*, a story by a dead man named Señor Cervantes. (The story is actually about a charming, wise man called Sancho Panza.) In my homeland, we do not have reading and writing. Our stories must be either memorized or newly invented, and they therefore have the virtue of being brief. They also have the virtue of relating the adventures of serpent-gods and monkey-gods, who are more clever and interesting than mere humans. Mr. Twee has offered to teach me to read and write, but I hesitate to learn a skill that can create pieces of paper saying that one person belongs to another.

*

Mr. Twee is sitting near the window, holding the dead man's book on his lap and reading to me of an encounter between some packhorsemen and the knight and his companion, Sancho (who cannot read and who rides a creature called an ass, which is not worshiped by these people the way the horse is). There is much talk of chivalry and knighthood, which apparently were rules that once determined how people fought and killed one another.

"I don't understand," I say, "why you changed the rules of chivalry."

"*I* didn't change the rules, my friend. *They* changed them. I think it's simply that they wanted to become better people, to improve their lives."

"I believe, Mr. Twee, that there are too many rules. There are the rules of Calvin, the rules of Luther, the rules of Pope, the rules of dead storytellers."

"That's only the beginning, Lenoir. There are the rules of the Spanish king, whose warriors are nearby. And worst of all, the rules of the lawyers, who are threatening to take me to bankruptcy court. You might end up belonging to the court instead of to me. It's all very complicated."

I say simply, "Yes, Mr. Twee." But I think to myself that it doesn't have to be so complicated. It gets complicated when you are fearful, when you tremble at names such as Calvin, Pope, or King.

After my conversation with Mr. Twee, I stroll out in search of snakes, which are highly revered in my homeland. Smiling, I greet the people I pass in the streets and along the canals — people who keep the grass too short for snakes to live in, and who have a story about a snake who encourages a naked lady to eat forbidden fruit. I think this would be easier to believe if a dog, not a snake, talked to the lady. The story supposedly explains why every human being is depraved from the time of birth. But before I was taken from my homeland, I became a father many times, and I did not notice that the babies my wives and I produced were depraved.

I see that many of the women who are out madly scrubbing their doorsteps on this fine morning cannot resist smiling at me and greeting me, maybe having forbidden thoughts. But the woman I am thinking of is the one in Mr. Rembrandt's painting, and I am determined that later today I will get to meet her.

As I stroll, I am careful to stand up straight and to move with grace, for behind the quarter-moon cutouts in the wooden shutters of the fortress-houses, I am sure many eyes are trained on me. These houses are places to hide in, and it is obvious that, despite the daytime gatherings at markets and in taverns, these people fear one another. I am surprised they even dare to place an occasional window in the thick stone and brick walls of their houses. Nevertheless, I must admit that the rows of buildings create a pleasing effect along the main streets and canals, even though I have to smile when I notice how the buildings must have straight lines and must be the same on either side of the center. If there is a window on the left, there must be a window of the same kind on the right; a certain angle to the roof on the left, the same angle on the right. In my homeland, where a house is mostly a roof, such matters are not important. One of the things I have learned in my exile is that almost anything can be deemed important by the flatlanders. In my homeland, one heard the phrase "It doesn't matter" many times a day. One seldom hears it among these people.

Carrying a forked stick, I wander to the outskirts of the city. I part the grass, looking for trails left by small rodents of the kind that would make a satisfying meal for a serpent. I look particularly for a black snake, which I think will make a fine present for the woman in the painting Mr. Twee got from Mr. Rembrandt. But I don't expect to find anything other than an ugly toad and a few scurrying insects.

Eventually I do find a snake — a small, handsome pale green creature that is unlike any other I have seen. Its color contrasts subtly with the greens of the grass that surrounds it. In my homeland, green surrounds us at every moment. I have taught myself not to feel homesick, but occasionally, in odd moments such as this, I want desperately to be among my own trees and snakes, and with my own people.

Increasing my feeling of sadness is the fact that this elegant little green snake is dead, its head crushed beneath a rock. I am deeply offended. A person who will kill a snake will kill anything. I am reminded that there is constant peril beneath the bland smiles of the people I now live among.

I apologize to the spirit of the dead creature and put its body in my pocket. On my way back to the inn, I stop at Calvin's church and drape the snake on the handle of the inner door. As I leave the church, a woman passes me — one who makes me grateful that it is the custom here to conceal virtually every part of one's body. I often regret that it is not the custom for the women to wear veils, which I understand is done in some countries.

After I am a few paces away from the church, I hear the woman produce a series of screams. Her shrieking sounds less than spontaneous to me, and I feel a great sympathy for the man who might have her for his only wife.

Mr. Twee is looking through the books in which he writes the numbers that represent his wealth. I do not understand why he does not buy houses or gold jewelry or even horses or paintings. It is flattering to think that I am the only thing of value that Mr. Twee owns. If he weren't fond of gaudy clothes, he would seem no more prosperous than the many people in this country who stand about selling flowers on street corners. (If Calvin or Pope allowed it, I think the flatlanders would worship flowers. I have noticed that they take a special interest in plants that have prominent male parts, although Mr. Twee says that their science considers it primitive foolishness to think that plants have sexual parts.)

I open the door of the birdcage, and Nghana, the red-and-green parrot, climbs out joyfully onto my shoulder and nibbles my earlobe. Mr. Twee looks disapprovingly at the bird, which refuses to speak words in any language except mine, and which has twice bitten Mr. Twee severely. Mr. Twee waits until Nghana says, as he always does, in his native language: "Life is good." I don't know who taught him the phrase. Mr. Twee is now trying, with no success, to teach Nghana (in the language of the Walloons) "Life stinks."

After Nghana makes his little statement about life, Mr. Twee says to me, "What's so good about the bird's life? What's so good about having your wings clipped and being at the mercy of someone of another species?"

I say, "Maybe it is better than being at the mercy of someone of the same species."

"Touché," Mr. Twee says. "Exactly right." Then, more quietly, "My investments are not doing well, Lenoir." He has the look of despair that only I am allowed to see, a look that will be replaced by a look of cheerfulness and energy when we leave our room.

"Perhaps," I suggest, "you should stop doing your investments."

"You don't understand."

It is true. I don't begin to understand Mr. Twee's investments, which have something to do with ships that carry things in trade from one place to another. I understand trading some of what one has for something one needs but does not have, but the flatlanders often seem to trade for things they do not need. Investment seems to involve trading pieces of paper for something one does not need. And it sometimes leads to buildings called debtors' prisons.

I say, "I understand that I would not like Mr. Twee to lose his freedom." He looks at me unpleasantly, and I realize that he thinks I am indirectly referring to my own lost freedom. But since I have belonged to Mr. Twee, I no longer feel in bondage, and I would never speak rudely to him. "I mean no ill," I say. "I am simply trying to help."

"You can't help me, Lenoir. That's one of your charms. You're not part of our game. Don't even try to help."

"Would you not like me to come to your assistance if someone attacked you?"

"Oh, definitely. I hope you will. You can *kill* for me. But don't *think* for me."

"Am I too stupid to think for you?"

"You're too honest."

"Not at all, Mr. Twee. I feel I am capable of great dishonesty. If dishonesty is helpful in the investment business, I would be a successful investment person, Mr. Twee."

My owner rises and pats my head as if I were a child. But his forehead wrinkles slightly, and I know he will think again of the offer I have just made. He says, "It's time for some honest exploitation."

I am not quite sure what exploitation is, but I am sure that Mr. Twee is, as he often claims, a master of it.

# 3

MR. REMBRANDT'S STUDIO is quiet again today as Mr. Twee and I stand looking at the picture the painter is making of himself. "Is the picture finished?" I ask Mr. Twee.

"You'll have to ask Rembrandt."

"That is one reason I could never make a picture," I say. "I would never know when to stop."

From behind us the voice of Mr. Rembrandt says, "Knowing when to stop is the difference between a good painter and a great painter."

I do not say so, but I believe the great painter would be the one who does not picture his nose as smaller than it is.

Mr. Twee has gone to a large picture that leans with its front against a wall. He peeks behind it and says to Mr. Rembrandt, "Then you *do* have a commission?"

The painter shrugs.

Mr. Twee turns the picture around. It is one of those portraits of many somber men. I ask, "Is this one finished?"

Mr. Rembrandt says, "*I* think so. But the *subjects* don't think so. They don't want to pay me."

"Perhaps," I say, "you have made them all look too much the

same. In my homeland, each man tries to look unlike other men."

"In *my* homeland," Mr. Rembrandt says, "we deal in fine distinctions."

So I suppose the reason I am here in this studio is to give Mr. Rembrandt a subject of large distinction. He asks me to pose wearing nothing above my waist but a necklace of colored beads that he has supplied. The studio is cold and damp, and I prepare myself for two hours of discomfort. Mr. Twee has apparently decided not to share this time with me and has vanished without saying good-bye.

Then I hear a terrifying sound. From another room, I hear words being spoken in a language from out of my past. It is the language of a people who live on the seacoast of my homeland and who send parties up the river to capture inland people like me and sell them to the captains of slave ships. My people have a saying: "The coastal people eat excrement and sell inland people for colored stones."

*My* people do not eat excrement, but they *do* eat the coastal people. That is, we eat them when we are fortunate enough to kill them. But coastal people have better killing devices, including the terrifying *donderbus*.

The king of the coastal people wears yellow-and-blue silk and has built many more than nine houses just to hold his wives.

I hear the voice again, this time speaking Walloon: "La, la. How beautiful!"

It is the dark-skinned woman from the painting. She rushes to me and runs her hands down my chest. She raises my arm and sniffs under it with her rather wide nose. "You smell like an inlander, my dear," she says. And then she adds a few words that are incomprehensible to me but that have the unmistakable coastal-people choking sound.

I cannot help but be annoyed, even though my short-arm, as we call it, has begun to be less short.

She says something in the flatlander language, and when I look puzzled, says in Walloon: "My name is Uba. Would you like to eat me, Inlander?"

Mr. Rembrandt says, "Later, Uba. This is my time with Lenoir."

"Lenoir?" Uba says. "They have taken away your name? What else have they taken away?"

I push Uba away. "You eat excrement and sell inland people for colored stones."

She reaches under my robe and grabs my short-arm, which is now decidedly unshort. She says, "You're in love with me, you rascal."

Love is not a thing her parents were familiar with. Uba has gone European.

"This is *my* time," Mr. Rembrandt shouts. He throws his brush — at Uba, I assume — and hits me on the chest, leaving a smear of bright blue paint. Uba picks up the brush and begins pressing it against my cheeks and forehead. She knows, I suppose, that my people paint themselves only before circumcisions and battles.

"Go away," Mr. Rembrandt shouts. He takes Uba by the shoulders and pushes her out of the studio. She laughs and doesn't resist. "Until tonight, Lenoir," she calls, and laughs again.

Uba forgets that I am not one of the flatlanders, who have no sense of honor. She thinks that I, like she, have forgotten the truths of life and have adopted the ways of my captors.

I prepare myself for posing. I look about the room. I notice the splendid little knife that Mr. Rembrandt uses to cut through the strong cloth on which he paints. After our session, I will slip it into the pocket of my robe. I will return it, of course, after I take Uba's life with it. I would not steal from Mr. Rembrandt.

"Lenoir. If you please. I am speaking to you." He is talking quickly, in Dutch. "I want you to smile, please, Lenoir."

"A big smile?"

"Not big, but strong. Very strong. Ecstatic."

"I do not understand *ecstatic.*"

He changes to his odd Walloon: "Very strong pleasure — the most common form is sexual — the moment of orgasm."

I understand that. But I point out: "I do not smile at that moment. I close my eyes and wrinkle my brow."

"Well, think of whatever pleases you enough to make you smile."

I do not hesitate. I think of the recent end of winter, the brightening of the sun, the blooming of the flowers. At first I did not understand how these people lived through the winter. Now I understand. They live in hope. They hope for the summer; just as in their religions they hope for pleasure after death. Their ecstasy is always in the future — with the exception of one activity. But I wonder if the solemn Mr. Rembrandt van Rijn even practices *that* ecstasy. There are no children's voices in his house.

I look across the room and through the small window. The sun is breaking through a cloud, changing the greens of the grass and leaves. I smile ecstatically.

And as Mr. Rembrandt works, he begins to smile; it pleases him to capture my beauty with his brushes. Perhaps it is an ecstatic smile. What is one to think of this activity? Two grinning men, one looking at the other, who looks out the window.

"You are an excellent model, Lenoir."

"Yes. I have great beauty."

"No. You don't. Your teeth are bad, and your little beard is uneven. But you have a great talent for remaining motionless but alert."

"It was our method of hunting — to stand and wait as the sun moved across the sky."

"The sun does not move, Lenoir. The earth moves."

How can one reply to such a stupid idea? How can such beliefs be held by people who can build big, handsome boats and direct them across waters larger than their countries? It is probably this belief that causes the sun to place so many clouds between itself and the Hollanders. They do not seem to realize that one must respect the objects of the world. How does one dare say untruthful things about the object that brings us light?

"Mr. Rembrandt," I say, "you make your living by imitating the sun. How can you speak badly of it? Are you not afraid it will punish you?"

Mr. Rembrandt's smile becomes a barking laugh. "Perhaps it *is* punishing me." He falls to his knees and raises his eyes and arms to the sky. "Forgive me, Sun," he shouts. "I see you move across the sky, bringing us warmth and light, banishing the blight of winter. Forgive me for speaking ill of you; forgive me my debts; make my wife healthy."

"Good. Very good. Do you not feel better?"

"I do, as a matter of fact. Much better."

I resume my pose. I have shielded his spirit from great danger.

I say to Mr. Rembrandt, "I feel fortunate to be not only beautiful but wise."

"Not to mention modest."

It is a term I will ask Mr. Twee to explain to me later.

After the sun moves a bit more, Mr. Rembrandt says, "Enough smiling, please, Lenoir. Look fierce now; look threatening and dangerous."

I turn from the window and think of Uba — of floating with Uba along the canal in a flat-bottomed boat as the sun moves below the hill-less horizon.

"Excellent, Lenoir. What do you think of to produce such an expression?"

"Blood blending into the slow-moving, dark water."

Mr. Rembrandt looks at me a new way. He stares at me, a brush held motionless and forgotten in his hand. I think he does not know whether to smile or scowl — an unusual experience for him but one that is commonplace for me, living in a country I will never understand.

Before I leave the studio, I look at the two sketchy paintings Mr. Rembrandt has done of me. I like the one with the expression he calls threatening. It has a seriousness that I do not see in the pictures made by most of these painters. I think this man has disturbed one too many spirits.

When I return to the inn, Mr. Twee is waiting for me. He wears the excited look that makes people think he has the falling sickness. "Busy day," he says. "Next we see Dr. Padmos."

"You are ill?"

"No. No. It's that Dr. Tulp thing of his. This could be big money, Lenoir. Very big."

"Am I supposed to know about Dr. Tulp?"

"Yes, you savage. Think."

*Savage* is one of Mr. Twee's secret terms of affection for me. I make an effort to recall Dr. Tulp but have no luck. I shake my head.

"That disgusting butcher scene by Rembrandt. *The Anatomy Lesson of Dr. Tulp.*"

Now I remember. A terrifying picture that only depraved people could admire. It shows a group of men gathered to watch Dr. Tulp cutting up a dead man's body. It made both Rembrandt and Dr. Tulp famous. My stomach contracts at the thought of it.

Mr. Twee's excitement is growing. He says, "Padmos hates Tulp . . . thinks he's a fraud . . . a quack who gets Rembrandt to do a sensational poster for him . . . who has students and would-be frauds flocking to him from everywhere."

"And what has this to do with us?"

"First we listen to what Padmos has to say."

"And then we arrange for an even more sensational poster?"

Mr. Twee smiles and raises his eyebrows.

*

As I suspected, Dr. Padmos speaks the language of Latin — which is apparently used in many countries by people who consider themselves wise. It does not seem to be a good language in which to call someone bad names, and soon the doctor switches to Dutch, which seems perfect for the purpose. As I watch him, I develop some sympathy for the person who has to paint his portrait. One side of his beard is longer than the other. He wears a brown robe that is stiff with dirt, and it is difficult to say whether his yellowish shirt was once white.

After ranting for a few minutes, Dr. Padmos seems to notice me for the first time.

He switches to Walloon. "Lenoir. One moment." He scuttles over to a cupboard and gets an armload of dried plants, which have been brought back from many countries by sailors. He thinks, correctly, that I can identify those that have medicinal qualities. He is hoping to find something like tobacco, which has become incredibly popular (if he had shown me tobacco, I would have said its only good quality is that it makes people slightly happy, which hardly makes up for its bad smell).

The doctor throws a plant to me. I examine it and sniff it. I have never seen anything like it before. I shake my head and drop the plant to the floor. He throws another. We do about a dozen, one of which I think has laxative qualities and another of which will make an acceptable love potion. Dr. Padmos hands Mr. Twee a coin in payment for my services.

The doctor stares at the wall for a moment, then says, "Any idiot can cut up a body. There are two problems: getting a supply of bodies and tolerating the stench. I'm good about the stench, but I can't always get the kind of bodies I want."

Padmos looks at Mr. Twee and me. I believe he is asking us — asking *me* — to get him bodies. A suitable occupation, he would think, for a dark-skinned man.

Mr. Twee asks, "How much?"

Is Mr. Twee's financial situation so desperate that there is no kind of activity he will not involve us in? While the two men haggle, I notice some small leather bags filled with what the doctor told me is dried blood. I get up and secretly drop one of the bags into my pocket.

In the afternoon, while Mr. Twee is having his siesta, Nghana sits on my shoulder and watches with great interest as I make a buxom female juju doll of straw, its belly containing the sack of dried blood I removed from Dr. Padmos's office.

Later, Uba sees the same expression on my face. She does not stop smiling; she never does. But her eyes become uneasy.

I have gone to her rooming house after leaving the studio. I wait outside the house while she finishes a sexual encounter with a member of Amsterdam's ruling council. With the wages of the encounter, Uba takes me to a tavern and buys me a meal — potatoes, which seem like a reasonable food to me, and sausages, which I find silly in appearance and taste. Uba has a naughty way of eating them. I drink enough beer to make the meal acceptable.

As we eat, we look at each other warily, gauging each other's power. Uba's sexual power is great. It is a power that, even though she is no longer youthful, is apparently felt as strongly — if not more strongly — by the men of this city as by the men of Uba's home village.

The power of my magic, however, has been weakened by lack of use. And even at its full strength, would my sorcery affect Uba, whose beliefs are so strangely different from mine? Perhaps it is time I found out. Perhaps it is time to regain the strength that I traded for this amusing but powerless life. I could begin to find the answer on this evening's boat ride.

There is no need to hire a boat, for Uba owns one: a simple-looking vessel draped — as are so many ordinary people in this city — with black cloth. But after we drift beyond the city and into the countryside — past the men who are for some unimaginable reason digging yet another big canal — Uba removes the cloth, revealing red-and-gold cushions. The black cloth is lined with red, and by attaching poles to its corners, we make it into a little roof. "This is my boat of ceremony," she says, "the ceremony of stir-the-seedpod." Or some such nonsense. She speaks in the language of her birth, which I know slightly, and which requires one to talk in pictures. For example, Uba would say that the sky now is the color of the mewbird and the early tree flower; whereas I would say the sky is dark gray, shading off to mauve at the horizon. We are not the same kind of people. Or rather, as I was taught as a child, I am a person and Uba is not a person.

Persons may do whatever they wish to nonpersons.

Nevertheless, I must admit I feel pleasure as we drift through the early evening. Now that I am away from the noise of horse-cart wheels against paving stones and the chatter of voices doing business, I can close my eyes and imagine I am a child again, listening to the comforting calls of birds settling into their roosting places, of frogs crying out for mates.

A breeze has sprung up, and in the distance there is the slightly frightening groan of slowly moving windmill arms. I open my eyes and see the black sails silhouetted against the sky, and I understand how Don Quixote could see this machine as a monster. Something as large as a windmill should not have the ability to move.

We have also passed five gibbets, from three of which hang dead bodies. The burghers like to keep the gibbets full, and when one commits a crime in this country, one must be prepared to feel the rope at one's neck. In my country, after an execution, we think it is best for the people to see not the victim but the executioner, who visits every home and shows his bloody ax.

Uba, after stroking my thigh and muttering insincere words of affection in several languages (including, I believe, the language of the hated and feared Spaniards), has fallen asleep. I am pleased that her life is not only one of simple pleasure but is also exhausting.

I reach into my robe for the knife I borrowed from Mr. Rembrandt. I whisper ceremonial words that I remember imperfectly.

Soon, just barely visible in the day's last light, there is blood on the water as I had imagined it earlier in the studio.

I feel a great satisfaction, as if I have made contact with the depths of the earth.

Then there is a cry of terror. Uba has awakened.

"Juju . . . juju . . . juju!"

"Hush," I say. "Simply a little sacrifice. A doll."

The juju doll — its arms, legs, and head hacked off, its belly slashed open — floats at the side of the boat. The water soaks up the blood, taking away the substance of life, leaving only pale straw.

Uba lapses into gibberish. She probably no longer knows which language to speak. She is terrified in a way no European could understand.

I can make out the name Egbo occasionally. Egbo is a man who walks at dusk in Uba's homeland, masked and carrying a whip and a sword. He wears a bell around his neck to announce his presence. He propitiates evil spirits by whipping people and cutting off their heads. I am not worthy of the honor of this name. I have merely dismembered a doll with a tiny knife. Nevertheless, this gesture helps keep alive the ways of my world, as does my selection of medicinal plants for Dr. Padmos.

Uba gradually becomes quiet. She has given up the idea of seducing me. She weeps quietly. I have won the contest. And I think I have made her homesick.

I wonder how much power I have retained. I wonder, as Uba must, whether she will soon suffer the fate of the little straw doll.

# 4

DURING THE NIGHT I am awakened by the sound of whispering. I get up to find Mr. Twee, in his nightgown, holding a lighted candle, whispering to a sleeping Nghana: "Life stinks."

In the morning, there is great confusion in the story of Don Quixote and Sancho Panza. The knight mistakes sheep for armies and says he is under the spell of an evil enchanter. I am saddened by this; Mr. Twee is amused. I ask, "Why do you laugh at the knight's enchantment?"

"He's not enchanted."

"How do you know this?"

"The author tells us. And Quixote's squire Sancho tells us."

"Perhaps they are lying."

"Everyone is lying, Lenoir. It's all imagined. It's not real."

"Among my people, there is not a difference between imagined stories and real stories. I don't understand how a thing cannot be real."

Mr. Twee sighs. He does not enjoy discussions that are not concerned with business and money. He says, "What if I told the notary that you stole money from me, and he had you put in jail?"

"You would be telling a lie."

"So, you see?"

"But it would be a *real* lie."

Mr. Twee closes his eyes and shakes his head. "Ask Dr. Padmos to explain. It's the sort of thing best explained by someone who speaks Latin. And we will be seeing the doctor again today. Some new business, new and different. We will be seeing everyone today. My ship was lost at sea."

Mr. Twee has spoken the phrase that every Hollander seems to speak sooner or later. It is part of the process of investment. One gives money to a syndicate; a ship is lost at sea; one loses one's money. It is a part of being a respected citizen. Notaries will begin to call. There will be talk of bankruptcy. We will go to another city.

I ask, "Will we be leaving Amsterdam?"

"Why not? There are no standards here. They'll publish anyone's book, paint in any style, and sink anyone's boat." Mr. Twee begins, in increasing excitement, to outline our day. In the morning, we will see two cloth merchants and Mr. Rembrandt. In the afternoon, we will arrange our "new and different" business with Dr. Padmos. Mr. Twee, who follows the local custom of wearing something on his head at all times, is featuring a wide-brimmed white hat decorated with a large red feather. As he speaks to me of business strategies, I wonder why anyone would trust him. Instead of the conventional black or brown costume, he wears an outfit of green velvet and satin, trimmed in fur.

He may be the thinnest person in this country, where even the starving beggars are plump. He wears jewelry and has neither a mustache nor a beard, habits that do not inspire confidence here. And he bathes as frequently as once a week, although it is a habit that many of these people believe can cause weakness or illness. He has documents proving he was born in eight different lands, but he is most often suspected of being a Frenchman — an assumption he denies because he claims it is bad for business.

My attention soon begins to wander. Mr. Twee removes one of the four rings he is wearing and throws it at me. It is one of the rings that makes a green circle on his finger. "Pay attention, Lenoir. I know why you want to leave Amsterdam. Exotics are ten for a guilder here — East Indians, West Indians, Scots. You can't stand the competition."

I think Mr. Twee may be right. I assume the ring belongs to me now. It fits the smallest child of my hand, as Uba would say.

Later in a café, I hear Mr. Twee ask a merchant: "Cork?"

"Cork," the merchant replies. "What could be safer?"

The merchant will give Mr. Twee a share in a shipment of cork in return for being included in the group portrait that Mr. Rembrandt is painting.

"Even if the ship's hull is cracked, it cannot be lost. The cork will keep it afloat. Cork being shipped from Lisbon to Cherbourg . . . a short, safe trip in any case."

"Two shares," Mr. Twee says. "In cash on delivery of the cargo. One share to go to Mr. Rembrandt (after deduction of my fee, of course); the second to be all mine."

The merchant looks at his partner, who beckons to him. They remove their massive hats so that they can have a mouth-to-ear, whispered conversation. They replace their hats, and the spokesman says, "My partner says Rembrandt's pictures aren't very good. Too many shadows, the paint too thick. What about something by young Mr. Flinck?"

"Flinck's a student. Rembrandt's a master. I'll ask Rembrandt to lighten things up, to give things more finish. But I'm not sure we can get your partner in anyway. It would be difficult. Rembrandt has already done much work on the canvas. Working two more figures into the group could spoil the composition. And it is customary for the subjects in a group to know one another, to be in the same trade."

"What is their trade?"

"I'm not sure."

The merchant shouts, "Messenger!"

A boy appears and is sent to ask Mr. Rembrandt who the men in the portrait are and what their trade is. In the meantime, we drink beer, which Hollanders drink not only between meals but *with* every meal, including breakfast. There is much belching and staggering in this country.

Fortunately, the boy returns quickly. Without hesitation, he recites the names of all the men in the unfinished portrait. They are warehousers. Fortunately, the merchants we are speaking to own warehouses and know all the men the boy has named. The boy holds out his hand. The merchants look to Mr. Twee, who looks back at them and nods his head toward the boy. Finally, I pull out my purse and give the boy a coin. He glances at me ungratefully and heads for the bar, where he orders some beer.

Later, as I pose for Mr. Rembrandt, Mr. Twee distracts us both by talking business. "Just two more people. Head and shoulders. No hands. For a full share of the cargo."

"Cork?"

"Can't sink; a sure thing."

"I need the money."

"Of course you do, Rembrandt. We both do. You don't buy big houses by painting self-portraits and little-known biblical scenes. You buy big houses by investing shrewdly."

"All right. Send the warehousers around. I'll fit them in. But I can't do it without permission of the others in the portrait."

Mr. Twee says, "I'll take care of that."

We all know he won't. He walks around to look at today's portrait of me. "A portrait of evil."

Next to business, evil is the favorite subject with these Hollanders. They are happiest when combining the two subjects.

And later in Dr. Padmos's office, I listen in amazement as he combines the subjects in a new way.

*

Dr. Padmos, Mr. Twee, and I stand around a table that holds an object covered by a white cloth. "You are about to see," the doctor says, "the object that will make Amsterdam wealthier and more famous." With a dramatic gesture, he removes the cloth. On the table is a strange, tiny building: round and roofless. I doubt that it will do what he claims unless it is used in doll-magic.

We stare at the object for a moment, Dr. Padmos in pride, Mr. Twee and I in confusion. Finally, Mr. Twee asks, "So what is it?"

"A theater. A combined anatomical-dramatic theater."

"No roof?"

"That's the beauty of it. Plenty of light, no trapped stench. We can do anatomies in the summer, not just in winter. Preceded by a parade. Followed by a banquet. And dramatic presentations featuring comedies and tragedies from various countries."

Mr. Twee asks, "How does anyone get wealthy with this?"

"Admission fees."

Mr. Twee seems skeptical. "People won't pay serious money to see actors . . . even if you throw in a corpse. You've seen those stupid plays they do here."

"The theater makes money in England, even without the corpse."

"The English are crazy; they've been in a mess since Queen Elizabeth died."

"A friend in The Hague tells me the English will soon follow our example and dispose of the monarchy."

I lose interest in the conversation. Hollanders will talk for hours about "the international situation." In my homeland, we saw no reason to discuss our neighbors. For each nearby tribe, we had one phrase that told us why they were not to be trusted, why they were not truly human. Aside from making occasional holiday death raids to assure them of our fierceness, we ignored them.

I also wonder why anyone would want to build a roofless theater in a country where there is so much rain.

Mr. Twee begins to lose his doubting expression. His deal-making expression is taking over. "It might work," he says. "Get the guilds to put up the money for the building . . . for the glory of the community, et cetera."

Dr. Padmos also changes his expression. I get the feeling that he is about to reveal his true reason for talking to us. He says, confidentially, "I want to perform some practice anatomies. I need a few bodies."

"That's not exactly a problem," Mr. Twee says. "They're hanging from gibbets all over town."

"The problem," the doctor says, "is that they are all male bodies. I need a few females. People will pay more to see a female body dissected."

By "people," I assume Dr. Padmos means men. I think it is odd indeed that women are allowed to appear as the subjects of dissections but not as players in the tragedies and comedies.

Mr. Twee is obviously becoming excited and enthusiastic. "You're right," he says. "Okay. That's no problem. We can dig up a few women — so to speak."

"It would be better," the doctor says, "if someone could get me a . . . fresh body . . . fresh and young."

The doctor looks at me. Mr. Twee looks at me. They both smile. I am a drowning man in a drowned country.

But I am forgetting that I know how to swim. I am forgetting that it is good when people need your services. I return the smiles and pretend I don't know what these men want. They will have to ask me, and I am not sure if they are ready to do that.

The doctor says to me, "I was summoned by Uba this morning."

So that's it. Uba. Well, I suppose she would have at least four advantages as an anatomical subject: she's female, healthy, exotic, and not too old. She has the disadvantage of being alive.

Dr. Padmos continues: "She tells me you've been naughty, Lenoir."

Mr. Twee says, "I hope so." His smile has turned to a leer.

"Not the sexual kind of naughtiness," the doctor says. "Rather, the kind that involves a doll and makes a person ill and sleepless. Uba thinks Lenoir is trying to kill her."

Mr. Twee now looks amused and respectful. "Could you do that, Lenoir? Kill Uba by doing things to a doll?"

I nod.

Dr. Padmos asks, "Could you also kill *other* people that way?"

I nod.

"Are you a witch?" Mr. Twee asks.

I nod and smile.

Mr. Twee now looks terrified. He says, "I've been told that the Calvinists hang witches."

Dr. Padmos produces a womanish laugh. "And who knows what they do to a person who *owns* a witch?"

"Very funny," Mr. Twee says. "Now let's just forget about witches and magic. No more of that. If any killing is necessary, it must be done in an enlightened way." He puts his hand on my shoulder. "Lenoir, you're living among rational people. You must do things our way."

"Then I should put the knife in *Uba's* body, not in the *doll's* body?"

Dr. Padmos is alarmed. "No knives," he says. "We need an unmarred corpse."

Mr. Twee is agitated. "Keep your voice down. We shouldn't be talking about it in this way. Simply refer to 'the merchandise.' The merchandise should not be damaged."

I ask, "A garrote, perhaps?" I make the motion of tightening the cord. "This is a skill that my people have perfected."

"I suggest poison." Padmos holds up a small bottle. "I have just the thing here. Very quick. The merchandise will be as pure and unblemished as a sleeping child."

Mr. Twee puts his finger to his lips. "Off to pose now, Lenoir. And say nothing about this plan to Mr. Rembrandt."

I nod. Mr. Rembrandt would not understand. I am not sure that I myself understand.

As I leave I see Mr. Twee take the bottle of poison from Dr. Padmos and pocket it.

I am relieved to be away from the doctor. But it is too early to go to the studio. There is not time to walk out to the countryside, so I decide to go into a church, where it will be quiet and where I can collect my thoughts about obtaining "merchandise."

I stand at the back amid the cool gloom. I see merchandise — mostly old — scattered about the church, praying. It seems fitting to think of these women as merchandise, for they are not given the many duties that women are given among my people. It must be tedious to have nothing to do but clean the house, cook, and pamper one's children. One of the women kneeling here in the church is young. I walk up behind her and imagine how easy it would be to slip a cord about her neck.

And then I am startled by the terrifying sound of the church organ. It is a noise to match the appearance of the windmills — a noise too large to be tolerated. I have noticed the man who plays this instrument. He has the look of madness in his eyes, and he speaks passionately about a Mr. Sweelinck, who was known in many countries for his skill with this monster sound machine. These musicians do not understand the dangers of complexity. The music in my country is made from five tones. Young people occasionally want to use new tones, but the elders discourage such thoughts. Young people do not understand that if the music changes, the dancing will soon change, and then the ceremonies. The gods will be offended. The women's crops will fail. People will vanish in the night. Thus, our saying "Five tones and nine wives are enough."

The church is now vibrating with the harsh, complicated sounds of the organ. I do not know why the vibrations have not caused the church to collapse. I put my hands over my ears and walk out into the streets, where the bright tulips have begun to appear.

Occasionally, when I pose for a painter, I get the feeling that I am truly taking part in a ceremony of magic. Today's session with Mr. Rembrandt is such a time. The noises that surround us — the ever-present screams of children, the *clop* of horses' hoofs on the cobblestones of the street, the squawking of seabirds — become muted, and I feel as though I am sending a type of power to the painter. Occasionally we speak — quietly, the way people speak in the dark.

"What do you think of us, Lenoir?"

"I forget at times that you are not just silly but are also dangerous."

The brush scrapes against the stiff cloth.

"Do you not find us noble once in a while?"

"Never. I think Mr. Calvin knew you well. You are all hopelessly damned."

"Not *all* of us. Calvin said *almost* all of us."

"In my homeland, we say, 'All things must be the same.'"

"But can't you see that all things are different?"

"Yes. We also say, 'No two things can be the same.'"

Mr. Rembrandt laughs. I laugh, too. This will be a good portrait, I think.

A few minutes later, Mrs. Rembrandt appears behind her husband. She does not look healthy. She carries an open bottle of wine, which she puts on the paint stand next to her husband.

Rembrandt says to her, "Saskia, this is Lenoir."

She smiles and nods at me. I think she, like her husband, is a melancholy person. But unlike her husband, she has a distinguished appearance. Perhaps she is melancholy because she is married to a picture maker instead of a burgher. Or perhaps she is sad because there are no children's voices in her big house. But she and her husband look fondly at each other.

They may not have had children, but I think they are still try-ing.

Saskia looks at the picture her husband is making of me. She smiles broadly and suddenly looks like the wife of a king. She looks at her husband again, and her expression of fondness changes to the strange one that these people call love. She kisses him on the cheek and leaves the room. She is still smil-ing, but she is shaking her head from side to side.

"Women," Mr. Rembrandt says. "They confuse me."

"You don't let them do enough work. Why, for example, don't you let them make pictures?"

Mr. Rembrandt goes to a stack of pictures in the corner and holds one up to face me. It shows a laughing man, holding up a goblet as if asking for a refill. The picture is like those Mr. Twee calls tavern art, but it seems more exciting than most I have seen. "It's by Anna van Cott," Mr. Rembrandt says. "She studies with Govert Flinck, who studies with me. I think soon they'll let her into the guild, like Jan Molenaer's wife, Judith. But like Ju-dith, Anna likes babies more than paintings. God lets men do frivolous things, but women must do the important thing."

"My gods let women do everything."

Mr. Rembrandt laughs. "What our gods seem to agree about is that women are more important than men."

I say, "I think women are exactly as important as men. Ex-actly."

"But you aren't a god."

I wonder if Mr. Rembrandt thinks he is a god, as many painters seem to do. We do not speak for the rest of the session.

As he paints, Mr. Rembrandt begins to look slightly drunk. And though he occasionally has a drink from the wine bottle his wife has left behind, I think he is drunk not from wine but from picture making.

In *my* imagination, I hear the drums and the five-tone mel-odies of my homeland.

*

That night, to impart wholeness, I make a flawless straw doll of Uba.

Nghana, upon my shoulder, chews pieces of straw. The pupils of his red eyes contract occasionally in pleasure, as he murmurs, "Life is good."

As I complete the doll, Mr. Twee returns from whatever business he has been conducting. "A doll?" he asks. "Is Lenoir feeling childish?"

"This is not a child's doll. It is a doll of great power. It has the power of juju."

"You should stop believing in juju, Lenoir. You should be like me and stop believing in everything."

"Most of the people of this land do not seem to lack belief."

"That's the thing. There's too much belief, Lenoir. Too many ways to believe. Reformations, counter-reformations, counter-counter-reformations. It's a mess. Learn to be reasonable, like me."

"To be reasonable is to believe nothing?"

"Unless you are a scientist. Or a philosopher. Philosophers say there is a time coming when everyone will be reasonable."

"Everyone will be like you, Mr. Twee?"

"Right. I'm the man of the future."

I have no answer for that, but I think I could not live without believing.

# 5

BETWEEN DAWN AND DUSK in this busy city, there is always at least one person standing in the background, observing. At first, I believed it was my striking appearance that attracted attention, but now I realize it is simply part of the distrust that exists among these people. They never know what a neighbor might do, and they stand waiting for the next event in fear or hope.

The person I see most often in the background today is Uba. When I approach her, she flees, not understanding that I wish to show her some kindness and dispel the mischief I subjected her to the other night.

Finally, while I have her attention, I produce the new, fat doll I created. I wave it and offer it to her. She stops fleeing and waits as I approach her. I hold out the doll to her, and she accepts it.

I say to her, in Walloon, "You and I are alike in one respect: we know where the true powers lie."

"And you and the pale people are alike in two respects, Lenoir. You are full of shit, and you think you are wise."

"You have not escaped your people's beliefs, Uba. Excrement is too much on your mind. But I am not offended." I am impressed at the quickness with which she replied to me. Perhaps I have been underrating her. I say, "Let me buy you a drink."

Uba cannot refuse. Mr. Twee has told me that she is under the spell of the drink called brandywine — a fact that confirms her lack of judgment. We live among people who are obsessed with drinking and who have uncountable beverages available. To choose sinister brandywine from all these truly shows bad character.

We look for a café — something that is never difficult to find. However, before we find a café, Uba stops, squats, and lifts her skirts. For although there are many places where one may go to drink, there are not many where one may go to piss. The streets reek of urine. In Mr. Twee's collection of pictures on paper, there are some (by Mr. Rembrandt, I think) that depict people pissing in the street. I cannot imagine why anyone would want to make or own such a picture.

When we are settled snugly at a chimney-corner table — Uba with a large brandywine, me with a small *porto* — I warn her: "It is not safe for you here, Uba. There are many other cities nearby. Go to one of them."

"I've been to them. They aren't safe either, especially not for people like you and me."

"I am not a woman. I am not a prostitute."

"Not being a woman is nothing to be proud of. And being a whore is nothing to be ashamed of. But at least you can't deny the fact that you're an African."

"I am no longer African. And I was not the same kind of African as you, in any case."

"You're *still* an African, Lenoir. You can fool *yourself*, but you can't fool anyone else. And if you're not an African, what are you?"

Uba has been speaking the language of the Walloons without hesitation, but in the accent of the men who work on the docks. I must remind her that I am not such a man. I say, "I am a beautiful man of the world. I have seen many parts of the

world, and I have not seen anyplace that is beyond my understanding or my abilities. I am as noble as any king or regent."

"Lenoir, you're a fancy swindler's houseboy-slave. There's
nothing noble about that. And I'm not sure you're not a whore.
I hear you sleep with that Twee."

I take these insults calmly, and I do not bother to deny the
accusation, for a plan is forming in my mind. I order another
brandywine for Uba. After she gulps it, I ask her, "Are you acquainted with many other women of your profession?"

"Do I know lots of whores? Oh yes."

"Close friends?"

"No. They don't stay around long."

"They sometimes disappear without explanation?"

"*Whatever* they do, it's without explanation."

"And do you think they would react to the sorcery of my
homeland?"

"Lenoir, I hope you're not up to what I think you're up to.
Let me ask you if you know what they do to murderers here.
They burn them alive is what they do. They don't have long
trials; they don't have lots of jails. If you do something bad to
someone, the magistrate gets someone to do something worse
to you, in a big hurry."

"Yes, yes. But what about magic?"

"There's witchcraft. But I've never heard of a witch-whore.
Witches are ugly, and they stink like frightened horses."

"Does their witchcraft have someone like your Egbo?"

"Satan, I suppose. The Prince of Darkness."

"And you could introduce me to some Satan-fearing prostitutes?"

"So could any man in Amsterdam, except your boyfriend and
possibly Mr. Rembrandt van Rijn."

"Why not Mr. Rembrandt?"

"He thinks whores are saints. He would like them to marry
and have many children."

Realizing what she has said, Uba pauses and blinks. She will probably never marry and have many children. I also blink. I will never again see my many children.

I order another brandywine for Uba, and I go to seek Mr. Twee.

I wonder how people could speculate about sexual activities between me and Mr. Twee. He says such people are truly evil. They could be the same people I sometimes see walking stiffly into Calvin's church, to kneel and stare at the walls, which go undecorated in this city, where some excellent picture makers are forced to live in the Home for Indigents.

I find Mr. Twee in our room at the inn, sitting at a table that is covered with sheets of paper, all of which contain numbers — long numbers, one above another. The room smells like cheese and tobacco smoke. Mr. Twee looks as though he is about to vomit.

I open the window. "The room smells like cheese and tobacco smoke," I say. I don't mention there is also the aroma of unemptied chamber pot.

"The whole country reeks of cheese. Cheese and piss and horses. That's what they like to smell. They don't make perfumes here. Even their fucking tulips either smell bad or don't smell at all. You won't catch a Hollander getting passionate about roses or lilacs."

I obviously don't have to worry about spoiling Mr. Twee's mood. I say, "You are forgetting about tobacco smoke."

"I'm not forgetting about it, my man. It's just that I don't share your unsophisticated aversion to it."

In his trunk, Mr. Twee has a few clay pipes, which I believe he puffs on when I am not present. But of more concern to me now is that he has called me "my man" — a term whose meaning I am not sure of. I say to him, "I think it is believed here that you and I do sexual acts together."

Mr. Twee shrugs. "Half of the men in this country are sailors, Lenoir. They are locked up in little floating prisons with other men for months and years at a time. East Indies, West Indies. They're buggers. They think about it all the time."

"There are many female prostitutes here."

"For the regents and clerks, the ones who put numbers on paper." He grabs a handful of papers and throws them into the air. "They want everything to involve payment, including sex."

I decide not to point out to Mr. Twee that *he* does not visit prostitutes (or the lonely wives) and that I have heard someone say that he smells and dresses like an unnatural Englander. He adds, "And besides, you and I *do* perform sexual acts together."

"Not often, Mr. Twee. Only when we have to sleep together in wall-box beds. And in any case, that is not the point. What disturbs me is that people should talk about such a thing."

"Forget it, Lenoir. It's meaningless. Didn't you have man-man or man-boy sex in your tribe?"

"Of course. We had every kind. But it is different here, where it is mixed with love and money. Sex is dangerous here."

Mr. Twee loses his temper. "The thing about sex is that it really doesn't help." He grabs pieces of paper and scatters them about the room. "I need help, Lenoir. You're supposed to help me. I need money. Remember, if *Twee* doesn't have money, *Lenoir* doesn't have money. Repeat after me . . ."

He is using the voice he used when he was teaching me languages. I interrupt him: "Here's some help, then. Mr. Rembrandt knows a female student who can paint better than most men. She will be admitted to the painter's guild. I would think she needs an agent."

Mr. Twee narrows his eyes. "Is she attractive?"

"I haven't seen her."

"She probably dresses like a man."

"Mr. Rembrandt says she will marry and have children."

"Excellent, Lenoir," Mr. Twee says, and kisses me on the forehead.

"If you will promise not to kiss me," I say, "I will tell you something else: Uba knows some young women who walk the streets at night and who would be sensitive to juju, who might expire in terror if they should see the Egbo or the Prince of Darkness lurking in the shadows."

"I wouldn't count on it, Lenoir. I wouldn't be surprised if it takes more than juju."

Mr. Twee might not count on it, but he is pleased. He has forgotten the numbers on the paper. In his pleasure, he forgets our little bargain and kisses me once more. I am glad my blushes are not visible.

The next morning I walk out before the sun has risen. The cold dampness of the air penetrates my robe. I need a new garment, one in gold and green, perhaps, for the spring weather — and shoes with soft leather tops and wood soles for slopping through the dirty puddles one encounters everywhere. Unless Mr. Twee reduces his debts, there will be no new robes for Lenoir.

With my drum slung over my shoulder, I stroll to the street of brothels, which is beginning to settle into its hours of morning quiet. Occasionally, a drunken man or prostitute emerges from one of the inns. Many picture makers live in this part of Amsterdam, where the rents are cheap and there are people who will pose in the nude. I wonder why there is so much concern with bodies among these people. Bodies are shown in pictures, dissected, hung from gibbets. And yet a prosperous person here — with gloves, hats, high collars — will hide his or her body except for the face. They show their faces, but only as a means of identification. Mr. Twee says the churches teach that the soul is more important than the body. But the pictures that people want are those that show their own uninteresting faces.

As I have this thought, a man emerges from his narrow house, carrying an easel and a paint box, and I am reminded of another strange kind of picture that is made here. I have seen this man at night in taverns, and he is much given to carousing. But on some mornings, to clear his head, he will walk to the edge of town. He will set up his equipment and wait until the beautiful colors of dawn are gone, and he will make a picture showing a tiny strip of flat land at the bottom and many gray clouds at the top. He is not the only painter to make such pictures, which also seem to be popular and must remind the respectable people of their own quiet lives.

But I am not concerned with the lives of respectable people this morning. I proceed to an inn where the prostitutes gather at dawn to have a final drink and discuss the evening's business before going to sleep.

The women greet me fondly, knowing that I have come to them out of friendship and that I would never visit them on a professional basis. I have enjoyed their favors occasionally, but never for money. I cannot imagine being degraded enough to pay someone to have a sexual encounter with me. Those who would do such a thing either are admitting to themselves that they have no beauty or charm or, as Mr. Twee has pointed out, are so given to doing business that they must bring this most delightful of activities down to the level of buying and selling.

I greet my friends, and two of them come wearily into my arms.

One of them asks me to sing a song. She speaks in French, which is the language generally used in the brothel when the women are not doing business. It is the language of sophistication, they say.

Tapping my drum lightly so as not to awaken those whose nights have ended, I sing a song I have converted into French. The song tells of Ngasa, the snake who loved the Chief Ghala's daughter:

> *Hiss, hiss, hiss.*
> My young beauty, do not fear me.
> Take me in your hand.

The night is hot, but is my body not cool?
Guide me to the entrance of the warm, moist cave;
let me enter and coil within the cave
while you sleep, smiling.
*Hiss, hiss, hiss.*

The song is popular with the men of my homeland, who, when trying to gain a woman's favors, have the expression "I wish I might sleep in Ngasa's cave."

When I finish my song, I look into the faces of my audience. The song has brought gentle smiles to their lips. Some of these women probably think the song was about love. They do not understand that they might one day be the center of attention in Dr. Padmos's Anatomical Theater.

But it is time to get down to business, as the popular expression goes. I say, in a confidential voice, "On my way here, I believe I caught a glimpse of your Satan."

My announcement is greeted by laughter. Katja, who is one of the establishment's more mature women, says, out of the corner of her mouth, "We see more than a glimpse of him every night."

It is a pleasure to look at Katja, despite her paleness. Two kinds of experience have shown me what her ample body is like beneath her clothing. I have seen it by candlelight — perspiration and shadows in the creases between the firm rolls of flesh. And I have seen it — pinker and smoother — in a picture Mr. Rembrandt made of her; a picture called Venus, a god-woman who is no longer worshiped.

I notice that at the mention of Satan, a young woman — one I have not seen before — raises her hand and, in the popish manner, touches first her forehead and then her breast. She is slender; no one would ask her to be Venus. Her eyes are fearful. I say to her, "I didn't mean to bring you fear."

Katja gets up and puts her plump, rough hand at the base

of the young woman's smooth neck. "Lenoir, this is Jeanne. She has come to us from Flanders, a land to the south, where the Sisters of Benedict taught her to fear Satan. They almost frightened her to death. Now she's *our* sister. We'll teach her not to fear anything."

Later, as I am leaving, I take Jeanne aside. I say, "There's nothing wrong with fear." She lowers her eyes respectfully. I continue: "You are just a child. I think you would rather be sleeping with dolls than with rough men like me." She looks up at me and smiles. "I will bring you a doll, Sister Jeanne."

Her eyes tell me she has a talent for trust, which is a talent that is as dangerous as it is rare.

When I arrive for my final session with Mr. Rembrandt, he has a student with him — a young woman I think must be the Anna he told me about. She does not, as Mr. Twee had feared, wear men's clothes. Beneath her painter's robe I see a skirt that at first seems like an ordinary black wool. But as it catches the light, I see that it is softly woven and has golden flecks in it. Although her skin is totally pale, her features are not the usual small collection but somehow remind me of the features of women in my home village.

When Mr. Rembrandt finally notices me, he says, "Lenoir, this is Miss Anna van Cott. We will be finished soon." (He calls her *juffrouw* rather than *mademoiselle*, which I am sure she would prefer.)

I reflect that my life — although it has not been as my parents and the gods had intended — could be worse. I have been introduced to two attractive young women this morning, and both smiled at me without effort.

I go to stand behind Mr. Rembrandt and Anna. She is holding a palette and brush, and they are looking at the picture I saw yesterday — the picture of a man who smiles and holds up a goblet. The painting seems complete and pleasing to me, but Anna is unhappy with it. She says to Mr. Rembrandt, "Flinck has spoiled it."

Mr. Rembrandt shrugs. "You must learn the difference between light and paint," he says to Anna. "You've been looking at things by Dou the Finisher, haven't you? He paints hairs, not pictures." Mr. Rembrandt speaks decisively but gently.

Anna says, "It is no longer my painting."

"It is a better painting now."

"I don't want it said that I merely imitate Flinck."

"And don't be satisfied with something just because it is yours. Soon your paintings will be both yours and excellent."

Anna still does not look pleased. "But this one is not mine," she says.

Mr. Rembrandt answers, "And it is not Flinck's."

Anna takes it from the easel and hands it to me. "It is yours, Lenoir."

"I cannot pay you," I say.

"That isn't necessary," she says. She stares at me for a moment. I assume she is admiring my beauty. Then she says, "You're not like us, are you?"

"Oh, no."

"Do people paint pictures in the country where you were born?"

I answer her in French: "Oh, no. We put colors on things to make them more enjoyable or when we cannot avoid it; everything one makes must have a color. Our doctors and sorcerers put paint on their dolls. But we make no pictures."

"You're sensible," she says, and turns and leaves the studio. I don't know whether she will become a good painter, but I guess that, like my people, she is too sensible to keep making pictures. I call after her, "Thank you, *mademoiselle*." I wonder if she, too, has made a picture of Katja's nude body.

In any case, Mr. Twee will be pleased with the picture Anna

has given me. I think he will be able to get a few guilders for it by claiming that it was made by Mr. Flinck, which is at least partly the truth. (I notice I have become more concerned with truth than I once was; the deranged ones are having their influence on me after all.)

Mr. Rembrandt fetches his latest portrait of me and puts it on the easel. The light in the studio is gray this morning, and there is an unhappiness in the portrait that displeases me. "You have not made me look happy," I say. "I notice that Mlle. van Cott's picture shows a happy man. All the men I have seen in your paintings look happy or pleased with themselves. Why should you make me appear unhappy?"

"With you, I simply paint what I sense is the truth."

"I have just been thinking about truth. It is dangerous to think about truth. You people have wars over truth. In my homeland, there was no word for truth."

"Did you not have wars?"

"Oh, yes. But about deeds, not words. Short wars. Eight hours . . . or perhaps eight days. Mr. Twee tells me that you have had wars that last longer than a lifetime."

"You should learn our numbers, Lenoir."

"And I should learn your music, too, I suppose. And your truths. Then I would not be Lenoir."

"Then you might look happier."

I am suddenly angry. I turn and begin to walk out of the studio. "I will not have it said that I am unhappy. Can't you see that I am happy? I am very, very happy." Then I remember I am leaving behind the painting Mlle. van Cott has given me. I return and pick it up. "I am happier than this pink-cheeked drunk."

"And now *I* am sad, Lenoir."

"Truth brings sadness," I say. I realize that what I have just said is like the things that Sancho Panza says in *The Ingenious Gentleman Don Quixote of La Mancha* — the proverbs that seem wise to me but that Mr. Twee, Don Quixote, and the storyteller find ridiculous. If Mr. Twee is at the inn when I get there, I will have him read to me, which will make my anger vanish.

Mr. Twee is pleased with the picture I have brought him. "A woman did this?"

"Her teacher, Mr. Flinck, did some parts."

"Nevertheless. And she is your friend?"

"Oh, yes. Yes. Miss Anna van Cott. Mlle. van Cott."

"If she can do a flattering likeness, there are many commissions here. Is she attractive?"

"Most."

"So if a man had the choice of spending a few hours having Mr. Rembrandt look at him or Mlle. van Cott look at him, we know which he would choose. Does she smell good?"

"Like mimosa blossoms."

"Is she engaged to be married?"

"Oh, no," I say, wondering if I speak the truth.

"There is another woman painter here: Judith Leyster Molenaer. She married a painter. He wasn't as good as she was, but he was the man, so she painted a few things for the general market and then, as far as I know, gave it up."

"Mlle. van Cott wants to make pictures more than she wants to make babies, I think."

"Some men might want to pose in the nude for her. Would she allow that?"

"She is a woman of the world."

Mr. Twee rubs his hands together and makes a high-pitched noise of pleasure. "Did you tell her about me?"

"Oh, yes."

"You must introduce her to me soon."

"A simple matter," I say, as I wonder where she might live.

"Good. But first, Dr. Padmos wants to see us. In about an hour."

"Perhaps there is time to read from the old book."

Mr. Twee reads to me of tricks played on Don Quixote; of enchantment and the Lady Dulcinea. I don't understand why the storyteller laughs at the misfortunes of the Don, who never laughs and is known as the Knight of the Sad Countenance. Why are these people pleased by the sadness of others? Why do they see sadness even in the countenance of Lenoir, where it doesn't exist?

# 6

"I WILL ENCHANT this young woman for you," I say to Dr. Padmos. "Even in the days of chivalry, before Sancho Panza, they knew about the power of enchantment."

"Forget the enchantment and juju," Dr. Padmos says. "I think there's a simpler answer. The plague is returning. I've seen several cases. I will soon have all the bodies I need. All ages, both sexes. Something for everyone."

Mr. Twee is frowning. "But they'll be *diseased*," he says. "Who will pay to see a diseased body?"

He is thinking about our commission, of course. The plague — the Black Death — supplies corpses at no charge. Perhaps it will even supply *our* bodies. Mr. Twee and the doctor obviously haven't thought of that. Money is more important than life to them.

Mr. Twee is thinking fast. "That's not a reliable approach," he says. "You have to plan ahead if you are to present a really spectacular public anatomical show. You must have a certain body at a certain time. There have to be certainties if you are going to attract a crowd of people and give them value for their money."

The doctor says, "This will be just a rehearsal."

"It's more than that. You need to make a good impression if

you're going to get financing for the outdoor theater. It has to be a good show — more entertaining than the tired plays the visiting theatrical companies present." He is excited by his own words. "How many people will be entertained by pustules? By swollen torsos? By blackened limbs?" Mr. Twee turns to me. "No offense, Lenoir." In his own way, he is a considerate person.

Dr. Padmos shakes his head impatiently. "Then what's the alternative? Juju death? That's pagan superstition."

The doctor is not so considerate. Of course, he doesn't realize that he is paying me a compliment. For I am honored not to be one of the people who say there is only one god and then fight about what he is like. And as for superstition, I think that is only a term for common sense.

The doctor sees that I am undisturbed by his remark, and he tries again to upset me. "Dolls are for children."

"And what of *that* doll?" I ask, pointing to the doll that hangs on his wall — the doll of the dead man nailed to the crossed posts. "You pray to that doll for miracles. You even prefer it to Venus."

Mr. Twee interrupts, as he often does when I talk about the nonpagan religions. He says, "Let's try to be businesslike about this. Lenoir, you have to prove to us that your method works. How soon can you get the job done?"

"The killing?"

Dr. Padmos puts his finger to his lips. "*Shh.* Let's just call it 'the job.'"

The doctor, like many other people in this part of the world, apparently believes that an action changes if you change the words that describe it. I think that is one of the reasons there is so much talking here; people are trying to cover up bad deeds with good words.

Mr. Twee says, "Let's use a modern approach to this problem." He turns to me with a pretended serious look. "Lenoir," he says, "we'll give you a chance to do the job. You deliver the merchandise here, undamaged and freshly obtained, at midnight, one week from tonight. Can you do that?"

There's almost no chance I can do that. I say, "Oh, yes. Is there any particular type of merchandise you want, Dr. Padmos?"

"Any healthy specimen would be acceptable for this test," he says. "But for the actual event, the quantity of blood will be important. A book has been published stating that blood circulates through the body. Round and round. I wonder how to demonstrate that."

I am sure that Mr. Twee is thinking not about blood but about money. There is a term I have heard, *bloedgeld*, or blood-gold, that combines these two subjects. It is an important term in the nonpagan religions. While my friends talk business, I walk to the back of the room and look at a cleverly assembled human skeleton, which is suspended from an almost invisible cord. I touch the skeleton and watch it swing and rotate. These bones are the bones of a male. They are not as delicate as those of Jeanne, who would have had a longer, if less enjoyable, life if she had remained with the Sisters of Benedict.

When Mr. Twee and I return to the inn, we find that we have a visitor. He is dressed entirely in black, and I think he is a clergyman. But although he has great patience and enjoys smiling at people who are in distress, he turns out to be not a minister or pastor but a sheriff's assistant from the bankruptcy court.

"I am Mr. Vlieg," he says, in Dutch, and he hands a sheet of paper to Mr. Twee. "Your creditors, who are listed in this document, request you to appear in court in the morning."

Mr. Twee does not seem surprised. He says, coolly, "At ten o'clock, I suppose."

"Yes."

"You see how predictable you are. I can anticipate your every move."

Mr. Vlieg says, also coolly, "Your anticipations don't matter to me." He is a person whose dull face has only one good feature: a set of perfect, very white teeth, which I must admit I greatly envy. He looks around the room with a disrespectful smile. I remember Katja telling me that good teeth are important in her profession. Vlieg says, "I am obliged to warn you not to dispose of any of your property — such as it is — before your appearance in court."

It occurs to me that Mr. Twee does indeed have very few possessions. He does not own land or a house. I remind myself that aside from some clothes and a few paintings, Mr. Twee's principal possession is . . . me, Lenoir.

Mr. Twee is beginning to look angry, as though he would like to remove Mr. Vlieg's gleaming teeth. But he simply says, "You're completely without imagination, aren't you? You wouldn't be willing to lose track of this summons for a few days until a certain ship docks and brings something of value for my creditors, for me, and for Mr. Vlieg? Something worth a year's wages to Mr. Vlieg?"

Mr. Vlieg asks, "Shall I add attempted corruption of an official to the charges?"

Mr. Twee reaches suddenly under the bed and grabs the chamber pot. He throws it at Mr. Vlieg. "How about attempted shit staining of an official? Not that anyone would notice." The pot does not even come close to Mr. Vlieg, but he leaves quickly.

I ask Mr. Twee, "If these people had a chief, it wouldn't be necessary to try to bribe people like Mr. Vlieg. You could bribe the chief himself."

"The point is, Lenoir, I can't bribe anyone. No one will take a bribery offer seriously when it is being offered by someone who is bankrupt."

"I would think that in this land, having no money is enough punishment. Why punish you any further?"

"My creditors — the people I owe money to — will feel better if I am put in prison."

"And will you be able to make money in prison?"

"No."

"Then that is the real punishment."

Mr. Twee looks at me impatiently, but he is calmer. He says, "The punishment is the loss of freedom."

"Tell me again what freedom is."

"I am free because no one owns me, the way I own you, Lenoir."

I say, "Ah, yes." But I think that Mr. Twee is actually owned by his creditors, who are unpleasant people. I am fortunate to be owned by one silly person who wishes me well.

There is no sleep for us that night. Mr. Twee says, "Let's not rely on juju, Lenoir. Let's get the merchandise in one of the reliable, old-fashioned ways. Money in the bank." Then he drinks a great deal of cheap wine and demands that I play my drum for him. Nghana begins to shriek. The innkeeper threatens to evict us because of the noise. Mr. Twee assembles his collection of number-covered papers, puts them in the chamber pot, pisses on them, and collapses.

I make a doll and then go for an early-morning stroll.

In the brothel, the glass of the window has the delicate green of a plant emerging from the soil of the forest. Filtered through the window is the first sunlight, which for a few moments has a red-orange hue I have seen in some of Nghana's secret feathers.

The colors of the window light show themselves subtly on Sister Jeanne's deathly white skin, which is stretched tightly across her delicate skeleton. Her breasts are small, in the European fashion, and her body would seem completely boyish if it weren't for a roundness to her belly.

"The stars are fading," she says.

"Among my people the stars do not matter. There are too many of them and they are too much alike."

"If you know where to look, the stars will show you animals and people."

"Will they show you a snake?"

"Yes. The serpent. Walk out with me some night and I'll show you how to find it."

Among the Europeans, everyone is willing to teach one something. I don't bother to tell Jeanne that among my people, "to look at the stars" means to waste one's time.

I prefer to watch the light become stronger against Jeanne's body.

I say, "I have brought you a special gift." I hand her the doll. It is faceless and unclothed. Because it is made of plant root and boar's hair, it has great power, but the power is unclear. The power waits for me to give it shape.

Sister Jeanne takes the doll from me with obvious gratitude and clasps it to her chest. "It will be for my child," she says, almost in a whisper.

"You have a child?"

"I am *going* to have a child. Katja thinks it will come in the late summer. It was conceived while I was living among the Sisters of Benedict."

"How can that be? It cannot be that one of your sisters fathered your child."

"No. That cannot be."

"Then I have it. I was told that these sisters are brides of your God."

Jeanne nods sadly.

I say, "Then your child will be a child of your God."

"No. It will be a child of a man — a Brother of Benedict."

"I do not understand," I say.

"Nor do I, Lenoir."

I think it better not to do a sexual act with this young mother to be. I stroke her hair and her body, which is like a pale ghost of the body of my first wife.

"I wanted to love the church," Jeanne says.

"Is there anything that can't be loved by your people?"

"No. I don't think so."

"Then maybe your loves are like the stars. They have no meaning because there are so many of them."

Jeanne takes my hand and bites it. Then she does many sexual things to me, sobbing, and with the concentration of a serious child at play.

Later, she says, "It is the first time I have had sex with anyone."

"And what is it that the father of your child did; what is it that your customers do?"

"They have sex with me, not I with them."

At full light, I hear my name being shouted in the street outside the brothel by Mr. Twee. I lean out the window and get his attention with a hiss. I put my finger to my lips. As I put my clothing on, I look at Jeanne, who is sleeping soundly — Jeanne, who has been confused and betrayed by love.

I run down the stairs.

Mr. Twee stands at the brothel's entrance, grinning. "You were with Katja?" he asks.

"I was with Sister Jeanne, who is with child by one of Benedict's large family."

I thought Mr. Twee had not been listening carefully, but he pauses for a moment. "With child?" he says. "Interesting. A day of good fortune for me."

"Very recently it was a day of *mis*fortune, I believe."

Mr. Twee takes my hand and holds it before him, palm up. He holds a purse over my hand and pours guilders into it — enough guilders, I would think, to make his creditors stop threatening him for a time.

I say, "And what terrible thing has Mr. Twee done to fill his purse so quickly?"

He says, "Never mind that for now. Just feel the guilders; you're feeling power."

"I feel only a metal. A metal that tarnishes."

"It tarnishes when you don't use it, Lenoir."

"Have you killed someone, Mr. Twee?"

"No, no. Nothing illegal. Come home. I'll explain as we go."

As we walk, we are joined by a dog, an ugly white creature with piggish eyes. If there were loose stones lying about, as there would be in a normal country, I would throw one at the dog. Instead, I kick at the creature. "Go," I say. A boy appears and shouts at me, "Leave him alone, black shit." He calls to the dog: "Baxter!" and they go off together, both looking back occasionally. The boy makes insulting gestures.

I believe this encounter is an omen of great misfortune, and Mr. Twee confirms my belief by saying, "There is no easy way to put this, so I'll just come out and say it. But I want you to understand that it makes me unhappy. I hope it doesn't make you unhappy. Maybe it won't. Maybe you'll be pleased."

"You haven't yet said it, Mr. Twee."

"No. Well, it might be better if I explained why it was unavoidable."

I stop walking. "Say it, please, Mr. Twee."

Mr. Twee doesn't stop walking. He says something I cannot hear. I run forward and face him. "Say it."

He looks down at the paving stones. "I sold you."

"You *sold* me?"

"To Dr. Padmos."

"Dr. Padmos? Why Dr. Padmos?"

"He has the money. He wants you."

"What about Mr. Rembrandt?"

"He doesn't have the money."

"What about Anna van Cott? Or Katja?"

"It's done, Lenoir. I sold your contract of ownership to Dr. Padmos."

"Have you no honor?" I ask. We walk the rest of the way to the inn without speaking to each other.

In our room, I ask Mr. Twee, "Did the doctor pay a lot of money for me?"

Mr. Twee cannot resist talking about money, even if it is money that bought his friend and companion. He says, "A good price, Lenoir. You brought a good price." Mr. Twee knows that there is no use telling me specific amounts. "Best of all," he says, "I got some very old coins."

"You couldn't get new money for me?"

"I got new money, too. But the old money is worth more than the new money. And the old money has naughty pictures on it. Naughtiness is always valuable, especially in southern countries."

"Why can't we flee? To the south."

"The sale is made, Lenoir. Business is business. The doctor expects you to report to him today. I will report to the magistrate. Why don't you just pretend that I have died?"

"But you have not died. I will see you walking about, making your deals. Or are *you* going to flee and leave me here?"

Mr. Twee frowns and looks at the floor. So that is it. He will pay his debts and leave Amsterdam, leave me. But I cannot accept this arrangement. I am not interested in the activities of Dr. Padmos, this old medicine man. Perhaps my dead body will soon lie on a table before many followers of Calvin who have paid to watch the doctor remove my heart.

I say to Mr. Twee, "If we cannot flee together, I will flee alone."

Mr. Twee shakes his head from side to side. "You would be caught, Lenoir. You can't disguise yourself. The doctor would demand his money back, and you would become the property

of the court. I would be punished. You would be sold. It's better this way. If you are unhappy with the doctor, maybe you can
persuade him to sell your contract to someone you would find
acceptable. Or better still . . ."

A pleased expression appears on Mr. Twee's face. He pulls
me to my feet and embraces me. "I will buy you back . . . when
my shipment of cork comes in. I will buy you back from the
doctor for more than he paid for you. He will make a profit,
and you and I will be reunited."

What I know — and what Mr. Twee will not admit to himself — is that his shipment of cork will not come in or will not
bring him a profit.

And yet there is truth in what he said about my fleeing. I cannot disguise my dark beauty. And even if my appearance were
ordinary, this is a land in which a person who is without a home
or other expensive property is treated with great suspicion.

At least for now, I belong to Dr. Padmos.

I have a great urge to kill someone: Mr. Twee, or Dr. Padmos. But there is only one death that would end my troubles:
my own death, and I have no urge to bring that about. There is
no word for self-destruction in the language of my people. If I
were to do such a thing, I would disgrace my ancestors.

As daylight grows stronger, Mr. Twee begins looking
through some unframed pictures that are stacked in a corner. I
think again of the horrible things that have happened in the last
few hours. I recall something important. I say to Mr. Twee,
"Mr. Vlieg warned you not to dispose of any of your property.
And you have disposed of me."

"But Vlieg doesn't *know* that you were my property, Lenoir.
He thinks we are just friends."

"Or lovers."

"Whatever."

The source of Mr. Twee's troubles — and my troubles — is
money. I have been told that Calvin's people believe it is evil to

love money. And yet they love to accumulate money. There is something here I do not understand. But of course, my people did not believe in either love or money.

Mr. Twee is looking at the painting Mlle. van Cott gave to me. It occurs to me that the painting belongs to me. When Mr. Twee first bought me, he told me that since I belonged to him, nothing could belong to me. But now, I do not belong to him.

I say, "That painting belongs to me. Mlle. van Cott gave it to me."

Mr. Twee hesitates, and then hands it to me. I gather my few articles of clothing together and place them in a bag. I take my painting, my clothes, my drum, and Nghana's cage, and I start to walk from the room.

Mr. Twee asks me, "Don't you have anything to say to me?"

"Just one question. How much did Dr. Padmos pay for me?"

"Eight thousand guilders."

I thank him, and I leave the inn.

But instead of going to Dr. Padmos's house, I go to Mr. Rembrandt's studio. Without explaining my situation, I ask him how to find Mlle. van Cott's house. And I verify, for reasons of my own, that nine thousand guilders is more than eight thousand guilders and that it is a respectable sum.

# 7

I SAY TO THE HOUSEMAID, "Would you tell Mlle. Anna van Cott that her good friend Mr. Lenoir would like to speak with her?"

In a moment, a heavy but muscular man appears. His face, in the shadow cast by the brim of his large black hat, is rough and lined. He says, "I am Captain van Cott, Mlle. van Cott's father."

I decide in an instant that he likes me and that he is fond of unexpected situations. I say, "I am Lenoir. Would you like to buy me, sir? I am yours for nine thousand guilders."

Captain van Cott laughs.

Mlle. van Cott appears behind the captain. Is she amused by this undignified scene?

I cannot tell. My vision is obscured by my tears.

These are the first tears I have shed since my infancy, and they could not have come at a worse time. Tears do not make a good first impression.

I step back, waiting for Captain van Cott to slam the door in my tearful face, as I believe I would do in his place. Instead, he laughs again and says a word that astonishes me: "Bulu." It is a word from one of the languages I knew when I was being taken from my homeland. The language was called boat talk — a babyish language that did not belong to anyone but could be understood by most of us who were taken from our homes. The word meant "misfortune," and it was heard often.

Fortunately, in my astonishment, I stop weeping immediately. I say, in boat talk, the words that mean "Misfortune brought by people without color."

The captain says, in Walloon, "If you look at my daughter's paintings, you won't say we are without color. In her eyes, we all have scarlet faces."

"I have looked closely at many pictures. Your painters do not paint what they see. They try to deceive our eyes."

Captain van Cott is no longer listening. He is looking distractedly over my shoulder. I turn and see an old woman standing in the road staring at us.

The captain looks at me again. There is some impatience in his smile now. He is not beyond caring about what his neighbors think. He says, "I'm sure it would be interesting to have you in our household, Lenoir. But it wouldn't be appropriate. I thank you for the offer, but it's no sale."

Mlle. Anna steps around her father, takes my arm, pulls me into the foyer, and shuts the door. She says to her father, "You're thinking about my reputation. That's ridiculous."

The three of us go to the room that Mlle. Anna uses as a studio, and she begins to speak to her father: "This is much too peculiar a situation to dismiss casually. You know we'll both regret it if we pass over a chance to do something original."

The captain says, "Originality means more to a painter than to a sailor. Let me think for a minute."

Mlle. Anna winks at me.

After what I assume is exactly one minute, the captain says, "I don't want to own a person, and if I did own one, I would want him to be an experienced seaman." The captain turns to me. "Are you a good seaman, Lenoir?"

"Very bad."

"What are you good at?" the captain asks me.

I hesitate. I have been useful to Mr. Twee, but Mr. Twee's needs are not those of this sea captain and his daughter. Perhaps I am no use to anyone but Mr. Twee. I feel the tears returning to my eyes. Quickly, I say, "I am handsome, as you can see. A man of the world. A master of the drum and juju. A good medicine man. Good at seeing colors. A good listener, yet energetic. Yes, highly energetic."

"I suppose some of this energy is sexual," the captain says.

"You are worried that I would try to perform sex with Mlle. Anna. I would be pleased to, of course. But only on request."

"What I am worried about," the captain says, "is that I am away from my daughter for months at a time, and I am a widower; there is no Mrs. van Cott to look after Anna. I want my daughter to be safe."

Mlle. Anna says, "And you also want me to be happy, don't you, Father?"

The captain is silent for a time. Then he says, "I told you I would not be comfortable owning another person. I can afford to choose my cargo now, and I no longer choose to work on ships that carry human cargo. I won't own a person."

Mlle. Anna is smiling. "Then don't own a person. Set Lenoir free. Buy his ownership papers and burn them."

"No," I say. "I have thought about this, and I know I cannot be free here. One can only be free with one's own people. In this land, if I do not have an owner, I am not a person. I would soon be on a gibbet."

The captain says, "You're mistaken, Lenoir. We are a tolerant people."

Mlle. Anna frowns. "No, Father, he's right. If he's not owned, people will fear him."

"People are frightened of my juju," I say. "Dr. Padmos wants me to do frightening things for him."

Mlle. Anna smiles slyly and raises her hand for attention.

"The problem is solved," she says. "Lenoir, you will be my guard, my protector. When my father is away, you will keep me safe."

Mlle. Anna and I look at the captain.

"No," he says. He says it in a way that I imagine he has to many frightened crewmen. But Mlle. Anna is not frightened. She goes to him and puts her arms around him. His arms stay at his sides. She holds her body tightly against his and says to him, "Think about it tonight. Please." She holds him more tightly. He looks uncomfortable. She looks at me and says, "Come and see us again tomorrow. At noon."

The captain looks at me and shakes his head no. But he doesn't speak. I suppose he loves his daughter. And I suppose his daughter is using his love as a weapon against him. I will return tomorrow and see how strong a weapon it is.

In the meantime, I am possibly a free man but certainly a homeless one.

At sunset, I take my belongings and store them beneath a bridge at the edge of the city. The evening is warm. It has been too long since I bathed. I remove my clothes and wade out into the cold, rain-dappled water. After I am clean, I squat shivering beneath the bridge and wait for the clouds to vanish. My thoughts are confused. I wonder if Twee is also confused. (I no longer think of him as Mister.)

In the middle of the night, the moon and stars appear. I search the sky for the ancient animals and beings that Sister Jeanne says are there. For a time, I look for the sky serpent. But I am obviously wasting my time. The serpent exists only in the heads of the Europeans.

I forget the star pictures, and I am comforted to see instead what the people of my homeland see when they look at the night sky: the moon, which has a lesson to teach us. The moon is also confused. It has offended the gods by not obeying their teachings and has been doomed never to be able to decide which part of the sky to stay in or what shape to have.

I sing my song, first in my own language and then in the Walloon language:

> Don't think I won't come.
> The path before me
> is a crooked line.
> But I hope it will lead me to a safe end.
> The loss of my people
> has confused the route for me.
> Wish me well with neither hatred nor jealousy.

A dog barks in the distance.

At noon, I am once more at the door of the van Cott house. The housemaid's expression is less fearful than it was yesterday. "Come in, Lenoir," she says, in Dutch. "I'm Karin. I'll tell the captain you're here." She reaches for Nghana's cage. "Let me take the beautiful creature." Her hand touches mine.

Karin returns soon and leads me to Captain van Cott's study, where he and Mlle. Anna sit. She is smiling. The captain looks displeased but resigned. I think love has defeated him. "Sit down, Lenoir."

I lower myself to the edge of an unsteady-looking chair that is carved to look as if flowers are growing in it. The chair is an example of the strange things that can happen when people are unwilling to simply squat on their heels.

The captain says, "I have spoken to Dr. Padmos about your ownership, Lenoir. We haven't reached a final decision, but until we do, the doctor doesn't mind if you stay as a guest in my house."

"But *I* would mind. I am not a guest in your country. I cannot be a guest in your house."

The captain looks at me impatiently. I think he does not dislike me but wishes I had not come to his door. Finally, he nods.

"I think I can see your point. And if you cannot be a guest, perhaps you should leave."

"Your house or your country?" I ask.

"Both. Go back to your homeland. I'm sure I could arrange it for you."

Before I can again say no, Mlle. Anna says to her father, "There's no need for that kind of talk. Lenoir can stay here as an employee — as my protector."

I am too tired to resist this offer. I hear rain being blown heavily against the windows. I don't want to spend another night under the bridge. I put out my hand to the captain. He takes it in his. "I am your servant, sir," I say.

I bow to the captain's daughter. "I am your servant and protector, Mlle. Anna."

She says, "You will have spare time, Lenoir. Maybe I could teach you to read."

Although I try to control myself, I think a look of alarm shows in my face.

Mlle. Anna, who is an understanding person, says, "Do what pleases you, Lenoir. But for now, I have an assignment for you. We will have a banquet next Friday at the inn to celebrate the return of a friend of the captain's. Maybe it will also be a celebration of your becoming free. You might want to invite your friends to attend: Mr. Twee, if he is not in prison; Dr. Padmos; a special woman friend, perhaps."

The idea delights me, although I can see that the captain is not pleased. I say, "And Mr. Rembrandt, if I may."

The captain asks Anna, "What about that Flinck person?"

"No. We've had a disagreement. But I will invite Jean, of course. He should get to know Lenoir."

"Jean?" I ask.

The captain says, "Jean Guelfe. A young man from whom my daughter doesn't want to be protected."

"It will be a pleasure to meet him." In truth, I think there will be no pleasure in it for me or for Mr. Guelfe.

"For now, Lenoir," the captain says, "Karin will show you to your room." I am sure he is wondering, as I am, why his daughter wants to have me in her household.

Karin leads me up a narrow, winding staircase — a pleasing structure that I have seen many versions of in the houses of Holland. We go through several rooms, some of which are on slightly different levels from others. My room is next to and, I'm pleased to see, somewhat larger than Karin's. She places Nghana's cage gently on a table near the window. I realize now that the affection I sense in her is for the parrot and not for me. Though my pride is injured, I am pleased for my pet, who is always seeking affection.

There is the usual too-small, curtained box to sleep in, but it contains a well-stuffed bag of feathers. I climb into the bed and smile up at Karin. She leaves the room.

As I get up and begin to unpack my belongings, the captain enters the room. He says, "You're not the kind of person who has regrets about his life, are you?"

"No, Captain."

"Nor am I. But I think Anna might be able to devote her life to sorrow. She regrets that her mother is dead. Otherwise, I have arranged it so that there has been nothing for her to regret. I have given her what she wants, and her wants have usually been sensible, if not always conventional." The captain grasps my upper arm and squeezes. He is dangerously strong. He says, "You won't give her reason for regret, will you, Lenoir?"

"Lenoir will not. But Lenoir cannot control the gods."

The captain smiles. "Leave the gods and the magistrates to me."

When I leave to invite my friends to the banquet, Mlle. Anna smiles at me, and the captain's glance is more friendly than it was earlier. They are substantial in a way that no person in my home village — not even the chief — could ever be. For the captain, storms at sea or the death of a wife are interruptions in the banquet. To my people, the banquet is an interruption in the storms and deaths.

I think of last night and my hours beneath the stars. I wonder if I was more comfortable crouched beneath the bridge than I am standing on the black-and-white squares of the captain's floor. I believe I miss the disorderly world of Twee.

Going to the bankruptcy court in Amsterdam is like going to a theater — one in which comedies, not tragedies, are being performed. Above the fireplace in the entrance hall is a large picture showing a winged person judging people and sending them either to a place of order, where they wear hats and white collars, or to a place of confusion, where their straight, dirty hair and their fat necks are revealed. In my homeland, we also were visited by winged people, but ours were people that flew at dusk and carried unwary villagers away. No one knew where the flying people took their victims, but we didn't think it was to a place of order.

Standing in the entrance hall of the court building are small groups of people who don't seem to be worried about being judged. They speak mostly in Dutch, but I can hear several other languages. In one of the groups is Mr. Vlieg, of the sheriff's office. He tells me that Twee will be meeting with creditors most of the day but that he will not be imprisoned or mutilated. My former owner is living once again at the inn, where I will try to see him later.

In the meantime, I go to Dr. Padmos's office. He does not mention that he may own me at the moment or that he may be going to make a large profit by having owned me for a short time. In a sense, I am more comfortable with the doctor's unsentimental, businesslike attitude toward me than I am with Mlle. Anna's mysterious affection. When I invite the doctor to the banquet, he says, "I don't approve of banquets." His stringy body has already told me that. He goes on speaking, more to himself than to me: "Dr. Tulp, who's more interested in government now than in medicine, has sponsored laws restricting the size of banquets. Excess is becoming unfashionable. And it's unhealthy, I believe."

"This banquet is given by Captain van Cott. I'm sure you don't want to displease him."

"I'll attend — and I assume, Lenoir, that you and I will still be able to do medical business together regardless of who owns you."

"Certainly."

"What about the merchandise we talked about?"

"That was between you and Mr. Twee."

"A contract is a contract."

"I don't know of any contract."

The doctor looks at me pleadingly, but without respect. "I need that merchandise."

I am about to say I can no longer help him when I realize that I need some new clothes. "We'll talk about it at the banquet."

He goes to his herbal cupboard and brings me a dried plant. He drops it in my lap. "This is poisonous, isn't it?" he asks.

I have never seen such a plant before. "How could it be otherwise?"

The plant is black.


"Will they have that Pérignon wine?" Mr. Rembrandt asks. "The one that tastes like stars?"

"I can't say."

"Saskia won't be able to come with me. Will I know anyone?"

"Perhaps. And I am sure there will be some people it would be profitable for you to know."

"Yes. All right."

But I think Mr. Rembrandt will be more interested in Katja than in wealthy merchants.

I stop at Katja's house on the chance that she might have arisen early. Fortunately, there are no red tulips in her ground-floor window, which means that she is available for social calls. When the flowers appear there, she is open for business.

She asks me, "Do I look like a *huisvrouw*, Lenoir? A *femme d'intérieur?* Like a woman in those silly paintings that everyone does — a woman sitting near the window, reading a letter? I should have a map on the wall."

"I will bring you a map. I'm sure Captain van Cott has many of them. I now work for that gentleman."

"Well, that's an improvement over that hustler Twee. And you'll have Anna's company."

"You know Anna?"

"And I know the captain. I was taken for a boat ride by him and painted by her. She works faster than he does. They both know what they're doing."

I invite Katja to the banquet and tell her that Sister Jeanne and Uba would also be welcome.

Twee, as I knew he would be, is overjoyed to be invited to the banquet. "I love a party," he says. "It is our greatest invention. Have a little fun. Make a few connections, do a little business. Lenoir, if someone asked me to tell the story of my life, I'd tell them about the parties I've attended."

"My story would be short if I told it that way."

"Your best parties lie ahead, Lenoir. Stay in touch with me, my friend."

On the night of the banquet, I find myself greatly excited. The proprietor of the inn has prepared a private room for the event. He brings platters containing shelled sea creatures and roasted animals and fish of various kinds, many of which I have never seen before. There are new kinds of beer and wine, including the wine that tastes like stars, which Mr. Rembrandt likes so much.

Many more than nine people — my friends as well as important-looking strangers — are at the table. Uba is here, looking more like the handsome women of my village than she had previously.

Before we sit down at the table, I see Captain van Cott talking to Dr. Padmos in a corner. After we are seated, I find myself across from the captain and Mlle. Anna. She winks at me.

The captain stands and takes out of his belt a handsome knife that has a handle someone says is made from the tooth of a vast fish. Banging the knife against the side of a tankard, the captain says, "The purpose of this gathering is first to welcome my friend Captain Wyck back from his long voyage and second to welcome Lenoir, who is a newly freed man, to the staff of the van Cott household. That is all I have to say."

As I try to overcome the feeling of terror that is sweeping over me, people raise their glasses to me and smile. The captain does not look at me, but he seems happy, and I suspect he has had more than one drink of rum. He suddenly stands and begins singing an undignified sailor's song:

> Rhenish wine, French wine,
> brandywine, and ale.
> These in my gut,
> a breeze in the sail.

Anna looks fondly at her father and says he is a bad singer. I say to the captain, "Sir, in my land we would not say you are a bad singer. We would say you sing with two tones. But that is not bad, for many of our songs also have two tones."

The captain does not smile but looks respectfully at me and says, "Thank you, Lenoir."

"Thank *you*, sir."

The captain nods and begins talking to his friend Captain Wyck, who sits next to him.

Twee quickly consumes most of a roasted fowl and many glasses of Rhenish wine. He takes me aside and, with tears in his eyes, says, "I will buy you back, Lenoir, my friend. Soon. We'll resume our journeys. Get out of this unimaginative land."

Then, drying his eyes on the ruffles of his shiny yellow shirt, Twee departs with a young sailor who has been sitting next to him and who is a stranger to me.

Dr. Padmos, after sipping a common ale and eating a potato, stops by to whisper in my ear, "Merchandise. Remember the merchandise. Come see me tomorrow." He puts a potato in his pocket and departs, glancing at me and nodding his head toward Uba.

Tobacco smoke is beginning to fog the room. Over the aroma of the roasted meats one can smell the perspiration of heavily clothed bodies. I notice that Uba is eating cabbage. Her skin glistens. She loosens the laces of her bodice. I remember banquets in my village, when bodies were only lightly draped, more for mystery than modesty, when the food was simple cassava.

I sing a song:

> Woman, if you want a calm and gentle man,
> pay a visit to Lenoir.
> No trouble, no bad words from the chief.
> Just true happiness.

While I sing, I tap the rhythm on the table.

After hearing the song only one time, Katja joins in with me and sings it perfectly. While we are singing, Uba says something to the captain and leaves. After our song, Katja says to me, "You should be kinder to Uba. Your kindness would mean more to her than ours."

"Sometimes it is hard to be kind to someone you know too well."

"It is also hard to be kind to someone you don't know at all. Uba and I both understand that."

"Are you and Uba friends?"

"More like colleagues. But I know she longs for her home. I think she'll go back there someday."

"Once you leave a home, it is no longer your home, Katja."

"Then is Amsterdam your home?"

"It is my parrot's home."

"Then your parrot is happier than you are?"

"My parrot lives in a cage."

After guests begin departing and the captain is having trouble staying awake, Mr. Rembrandt produces some sheets of paper and sticks of charcoal. He gives some of them to Mlle. Anna. Then he kisses Katja and asks her to sit on a table, around which he arranges some candles. She raises her skirts slightly, smiles, and leans back on one arm. Although Katja's pose is not much different from one that might be struck by one of the more proper women who are at the table, it is very exciting to me.

Anna and Mr. Rembrandt quickly make pictures of Katja. Can it be that they do not have all the spirit they want and must copy the spirit of their model? As my former owner Twee knows, there are people who would buy these pictures and would even pass them on to their children and their children's children as reminders of the spirit of Katja on this drunken evening. Twee says the people who buy pictures of Venus often develop the condition called love.

\*

As Mlle. Anna and I help her father walk unsteadily out of the tavern after the banquet, I notice that one of the pictures of Katja has fallen on the floor. I pick it up and place it in the pocket of the captain's jacket.

Before I sleep, as I lie on my bed of feathers, I try to remember the events that have led me here. I try to explain to myself how the happenings of this day will change my life. But I find I cannot think of myself. I can think only of certain delicate colors. Then I realize that the colors are those that I saw on the skin of Sister Jeanne. I wonder if Mlle. Anna could make a picture of Jeanne for me. I think it would be good for both me and Anna to borrow some of that young woman's spirit. Jeanne is becoming my Venus.

# 8

KARIN PLACES a blue bowl on the table before Anna, who puts a piece of white bread into the bowl and pours thick, yellowish milk over it. Karin pours fragrant, almost black coffee into two smaller bowls and gives one to Anna and one to me. The room is bright with morning sun.

Anna holds her palms against the bottom of the coffee bowl for a few moments, then raises her warmed hands to the pale skin at the base of her throat. I think the sun has never shone on that skin. She is wearing a collarless, dark blue robe that reveals her throat but stops well short of her bosom. Her long hair, which is twisted and pinned close to her head, is a brown so dark that it might seem as black as mine by candlelight. I wonder if she is beautiful by the odd standards of the flatlander men, who seem to think that a beautiful woman is not the same thing as a sexually attractive woman. I think she is both beautiful and arousing, but I am wise enough to know I must ignore both those things. I must see only her intelligence, kindness, and good humor. I am sure I will find that she is not the perfect person she now seems to be. But as her servant, I will respect her flaws as I did those of Twee.

She smiles at me for a moment in what might be embarrassment, probably sensing the esteem I have for her. She says,

"This is the arrangement we would like to make with you, Lenoir: You may sleep here and share our meals whenever you like. When my father is here in Amsterdam — when he is not away on a voyage or a business trip — you may do as you please most of the time. But when Father is away — which will be often — I would like you to be available to me. Generally, I'll want you to go on errands or to be my escort. We won't be able to pay you a salary, I'm afraid."

I say, "I will need clothing and boots. I don't want you to be ashamed of your protector's appearance."

"There will be time for you to earn some money by working for someone else — Mr. Twee, perhaps."

"Oh, I don't think Twee would want to pay me even if he could afford it. But Dr. Padmos might pay for my help."

"Then our offer is acceptable?"

"Certainly. You and the captain are most generous."

"And what about language?" Anna asks. "I take it you would prefer to speak in Walloon French?"

"Yes."

"But you will need to practice your Dutch. So I will speak Dutch to you, and you may reply in French."

"Excellent. I will be proud to be in your service. And, of course, I will be pleased to model for your pictures — even without my clothing if that should become necessary."

Anna smiles at me. I would say it is still a fond smile. She says, "I don't think that will be necessary, Lenoir. But our family motto is 'One never knows.'"

"If my family had a motto, it would be 'One usually knows.'"

"And yet here you are."

"Yes. Quite true. Here I am."

Where I am is in a room that has books where the walls should be. Some of the books are covered in red-and-gold leather that would make fine boots. Anna notices my envious look but doesn't understand it. "You could easily learn to read, Lenoir. I'd be glad to teach you."

"It is not a matter of easy or not easy. It is a matter of danger."

"What danger could there be in reading?" Anna asks.

"One never knows," I say.

But I wonder if one of these books is *The Ingenious Gentleman Don Quixote of La Mancha.*

On my way to see Dr. Padmos, I stop in the market square, as I frequently do, to listen to the people discuss the public announcements that are posted there. Today they are talking excitedly about the new demonstration that Dr. Padmos will be presenting in his little Anatomical Theater. As the main attraction in the demonstration, the doctor plans to dissect the corpse of a pregnant woman and pass the unborn child around for the spectators to examine. The presentation is to be called "Life — God's Miracle."

Most of the people I overhear pretend to disapprove of the planned show. But as they speak, their eyes glitter with excitement. I sometimes think these people have too great an interest in death. Yet at the moment, the plague cart passes in the distance, carrying the morning's collection of victims. The cart avoids the square so as not to attract attention, but everyone who is not deaf hears it rumble over the cobblestones, and even the beggar who is deaf and blind shows by the flare of his nostrils that the cart's stench has not escaped him. The beggar, like most of the men about me, probably spent some months or years on corpse-littered battlefields. One is not allowed to forget death in this country. In the churches, it is apparently taught that a new, better life can follow death. In my homeland, such a thought would have been laughed at. Death was discussed only by the chief and a few elders; it was not something for general conversation, and it was not considered entertaining.

In Dr. Padmos's waiting room, I encounter Twee. "Lenoir," he says. "My savior. You saved me from prison. I won't soon forget it."

A moment later, he has forgotten it. He says, "Did you hear about the new Padmos show? The miracle of life show?"

"Everyone is talking about it. Everyone wants to see it," I say. I am exaggerating because I suspect it is his idea.

Twee points a thumb at his chest and nods his head. "Mr. Twee's idea," he says.

I say, "Will Twee also supply the merchandise for the exhibit?"

"You know that's not my line of work, Lenoir. That's what I'm here to arrange with Padmos. You couldn't have come at a better time."

While we wait to see the doctor, we find we have little to say to each other. I wonder whether the young sailor spent the night with Twee.

Cries of pain emerge from the doctor's examining room. And soon an unbelievably pale man emerges from the room. His white ruff is spattered with blood.

When we enter Dr. Padmos's office, he is putting leeches into a jar. His hands are wet with fresh blood. He smiles. "Welcome, my friends." He takes some collapsed tulips from a vase and throws them into a corner. He pours the vase's foul-smelling water over his hands and wipes them on the skirts of his robe. "Let's do some business," he says.

I half-listen while the two men discuss numbers: the number of spectators they can fit into the small surgical theater they have reserved in an old gate tower, the price they will be able to charge for admission to the demonstration. This gives them an amount called their income, from which their expenses must be deducted to reach the most magical number: the profit.

When they begin discussing expenses, I give them my full attention, for my name is mentioned. The doctor says, "One expense I am not sure of, Lenoir, is the cost of obtaining the merchandise for the demonstration."

"Why ask me?"

"Mr. Twee tells me you have great influence over a certain young mother-to-be called Jeanne."

"I don't know what my influence is. But I know she is not merchandise."

Twee says, "A whore is usually considered merchandise."

"She is a sister of the god Benedict."

Twee and the doctor look at each other and smile. Twee says, "Then you won't help us, Lenoir?"

"I will help you in some way. I must have some new clothing. But I cannot help with Jeanne."

"But it's Jeanne we want," the doctor says.

I shake my head.

The doctor looks at his hands and sniffs them. "Then there's no deal," he says.

"Some other merchandise," I suggest. "I could obtain someone else. Someone much larger."

Twee says, "There's no time to find the right person — someone who's pregnant, who won't be missed."

"Jeanne will be missed."

"Not by anyone who will complain."

I try again: "Why must there be an unborn child?"

The doctor says, "Our people are fond of children."

"I have not noticed such a thing," I reply. "You and Twee don't have children. No one I know has children, and no one wants to have them except Mr. Rembrandt." I am angry. I stand up.

Twee stands too, and embraces me. "Be calm, my old friend," he says. "Leave this matter to us. You can help us with other matters." He pulls out a purse from under a new cloak he is wearing. "In the meantime, here is something on account." He hands me a few coins that would probably not even buy a decent shirt.

Dr. Padmos says, "Come and see me after the presentation, Lenoir. We will work something out."

As I leave the doctor's office, I see Mr. Vlieg, the sheriff's man, lurking a few doors away. I assume he is waiting to follow Twee. After I walk a block or so, however, I become aware that Mr. Vlieg is following me. I decide to ignore him, for I have nothing to hide from him or anyone else. I am a well-behaved, free person.

On my way back to the van Cott house, I encounter a man who is displaying some old books along the top of a short wall. I pick up a small volume and run my fingers over its stained leather cover. I open it and admire the neat blocks that the black words form on the white paper.

The man asks me if I am looking for something in particular. "Yes," I say. "Do you have a book entitled *The Ingenious Gentleman Don Quixote of La Mancha?* In the French language?"

"Of course, of course," the proprietor says, and reaches for a book with no front cover and many bent pages. It is much smaller than the book Twee used to read to me from. I bargain with the proprietor until he agrees to let me have the book for the coins Twee has just given me.

When I get to my new home, Mr. Vlieg stands at the end of the street. I frown at him before I go through the door. He flashes his teeth at me.

I find Anna in her studio. She is smoking a long-stemmed clay pipe. I raise my eyebrows in surprise. "Medicine," she says. "They say the plague is fended off by tobacco."

"That would not surprise me," I say.

I do not want to discuss the kind of medicine that is practiced by foolish men like Dr. Padmos. To change the subject, I hold up my new book and say to Anna, "Perhaps you could read to me from this occasionally."

She looks at the book and then looks at me. "From a book of prayers, Lenoir?"

I cover my confusion by saying, "I am making a joke."

Occasionally I forget that one cannot trust these people.

"Stay with me, while I work," Anna says. She is making a foolish picture of some household objects arranged on a table. She works carefully, holding her pipe in one hand and a brush in the other, mixing paints on the top of a little table. Her hair is hanging down her back, almost to her waist, gathered by a golden loop at her neck. As she works, I think of my homeland, where the men believe there are few things more satisfying to see than a woman at work.

After a few minutes, during which I look more often at Anna than at her painting, she says, "Father is going away tomorrow. To Haarlem. For a week or so. He'll expect you to be in the house whenever I'm here alone." She pauses to place a thin line of blue-white against — naturally — a black background. An empty glass tumbler is appearing miraculously in the picture. I say to Anna, "Picture making is like magic." She nods in agreement. "But," I continue, "it is a magic with no purpose, I believe." She does not answer. "In my homeland, magic always has a purpose; it makes people sick or well; it makes them live or die. It is not for amusement."

Anna continues to paint, but she says, "It isn't just amusement, Lenoir. Paintings have meanings, hidden meanings. This empty tumbler, for example, has a sexual meaning. It is something to be filled." As she draws the brush carefully across the picture, she takes a deep breath and holds it. Her breasts rise and push against the laces of her bodice. She exhales and says, "Mr. Guelfe — Jean — will visit me occasionally. There's no need for you to be here at those times, if there are other things you want to do."

"Very good." But I do not think it is very good. She doesn't want me to hear this Guelfe person grunting and puffing over her — or behind her — or under her — or whatever they do.

She continues making the picture. The more she does to it, the less purpose it seems to have. Eventually she says, "Mr. Guelfe will be spending the night here tomorrow, I think."

"Excellent," I say. "There is a young woman I must give a warning to."

Anna smiles. "An all-night warning, Lenoir?"

"She will want to thank me for the warning, I believe."

*

After breakfast the next morning, Anna lights her pipe.

The captain says, "That's an unnecessary stink, Anna."

"Dr. Padmos says it will prevent the plague."

"And *I* say that *Padmos* is a plague. I've seen cartloads of tobacco smokers dead of the plague. Or maybe they're dead of tobacco. Smoke if you *like* to smoke. That's the only good reason to do anything. But don't do it just because that charlatan recommends it."

Then Anna and I accompany her father in the carriage that takes him to the boat that will take him to the nearby city of Haarlem, in which — according to Twee — there are many makers of bad pictures and in which an African person would not enjoy living. When we enter the carriage, he asks, "Who is that weasel who is lurking at the corner, Lenoir?"

I say, without hesitation, "That is Mr. Vlieg of the sheriff's office. I don't why he is lurking, but I suppose it is part of his job." I hope the captain is impressed with my knowledge.

We pass one of many large posters, illegally placed (probably by Twee), which I am told announce the upcoming anatomy lesson. The captain says, "Lechery hiding behind Latin."

Anna says, "You'll probably find the same kind of displays in Haarlem. They're a sensation. Padmos has asked Rembrandt to paint the exhibition that's coming up here." And then Anna looks slyly at the captain. "I thought I might go to see this one. It's helpful for a painter to understand anatomy."

"It's also helpful for a painter to understand how charlatans exploit people's lower impulses. But go if you will. Just be sure to take Lenoir along."

Anna puts her hand on mine for a moment and says, "I hope I'm not going to corrupt you, Lenoir."

I smile even though I think Anna has just made her first insincere statement to me.

When Mr. Guelfe arrives, I leave the house so that he may be alone with Anna.

I think I must expand my circle of friends. When I was with Twee, I seldom had time of my own, and then only when I asked for it. I realize now that with my new life I must find people who would be willing to share their time with me. At the moment, the people who are closest to being my companions are the women who work at the brothel. But it is sometimes difficult to make it clear to them that my visits are social and not professional. In any case, I do not have the money for a professional call. Nevertheless, I decide to go and knock at Katja's door and perhaps spend some time with Sister Jeanne.

As I enter the building, an increasingly familiar figure is leaving: It is Mr. Vlieg. I am sure he cannot have been here for pleasure. Most likely he has been threatening to arrest someone. Now that I consider it, I don't know how he could be here at all, for I believe I saw him on the street a minute or two ago. Is he a devil who can be in two places at once?

Katja seems genuinely happy to see me. We sit on the edge of her bed, and I say, "Is Jeanne able to read?"

"Yes."

"Perhaps you can give this to her." I hand Katja the prayer book I mistakenly bought.

"She couldn't read this, though. This is in Dutch. She doesn't read Dutch. She reads French."

"And *you* can read Dutch, Katja?"

She opens the prayer book at random and reads slowly and haltingly:

> We humbly commend the soul of this thy servant, our dear brother, into thy hands, as into the hands of a faithful Creator, and most merciful Savior; most humbly beseeching thee that it may be precious in thy sight. Wash it, we pray thee, in the blood of that immaculate Lamb, that was slain to take away the sins of the world; that whatsoever defilements it may have contracted in the midst of this miserable and naughty

world, through the lusts of the flesh or the wiles of Satan, being purged and done away, it may be presented pure and without spot before thee; through the merits of Jesus Christ thine only Son our Lord. Amen.

I say, "There is much I don't understand in those words."

"There's a lot I don't understand either," Katja replies.

"Perhaps you got some of the words wrong. The brother, would that be Brother Benedict? What is it again that is done with the lamb's blood?"

"Never mind those things, Lenoir. It's right about one thing; there are definitely lusts of the flesh. That is definitely true."

"And is it right about the world being miserable and naughty?"

"I think maybe you'd better take those kinds of questions to Sister Jeanne. But maybe not tonight. She's not well."

"Is it something serious?"

"I don't think so," Katja says. "It may just be the effects of her last encounter — which was governmental, not sexual."

"I saw Mr. Vlieg leaving."

"Yes. He does not improve the morale — or the income — of my staff. But if I didn't cooperate with him, I could find myself out of business."

"What does Mr. Vlieg want from Jeanne?" I ask.

"Trouble. But probably not for Jeanne or me. The two things that interest Mr. Vlieg are trouble and punishment. What he gets from women is information, not pleasure."

Katja extends her arms toward me and puts her hands on the back of my neck. She says, in a whisper, "But you like a little pleasure along with your information, don't you, Lenoir?"

"The pleasure I would like now is a visit with Sister Jeanne."

Katja looks displeased. "You know, Jeanne is not really here to talk to people."

"Do not be jealous," I say. "She is our friend. I will make her well with my juju."

Katja is smiling now. "That's what they all say, Lenoir. Only they don't call it their juju."

Sister Jeanne's room is dark. The heavy drape is drawn across the window, and a single candle is burning. She is naked, lying on the floor, her knees pulled up to her stomach, her arms around her knees. I think she tries to smile at me, but her face shows only pain. I say, "It is not yet time for the child, is it?"

She closes her eyes and shakes her head. There are no pale colors against her body now as there were when we were first together. Now there are deep shadows that emphasize her paleness. I kneel beside her and put my hand on her forehead. I say, "You will soon be well. Your child will be well. I have come to tell you that if you wish, I will act as the child's father."

Jeanne's eyes do not open. Tears begin to flow from beneath her eyelids.

Perhaps the prayer book is right. Perhaps it is a naughty, miserable world.

The doll I made for Jeanne is on the floor next to her. I take it in my hand and ask it and the serpent-god to make Sister Jeanne well.

As I walk home, I drop the prayer book in a canal.

My life in the van Cott household is kept from being pleasant by my concern for Sister Jeanne. But life is very pleasant for Nghana the parrot. Two weeks ago I would have said *my* parrot, not *the* parrot. But Nghana's heart now belongs to Karin. He has completed a molt that began before the spring months arrived, and his feathers have a new sleekness and brilliance. He wants only to sit on Karin's shoulder and run his dry, black tongue along the rim of her ear. I watch as his scaly feet clutch the muscle of her shoulder. As the needle-sharp points of his claws pierce the wool of her dress, she winces and brings her hand to the shoulder. When she brings the hand away, there is blood on her fingers. She is teaching Nghana new words — words that he doesn't scream out but mutters softly to his new friend.

Twee once told me that when a parrot is in love with someone, it will regurgitate its food for that person. I have seen Karin look secretly into the palm of her hand and smile.

Dr. Padmos's anatomical demonstration is being spoken of by everyone, partly through the efforts of Twee, who has cleverly persuaded many prominent citizens to condemn the event as unacceptable to the God of the naughty world. But because Padmos is a doctor, he is able to claim that what he is doing is scientific, and science is sometimes allowed to be naughty.

The theater consists of a small, round room with a platform in its center. The platform is surrounded by seats on rising levels. Twee arranged — for a price that made Anna gasp — to reserve seats for her and me in the center and front, just behind Mr. Rembrandt, who has set up an easel with charcoal sticks, brushes, paints, and many large pieces of paper.

It is a cloudless day, and the half-risen sun shines brilliantly and clearly through the room's many small windows. But soon, the usual fog of tobacco smoke accumulates, its aroma blending with the smells of ale, wine, and unwashed bodies. I believe Anna is the only woman in the audience — a situation that I suspect does not displease her.

The audience gradually becomes impatient and noisy. Men who have had too much to drink begin to stamp their boots on the floor. I doubt whether their behavior is scientific.

Then four young men enter the room. They are carrying a long, wide plank draped with a white sheet that obviously conceals a body. The room quickly becomes silent. The young men place the body, feet forward, on a table and leave the room. Murmurs begin.

Then Dr. Padmos enters. He stands at the side of the table and takes the edge of the sheet in his hand. He is wearing a new black suit, glossy black boots, a clean ruffed shirt, and a black cloak lined with red silk. I suspect much of the proceeds from the ticket sales will go to the doctor's newfound tailor.

"The human body," he says, "is one of God's great miracles. And the way God has chosen to reproduce the human body is complex and mysterious. We are gathered here today to come closer to God by coming to a better understanding of the way a new life is formed in the female body." The doctor pauses. He has been speaking Dutch, occasionally also using a word or two in Latin.

The room is absolutely silent. Then he continues, in a confidential voice, "I don't think there is any need for me to comment on the events that lead up to the creation of a new life." There are not as many laughs as the doctor had probably expected. If the rest of the audience is staring as intently as I am at the doctor's hand at the edge of the sheet, they will not pay much attention to his words.

Then the doctor drops his hold on the sheet and turns away to another table on which are displayed odd knives and other instruments. He picks up a knife that has a short, shiny blade. He returns to the other table, takes the edge of the sheet in his free hand, and pulls it slowly from the table, letting it fall to the floor.

On the table lies the body of a slender young woman. My eyes travel slowly upward along the body, not wanting to show me what I know in an instant: It is the bloodless corpse of Sister Jeanne, who is free from this miserable and naughty world. God will presumably wash her soul in the blood of the Lamb — although no one bothered to wash the soles of her feet.

I rise and leave the room. I do not want to see Jeanne's unborn child, the child of Brother Benedict. And in any case, my tears will not allow me to see. But they do not prevent me from hearing the laughter that accompanies my quick departure.

Then I notice that I am not alone. Walking just in back of me is Mr. Rembrandt. As he pushes past me, he says, "My wife gave birth to a dead child three months ago." He begins to run, and as he reaches the stairway, he vomits. I wait until he has recovered, and I follow him down the stairs.

When we are outside, Rembrandt quickly disappears along one of the small streets off the square. I stand holding my hands over my face for a time, wondering if I could have felt love for Jeanne. When I remove my hands from my eyes, I find myself facing Mr. Vlieg, who says, "I wonder if we could go somewhere and talk about the death of Sister Jeanne."

At any other time I would have refused to speak to this person. But I am unsettled. And I am inquisitive.

Soon we are seated on a bench before a bed of deep scarlet tulips glowing so dazzlingly in the sunlight that I must close my eyes against them. Even with my eyes closed, I still see the scarlet color.

"The flowers are the color of fresh blood," the weasel Vlieg says.

I look at him angrily. As he speaks, his teeth glint in the sunlight. And I notice that his eyes are not both the same color. How could I, who am proud of knowing colors, not have noticed this before? It is a disfigurement that would be inconceivable among my people, whose eyes are all exactly the same dark color. But this Vlieg has one eye the color of horse droppings and another the color of an unripe apple. It could only be an ill omen, and I am surprised that the midwife allowed him to survive. Obviously the reason he whitens his teeth is to distract one's attention from his eyes.

Vlieg opens a large leather pouch that hangs by a strap from his shoulder. He removes the doll I gave Jeanne. He says, "Did you not make this doll?"

"No," I say. As is usual when I try to deceive someone, I cannot help smiling in an odd, strained way.

"The woman Uba says it is the kind of doll you make; and it is the kind of doll a witch-man can use to cast a spell on someone."

"Uba is from people who betray their neighbors for pieces of colored glass and who eat shit."

"I don't care about her diet. I want to know if the black arts were used to cause the death of the young woman Jeanne. We do not encourage the practice of the black arts in the city of Amsterdam."

"A black skin and the black arts do not necessarily go together. I know about your white witches." Actually, all I know about the white witches is that they are usually women, that they are often displayed with their heads and hands locked in the three-holed pillory or are seen dangling from the gibbet rope. But I remind myself that I have no guilt in this matter and that there is no need for me to defend myself. I say, "If you want to know about this woman's death, you should ask Dr. Padmos. I would never have harmed her. I have tried to make her well."

"What I am concerned with is not the woman's death but the *cause* of her death."

"What does the doctor say about the cause?"

"The doctor is stupid and dishonest."

"Perhaps you think I am also those things."

"*Most* people are those things."

"But you are not?"

"I am not stupid. The doctor says Sister Jeanne died of the plague. But I have seen people die of the plague, and she did not die in that way."

Although it pains me, I say, "Her death is of no interest to me." I don't know what else to say. I don't understand what kind of man this is. There are too many different kinds of people in this country, just as there are too many colors of eyes.

"I thought you were a special friend of Sister Jeanne's," Mr. Vlieg says. His face, which has had too much of the infrequent but strong springtime sun, reflects the scarlet of the tulips that surround us. His skin is the color of Satan's cloak, which I have seen in pictures that Twee calls old-fashioned.

When I don't respond, Mr. Vlieg continues, "Do you make dolls for just anyone, Mr. Lenoir?"

"Just for special people, Mr. Vlieg. Just for people who are especially good or bad."

I get up and walk quickly away. I don't look back, but I assume I am being followed by this unpleasant man who can be everywhere at the same time and whose eyes change color.

Outside the city, I find a field thick with dried reeds and grass, which some untidy person has allowed to survive into the new season. It is in such fields, beneath the dead plants, that a snake may make a nest and lay its eggs. And as I look carefully through the weeds, I have the good fortune of finding such a nest. The eggs have recently hatched, and many little snakes squirm about in the warming earth, making their way without the care of their parents. I hold several of the sacred infants in my palm for a few minutes, admiring the gaze of their never-closing eyes and the subtle marking of their bodies. My spirits rise. This can only be a favorable portent. I put the snakes back in the nest and take one of the abandoned eggshells.

I squat in the dried grass and quickly assemble a Vlieg doll. Concealed in its belly is the empty egg of the serpent, over which I have sung a song:

> It's best that you go away, threatening person.
> For although it's not in my nature
> to wish any person ill,
> neither do I let someone's evil deeds
> go unpunished.
> So it's best that you go away, threatening person.

Back at the van Cott house, I go to Anna's studio and use her paints to make the doll's face and eyes. I find it is not difficult to remember the colors of Mr. Vlieg's eyes and to mix the correct colors from those on Anna's worktable.

As I work, I suddenly hear loud voices in the entrance hall. And then, from nearby, Anna's voice says to me, "Excellent."

"The doll?" I say.

"I'm too old for dolls. And you should be, too, Lenoir. What's excellent is the color. That's a doll of the weasel Vlieg, isn't it? I just saw him. You've got the colors of his eyes exactly right."

"That will make the doll more effective, then."

"It would be wise to stop making dolls, Lenoir. Stop making them as long as you live in this land. Dolls will get you in trouble here."

"They are part of what has been passed to me from my ancestors."

"I'm not asking you to forget dolls. Just stop making them and using them. Let me show you something that will be more useful to you. Come with me."

Anna takes me by the hand and leads me to the dining room, where we find my former owner Twee sitting at the table drinking brandywine. I am offended to find Twee here. He gets up and embraces me. The brandywine has apparently gone to his head. "My old friend," he says. "You should have stayed at the show. A great success."

I say, "I'm pleased for you." And I realize that I have not said this to be courteous. I am beginning to feel the pleasure I have so often felt at Twee's childish enthusiasm for things.

Anna says, "Lenoir and I are playing a game, Dom — a serious game."

I had forgotten that Twee's other name is Dom.

Anna asks Karin to bring a lighted candelabrum, then she takes me and Twee to a corner of the room away from the window. She holds the candles near his jacket, which is new and made of a shiny material the color of a certain blue flower I can remember from my childhood. Anna says to me, "Look carefully at this color. Keep it in your memory while we pay a short visit to Rembrandt."

She says to Twee, "You can look through the paintings in my studio while we're gone, Dom. See if there's anything you think you could sell. We'll be back soon, and Karin will give us all some soup and bread."

On the way to Mr. Rembrandt's house, I ask, "Is Twee to become a friend of yours?"

"He's my agent. And he's your friend. He's fond of you, Lenoir. He only sold you to keep from being sent to the House of Correction."

"He could have fled with me."

"Isn't this better? We're all together. Old friends, new friends."

"I am not sure Mr. Rembrandt is our friend after today."

"I don't understand why he was so upset. He's painted dissections before."

"This one was of a pregnant woman. And his wife lost a baby at birth recently."

"Of course. I knew that. I'm becoming insensitive, I think."

"Or Mr. Rembrandt is becoming more sensitive."

In his studio, Mr. Rembrandt is looking at a charcoal-and-paper picture that seems to show Dr. Padmos standing next to Jeanne's smooth, small-breasted, open-bellied corpse. The doctor is holding the unborn child in his cupped hands.

There seem to be tears in the painter's eyes.

Mlle. Anna says, "I came to apologize, Master. I should have known the dissection would upset you."

"I'm the one who should have known. I no longer know my own feelings."

"It happens to us all, I think," Mlle. Anna says.

"We shouldn't let it happen." Mr. Rembrandt takes the picture off the easel and tears the paper slowly and carefully in many small pieces, which he drops on the floor. "That ends that . . . What can we discuss that's more wholesome?"

Mlle. Anna says, "Lenoir."

Mr. Rembrandt smiles. "Are you wholesome, Lenoir?"

"Should I be?"

Anna says, "Lenoir has a wholesome talent for color memory."

"Like yours?" Rembrandt asks.

"Better than mine. Perfect recall, perhaps. May he use your palette?"

Mr. Rembrandt hands me a palette containing a strange, muddy collection of paints. Anna picks up a piece of paper from the floor and gives it to me. She says, "Please make the color of Dom's new jacket. Make it by the light of a candle."

I go to a lighted candle in the corner of the studio, and I make the color on the paper. When I have finished, I show it to Anna. She says, "I would have made it a bit darker. Lenoir's probably right."

Mr. Rembrandt is smiling now. He has forgotten his gruesome pictures. "Remarkable."

And for a few minutes, we play a game. I go to another room and look at the color of something. Then I come back to the studio and make the color with paints. Then we compare the color I made with the color of the object I looked at. The colors are always the same. Anna and Mr. Rembrandt are surprised and delighted, but I am surprised only to find that not everyone could do the same thing.

"A very rare ability," Mr. Rembrandt says. "Perfect color recall."

I ask, "And what can I do with such an ability besides play games?"

"Probably nothing," Mr. Rembrandt replies. "Probably nothing."

"I'm not sure," Anna says. "In a big studio, like the one Rubens has in Antwerp, where students and helpers fill in the background or make copies or enlargements of the master's original, Lenoir's talent could probably be useful."

"But not in my studio at the moment," Mr. Rembrandt says. "Just keep in mind, Lenoir, that if you ever find yourself unemployed in Antwerp — which is true of many people there now — let Mr. Rubens know about your talent."

When Anna and I get back to the van Cott house, we compare the blue color I made at Mr. Rembrandt's studio with the color of Twee's jacket. The colors are the same; precisely the same, according to Anna. I don't understand how it could have been otherwise.

In the dining room, Karin serves us a soup that contains cabbage and potatoes. With the soup, we drink a wine from a place called Bourgogne. Twee says he can taste many flavors in it, such as mushrooms and blueberries. I taste only freshly turned earth. I am not as good with flavors as with colors.

After dinner we drink brandywine, while Anna and Twee talk of making large amounts of money in various ways.

I am on the verge of falling asleep when there is a pounding on the door. Karin announces that Mr. Vlieg has arrived with a paper that he is required to hand directly to me. Anna, Twee, and I go unsteadily to the door.

Vlieg is waiting outside. He removes a black, broad-brimmed hat with one hand and gives me the paper with the other. It is the same type of paper I saw him hand to Twee recently.

Anna says to him, "Is there anything else?"

Vlieg is looking past us, into the house, obviously trying to snoop. Suddenly his weasel-like expression changes, first to fright, and then to a smile. I turn to see what has caught his attention. The door of Anna's studio is open, and in what is left of the daylight, I can see my Vlieg doll lying on a table.

There is silence for a time. Then Vlieg bows, replaces his hat, says, "See you soon," and goes away.

Anna takes the paper from me and reads it to herself. "Lenoir, you are to appear before the magistrate on Monday morning and defend yourself against a charge of sorcery and of bringing about the death of one Jeanne Morel."

Twee puts his hands on my shoulders. "This is nothing to worry about, Lenoir. I'll testify for you. You didn't bring about the death of Jeanne. Vlieg did. Dr. Padmos told me about it. Padmos gave Vlieg the poison (one of the poisons you identified for him, I'm afraid). Padmos paid Vlieg to do the poisoning."

"And Vlieg is accusing me of the murder?"

Anna says, unbelievingly, "They killed her just to use her body in today's show? Would Dr. Padmos actually do that?"

Twee doesn't seem to understand Anna's shock. He says, "Jeanne was very effective. You saw that. The audience loved her. She brought an innocence and spirituality to the show."

"She couldn't have brought anything," Anna shouts. "She was dead."

Twee says, "The important thing now is that Lenoir didn't kill her. I can testify to that."

Anna walks quickly back to the dining room, saying, "And who's going to take your word for anything, Dom? You're a notorious liar."

Twee looks hurt, but he must know that Anna is right.

Anna continues, "I'm afraid your friends can't help you much with this problem, Lenoir. The people who can vouch for your character are painters, prostitutes, and a painter's agent — not the sorts of people who inspire confidence. Don't you know any clergymen or merchants?"

I shake my head and look at Twee. He has had dealings with many important people, including regents and burgomasters, but I don't think he has gained their respect. He shakes his head.

"Then we can only hope that Father gets back in time. His confidence in you will mean something."

Twee says, "Tomorrow is Sunday. The captain isn't likely to be traveling, and that means he can't get here in time."

Suddenly I resent everyone's concern for me. "Why does everyone think I will not be able to defend myself? Let me talk to the magistrate. I am sure he will be more reasonable than that weasel Vlieg."

Anna and Twee look at me doubtfully, but I think they are relieved to have me take the matter off their hands.

Twee says, "Maybe you're right. I forget that you're a free man now. You're intelligent, well-spoken. But just one piece of advice, Lenoir. Tell them you're a Christian."

"But that would be a lie."

Twee rolls his eyes in exasperation. "It's a lie, but it will make you more believable."

Anna adds, "Dom is right. They may ask you to take an oath on the Bible, anyway."

I say, "And what kind of Christian should I say I am?"

"Calvinist," Anna suggests. "Definitely Calvinist. That's what the magistrates are."

"And what," I say, "do I tell them if they ask me what I believe?"

Twee says, "Just change the subject. But if they insist, say you believe in Jesus Christ but that you don't believe in the Pope or the Spanish Inquisition. Now that I think of it, you should bring the subject up yourself. Say that inquisitions are not appropriate in this great and free country. Tell them how happy you are to live in this enlightened land. Say that —"

Anna interrupts. "Never mind, Dom. I think Lenoir will do all right without our help." She turns to me. "Tell the truth. Answer their questions. Make sure they know you live in Captain van Cott's house. And call them sir." She pours a large helping of brandywine.

"May I tell them that I might have been in love with Jeanne Morel?"

Twee and Anna look at me as if I am insane. Anna asks, "You loved her?"

"I could not forget the few moments we had together."

Twee says, "That's not necessarily love, Lenoir. It could be many other strange things. But whatever it is, don't mention it. The magistrates would be either embarrassed or angry. Say you respected Jeanne's spiritual qualities."

"Yes," I say. "I think that is the truth."

"Well, whatever," Twee says. "Remember that with magistrates, spiritual is good and physical is bad. And one more thing: tell them you prefer to speak in French. They might have to use a translator, which will give you more time to think. And even if they don't use a translator, answer their questions slowly. Think before you talk."

I suspect Twee, who is not noted for thinking before he talks, is telling me something he learned at the bankruptcy court.

Anna is showing the effects of the brandywine. Her cheeks are a deeper shade of red, and her eyes are squinting. She is not feeling spiritual. She rises unsteadily, goes to the corner of the dining room, and brings back a handsome object that I had assumed was an old-fashioned weapon of some kind. She sits down and cradles the device in her lap. "Hurdy-gurdy," she says. She turns a crank on the side of the device, which begins to make a whining noise. "I'll teach you a song." She begins to sing, in Dutch:

> In Amsterdam, we prostitutes
> are fine erection builders.
> The hypocritical magistrates,
> they fine us many guilders.
> Nevertheless, our worries are slight,
> for the fines we pay
> to them during the day,
> they pay us back at night.

Although I am aware that Anna is a woman of the world, I am a little surprised that she knows such a song. I wonder if she would sing it if her friend Jean Guelfe were here.

And I wonder if the magistrate will see me as a bad and dangerous person.

When I belonged to Twee, Sunday was truly a day of rest for us. We slept late and never ventured far from our beds (or bed, as the case might be). We listened to the chiming of bells and the sound of shoes and boots scraping against the cobblestones as people went to their many churches. In Amsterdam, there are followers not only of Calvin and Pope but of Luther; there are some called Baptists, some called Remonstrants, and many others. And although the people argue about their beliefs, it seems that they are proud to have so many types of belief. There is even a place for the non-Christians called Jews to worship.

I am not yet certain how I will spend my future Sundays, but I will spend today wondering about my encounter tomorrow with the magistrate. I am up early so that I will be available for Anna whenever she wakens.

I pay a visit to Nghana the parrot, who is whistling a new little tune that I assume he has learned from Karin. I go to the kitchen and find some grain for him and put some watered milk in his bowl. He is, as usual, more interested in affection than in food. I take him on my finger and stroke him. He raises the feathers of his head, and he bows, inviting me to scratch. As I run a fingernail across his scalp, he murmurs, "Good life . . . good life."

From behind me, Anna says, "Do you agree with Nghana, Lenoir?"

"I agree this morning. I hope I will also agree tomorrow night."

"You will. Don't worry. Relax today. See your friends. I'll paint today. I'm starting a portrait of Jean Guelfe. I'll be safe."

I decide that if I am to follow Twee's advice and represent myself to the magistrate as a Christian, it would be a good time for me to attend a church service. And I admit to myself for the first time that I am afraid of these churches. The buildings are too large, and from what Twee and others have told me, there is too much talking in them and not enough dancing.

I wait near the Church of Calvin and watch the solemn, proud-looking people enter. I am surprised, however, to see several painters among them, including Mr. Rembrandt. Eventually the bells stop clanging and the people stop entering. Then I hear them begin to sing. Many of the people would do better singing the simpler songs of my homeland.

I go quietly and, I hope, unnoticed through the large doorway and stand in the shadows at the back.

The singing seems to be about sleep, and I recall the words that Katja read me about the blood of a lamb. When the sour singing ends, a very pale man stands in a box and reads from a large book, which I assume is the Bible that I have heard mentioned so often — the Holy Bible. I do not know if anything made by people can be Holy. In my homeland, only natural creatures may be worshiped.

A few wealthy-looking people sit on chairs and in wooden enclosures in front of the pale man, but most of the people stand, staring up at him as he tells how some people with strange names had children and gave these children even stranger names. I don't know why everyone listens to this with such apparent interest.

Next, the man in the box tells us how the unseen is more important than the seen. I wonder how this sounds to Mr. Rembrandt, who is gazing up at the frighteningly high, white ceiling, which reflects the sunlight streaming through the tall, clear-glassed windows.

I am more interested in the floor, which is made up of slabs of stone, each about the size of a person. Writing is carved on the slabs, and I believe the bodies of many Christian people are buried under the floor. The thought of such a thing, combined with the cold air in the church, makes me shiver.

I look around at the many large black hats, which are like giant flowers in a garden of death. Then I see a figure in a shadowy corner opposite me. It is Mr. Vlieg.

I begin to feel the way I felt in a childhood dancing game in which we tried to see who could spin about the longest without falling over in dizziness. It was a game I never won.

I turn and walk gratefully out of the cold building.

Outside, I resist a desire to go and see Twee to ask him if he might be in the mood to read to me from the Spanish book, which — unlike the Bible — makes me want to know what comes next.

As I am about to head for my new home, I am astonished to see Katja and several of her co-workers walking proudly toward me. They are plainly dressed, for them, but their hats are not black. They greet me warmly, but less warmly than usual.

"You are out early," I say.

"It's Sunday," Katja says. "We're on our way to church."

"You're not early enough for that. The pale man is already talking."

"We go to one of the secret churches," Katja says. "Come along. You'll like it."

I join them. On the way, they tell me about the secret church. It is the church of the Catholics, who are led by Pope. For many years it was the only church, but after lots of complicated events, people in the North are now forbidden from going to this church. But people go, and everyone knows they go, even though it is supposed to be a secret. We make our way to a building in the warehouse section of the city and climb winding flights of narrow, dark stairs that suddenly open up to a bright, richly colored room with a stage at one end. At least the Catholics have benches to sit on.

Katja says, "It's called God-in-the-Attic, Lenoir. It's where we have our ceremonies. What do you think?"

"I think it's beautiful. Do you have serpents in your ceremonies?"

"Not lately."

The music is much better than it was at Calvin's church. A few brightly dressed singers sit at the side of the stage. They all sing the same song, and it has a satisfying simple melody. But the words are hard to understand. Then I realize they are singing in the Latin language that Dr. Padmos sometimes speaks.

Soon there is a little parade of people wearing robes that I would be pleased to wear. Someone swings an object that releases delightful-smelling smoke. A beautifully robed man begins to sing in Latin. I now understand the purpose of speaking an incomprehensible language. It disguises dull speeches or stories.

The man sings a song with a simple, attractive melody. It would sound quite like a song of my homeland if accompanied by drums. I like in particular a part with the word "Ky-ri-e-e-le-i-son."

I am never quite sure what is happening, but I am not bored. I look at pictures, made of colored glass, that Katja tells me were saved when people smashed the Pope's big church. And my attention is soon rewarded when a robed man begins speaking in French. He asks us to pray for people who have died of the plague. One of the people he mentions is Jeanne Morel, who, he is pleased to say, had asked for and received the last rites despite her recent troubles with the Roman Catholic Church.

Later, in her room, I ask Katja if she is a member of the Roman Catholic Church.

"Yes," she says. "Always."

"What does the word 'Ky-ri-e-e-le-i-son' mean?"

"Two words: 'kyrie eleison.' They mean, 'Lord have mercy on us.'"

"Ah," I say. "The Roman Catholics have excellent music. And excellent robes."

"The best thing they have is absolution," she says.

"And what is that, Katja?"

"They'll forgive you for being a whore ... for being just about anything."

"I don't suppose there is a chance that the magistrate is a member of the Roman Catholic Church?"

"No chance, Lenoir. Not in this town."

"Then maybe it would be better to live in another town — a town where it is warmer and where there are more Roman Catholics."

"Cold weather and Calvinism are good for my business, Lenoir. People need a little secret warmth without judgment."

"I think cold weather is good for all kinds of business. People must keep moving to be warm. Business is a way to keep from sitting still and shivering."

"It's also a way to make money, Lenoir."

"Soon I will also make money. Mr. Rembrandt says I could make money to the south in Antwerp with Mr. Rubens. You could come with me, Katja."

"You think you and I would be good traveling companions for each other?"

"I think we would make good companions altogether. I guess we are of the same age. Unfortunately, my teeth are not excellent like yours."

Katja smiles, showing me that she indeed has all her teeth and that they are clean and white. She says, "That might be as good a reason as any for companionship, Lenoir. You might have noticed that all the women who work for me have excellent teeth. They might have other flaws — crooked legs, no bosom — but they are clean and have good teeth."

Katja moves close to me. "Many people don't realize what an important sexual organ the mouth is."

I nod and look at the picture windows. I wonder if God-in-the-Attic is pleased with Katja.

# 9

THE MAGISTRATE AND I sit facing each other at either end of a long table. At the side of the table is a young man who writes as we talk. At each of the room's two doors stand men holding metal-pointed poles and wearing metal hats and vests.

I cannot see the magistrate's face clearly. His hat appears to be old, and its wide brim droops over his forehead. He has a neatly trimmed gray beard, and tied under his chin is a bandage of the type people wear when they have a toothache.

Lying unopened on the table in front of me is a heavy book.

The room, which has many large windows that face away from the sun, would be excellent for a painter. And it makes me feel less frightened when I see on the wall a big picture of some magistrates sitting at the very table at which I am sitting. And one of the magistrates in the picture is the man I am facing.

I say, in French, "This picture was made by Mr. Rembrandt, I think. Mr. Rembrandt, who is my friend, has also made pictures of me. He is the teacher of Mr. Flinck, who is the teacher of Mlle. Anna van Cott, whose father, Captain van Cott, a noted seaman and trader, who I'm sure is no stranger to you, employs me to protect Mlle. Anna."

The magistrate looks at me without expression. "This is not a trial but only an inquiry. I will ask questions that require simple answers, usually yes or no. First, I assume you would prefer me to conduct this inquiry in French rather than Dutch."

"Yes."

"In front of you is a Bible. If you are a Christian, please place your hand on it."

I smile and put my hand on the thick leather cover, which is worn smooth and shiny from being touched.

"Do you swear by the Bible that everything you say to me will be the truth?"

"Oh, yes." And although I do not say so, I also ask the Bible to use its powers to keep the magistrate's tooth from aching while he is questioning me.

"Your full name is Lenoir?"

"In my homeland I am called Mbatgha."

"You were brought to this country against your will?"

"Yes."

"Do you know anything about the laws of this country, Mr. Lenoir?"

"I know that you have many laws, but I have not learned them."

"Do you know that some of them are concerned with the taking of human life?"

"I know it is only safe to take a life if you are a soldier or the hangman."

The magistrate does not seem pleased with my answer. I wonder if his tooth is aching. His voice is louder when he asks the next question: "What do you know about the Devil?"

"I have never seen him, but I have often heard him spoken of in church."

"And what church is that?"

"The Roman Catholic Church," I say without intending to.

"You are a Roman Catholic?"

"I am not Roman, of course."

"And you are aware that there are laws in this country forbidding the practice of your religion?"

"I seldom practice it."

"You were seen practicing it yesterday in the company of some prostitutes, I believe."

I cannot stop myself from saying, "By that weasel Vlieg?"

The magistrate pauses. I wonder if I detect the beginning of a smile. He adjusts his bandage and asks, "Were you acquainted with a prostitute named Jeanne Morel?"

"Very much so. Yes."

"And what do you know about her death?"

After a moment of confusion, I say, "Nothing."

The magistrate opens a drawer in the table and takes out the doll I made for Sister Jeanne. "Did you make this?" he asks.

"Yes. A childish gift I gave Sister Jeanne."

"And could this be used in a ceremony known as juju?"

"I would not have harmed Sister Jeanne."

"What I am concerned about is not the taking of a life but the way in which it was taken. A life is a small thing, but the realm of the Devil is infinitely large."

"Yes . . . sir. But juju is not of the Devil's realm. It is of God's realm." I do not think it would be helpful to explain that the god involved is a snake-god. But it seems worthwhile to add: "Those who do juju can use it for many good things. They can take away pain, for example."

"God is not approached through juju. He is approached through prayer — as any Christian knows."

"Yes, sir."

The magistrate is silent for a moment. Then he says, "And how would a person use juju to take away pain? The pain of a toothache, for example?"

We stare at each other. My mind is moving too slowly to know how to answer this question. Is it a trap of some sort? Finally I say, "A person would have to be free to work on the problem for a time."

"All right. But I expect you to complete your work before I leave here this evening."

"Yes, sir."

When I get home, Anna is in the studio with a man I assume to be Mr. Guelfe. She is making his picture. She seems to be trying to make him look jolly, but I think she is not successful. I realize for the first time that she is an excellent painter. There is truth as well as likeness in her portraits.

She puts her palette aside. "How did it go?" she asks.

After I tell her what happened at the magistrate's, she says, "It's very strange. If the magistrate's toothache goes away, it will be proof that you can do juju, which is bad. But he will be grateful, which is good. On the other hand, if his tooth still aches, you will have proved that you cannot do juju and therefore did not cause Jeanne's death, which is good. But he will be in pain and will have no reason to be grateful to you, which is bad."

"I think I would like to have his gratitude."

"That raises another question, Lenoir. A basic question: Are you sure you could make the pain go away even if you tried?"

"One cannot be sure."

Anna sighs. "Then it doesn't matter what you do tonight. What matters is how the magistrate feels in the morning and whether he thinks you are a threat to the people of Amsterdam."

"I wish the captain were here. He said to me once to leave the gods and the magistrates to him."

"Then leave them to him. Let's go shopping. Let me buy you a present.

"The weasel Vlieg may be watching."

"Let him watch."

After Mr. Guelfe leaves us, Anna and I go to a shop where one may buy cloth from many parts of the world. The largest display, of course, is of woolen materials in blacks, browns, and grays. But in one corner of the shop there are some brilliantly colored fabrics, including silks, which I have seen worn only by Twee, Katja, and a few young and wealthy women. My spirits rise immediately. I choose a soft wool the color of the seeds of the rare pomegranate fruit, which I have seen in the market. And to decorate the cloth, I select some golden braid. Anna buys it for me, pretending it is for herself. It will be up to me to have it made into a garment.

As I admire the cloth and think of the pomegranate, I recall a similar fruit that I knew in my homeland. And I remember that the leaves of the fruit's tree were used by our medicine man to remove pain. And then I remember that I have seen some of those leaves among those that Dr. Padmos recently asked me to identify.

After thanking Anna, I tell her I must run an urgent errand.

As usual, there are no patients waiting to see Dr. Padmos in his surgery. However, he is not alone. He is sitting at a table with Twee. In front of them are two wine bottles, one of them empty.

The doctor says to me, "You walked out on my show, Lenoir. No stomach for it, so to speak?" He does his little cackling laugh.

"You are quite right," I say. "How clever of you to know. My stomach has been in great pain for several days. I have come here to use one of your medicinal plants if I may."

He waves his hand toward the cabinet where the plants are stored, and he nods his head.

As I search through the plants, Twee says to the doctor, "Well, you can't expect your surgery business to thrive after one of these shows. People are going to wonder if they'll end up starring in the next show. Forget about your medical business. You're in entertainment and education now. Any clod can feed leeches or mush up some kind of poultice or give an enema. But you've got dramatic ability."

The doctor doesn't reply.

Twee says, "Padmos?"

There is still no reply, and Twee says to me, "His drinking might be a problem. Being drunk is no problem when you're dealing with terrified sick people one at a time . . . people who aren't going to pay you anyway. But when it's a crowd who paid good money, you've got to be alert."

I search desperately for the leaves.

Twee says in a quiet, almost affectionate tone, "So how're things, Lenoir? Enjoying your freedom?"

"I have trouble with a magistrate."

"That's one of the privileges of freedom."

"That sheriff's spy-weasel Vlieg told the magistrate I do black magic."

"How did Vlieg know that?"

"Uba told him, I think. And he has seen some of my dolls."

"You should try to be more European, Lenoir, especially now that you're free. Learn the numbers, learn to read."

"So that I may become like Dr. Padmos or Mr. Vlieg?"

"So that you may become like me. I think you're basically like me. That's why I bought you in the first place."

"I am more like Sancho Panza than like you."

Twee smiles. "I think you're right. Is anyone reading *Quixote* to you now?"

Before I can answer, I discover the leaves I am looking for. Fortunately, the doctor is now asleep, slumped forward on the table. I pour some kind of oil from a bottle into a heavy mixing bowl. I crumble some of the leaves into the oil and gradually blend the mixture into a paste.

As I work, Twee says, "They give Sancho a little kingdom to govern. Or so he thinks."

"They deceive him?"

"Yes."

"They could not have deceived him when the story began."

"No. He learns how to be deceived."

"And is that a good thing?"

"His deceivers enjoy it. He enjoys it. We enjoy it."

"I would like to live without deception."

"I think you're trying to deceive me, my friend."

The paste is ready. I touch some of it to my lip, and at once my lip loses all feeling.

"This will deceive your lip," I say, and I touch some of the paste to his mouth with my finger.

In a moment, his eyebrows rise and he grins. "Still full of surprises," he says. "Come visit me tonight. I'll read to you."

I am kept waiting, but I am finally allowed to see the magistrate before he leaves his chambers. He greets me impatiently, and his eyes are moist with tears of pain. He still wears the bandage, which is now stained with what looks and smells like tobacco juice, and he is drinking from a large tumbler of brandywine, which he has just refilled from an exceptionally large bottle.

I give him a small jar of the paste. I tell him it is part of the juju and ask him to rub some of it at the base of his painful tooth. He hesitates, but apparently his pain overcomes his mistrust. He puts a finger into the paste and then into his mouth. Within a minute or so, he takes my hand and thanks me. There are still tears in his eyes, but I think they have become tears of gratitude.

When I get back to the van Cott house, there is reason for me to be grateful: a carriage is being unloaded: the captain has returned. I help the driver and Karin carry many boxes and barrels into the house. Before the driver leaves with the carriage, Captain van Cott gives him some money, along with three bottles of wine.

Then the captain and Anna and I settle about the dining room table and sample a bottle of brandy made not from grapes but from French apples. And even though the brandy is old, it is less harsh than these drinks usually are. But even though I take only tiny sips, my head soon begins to feel numb as my lip felt when I put my medicine on it.

I wonder how these Hollanders can conduct their businesses as efficiently as they supposedly do while at the same time drinking all these brain-numbing liquids. It may be that their brains are not affected in the same way as mine is. Or perhaps a muddled head is an advantage in the world of their business.

Being a considerate person, the captain does not begin by telling us about his trip but asks Anna and me what we have been doing.

Anna says, "Lenoir has had a talk with a magistrate. The sheriff thinks Lenoir's juju is the work of the Devil."

The captain looks amused. "The Devil is what they're really interested in. They're jealous of Lenoir's Devil. But they're most dangerous when they're jealous. What have they threatened to do to you, Lenoir?"

"Nothing as yet. I am trying to cure the magistrate's toothache."

"Don't cure it. Don't do anything. I'll talk to him first thing in the morning. What's his name?"

I shake my head.

"I'll find him. But if you don't know how to ride a horse, you should learn right away. You might have to get out of town in a hurry."

I hope the captain is not being serious. I could never sit on one of those monsters.

The captain turns from me to his daughter and asks, "And what's new with Anna?"

"I'm painting a portrait of Mr. Guelfe," she says and winks.

For an instant, the captain looks at his daughter with a pained expression. I wonder if he is jealous of Mr. Guelfe. But the captain quickly smiles and says, "I've got myself a ship — to the West Indies. A short trip." He puts his hand on mine. "Anna will probably want to have you here, Lenoir. But you should know this: I met a captain who would take you to your homeland, or close to it, if you want to go there."

My stomach tightens, and I don't know what to say. I am reminded that I am free now. I wonder if it would be easier to act as a free person in my homeland than it is among these flatlanders.

I think the captain simply wants to get rid of me. I think he wishes I had never knocked on his door. He continues: "Think about it. But not too long. The ship sails in a week."

"Would this captain take my friend Uba to her home?"

"I think he would be glad to have her as a passenger, Lenoir . . . I think he would be delighted. But what would delight me now is some sleep. I must excuse myself."

I, too, am tired, but I am also agitated and do not think of sleeping. Anna gives me permission to leave the house, and I go to see that rascal Twee.

"The captain thinks I should learn to ride a horse," I tell him.

"People always want you to learn things. But I let you learn what you wanted to learn."

Twee pours two glasses of wine. I accept one to be polite, but I have had enough to drink for one day.

"So," asks Twee, "do you want to learn to ride a horse?"

"No. Those creatures are too large and terrifying."

"Don Quixote was devoted to Rocinante."

"But Sancho Panza preferred another creature."

"An ass. There are plenty of asses in Amsterdam."

"I haven't seen one."

"A way of speaking, Lenoir. A dolt, a dunderhead, an oaf."

"Plenty of those, yes. But I came here to hear about Sancho Panza governing his kingdom."

And for a few pleasant minutes I heard of Sancho's wisdom as a governor. As always, the people who try to treat him as an oaf are surprised at his good sense and intelligence. He makes many excellent decisions in cases that are brought to him for

justice. I wish he were going to be my magistrate in the morning. Twee continues to drink wine as he reads, and he obviously
is becoming excited about the world of Sancho Panza, as any
normal person would. As he closes the book, Twee gets unsteadily to his feet. "Let's have a riding lesson," he says.

"Oh, no. For one thing, it is late. For another we do not have
a horse or even an ass. And I have no desire to have such a lesson."

"Those problems are easily overcome," Twee says. He lights
a lantern, and he takes my arm and drags me out into the cool,
damp night. We walk quickly through the quiet streets. I hold
the lantern and also try to keep Twee from staggering into a
canal. I realize that I am no longer obliged to go along with
Twee on his silly forays. But I must admit that I am enjoying
myself. It is better than sitting at home and thinking about tomorrow.

There is a stable attached to the brothel where Katja lives,
and I steer Twee toward it.

There is no attendant in the stable, and Twee opens one of
the horse stalls, which contains a large horse that has a brown
body and a yellow mane and tail. It is the type of horse that is
not for riding but for pulling carts loaded with bricks or barrels. "He has no saddle," Twee says, "but I can help you up on
him. Just to get the feeling of sitting." He says to the horse,
"Come on, big guy." Surprisingly, the creature follows us quietly out into the street, where it stops and relieves itself of a
seemingly endless stream of piss. While we are waiting for this
display to end, I watch the steaming liquid make its way quickly
along the gutter. It moves among the cobblestones like a snake.
And suddenly it stops. It has encountered not a cobblestone but
a boot.

Wearing the boot is the sheriff's weasel Vlieg. He asks, "Do
you have the owner's permission to take this horse?"

"Of course," Twee says. "*I* am the owner."

In my surprise at Twee's answer, I drop our lantern, breaking its glass and putting out its light. The noise startles the horse, which rears up, lurches forward, and knocks Vlieg to the ground. Then the stupid creature begins trotting about in circles.

Twee and I stumble after the horse and are about to despair of catching it when it stops and allows us to lead it back to the stable.

Vlieg has not moved from where we left him lying in the gutter. I bend over him. His hat has been knocked off, and his head lies against a large cobblestone. His hair is matted with blood.

I say to Twee, "He is hurt."

Twee opens Vlieg's clothing and puts his ear against the injured man's chest. "I can't hear his heart beat. Maybe you can." I put my ear against the hairless, bony chest. I do not hear a heartbeat. Twee says, "Lift his eyelids, see if the pupils of his eyes can change."

I sit up and lift one of Vlieg's eyelids. The eye stares lifelessly ahead. But what interests me most is its color, which isn't either of the colors I had seen before.

Twee's head is next to mine. "He's dead, Lenoir. Good riddance, I'd say. And it isn't as if there isn't another."

"Another what?"

"Another Vlieg. Didn't I tell you? There are twin Vliegs. Or there were."

Before my astonishment allows me to answer, a window opens across the street. A man's voice says, "Who's there? What's happening there?" A woman's voice says, "Never mind. Stay out of it."

Another window opens, this one in Katja's building. I think it is Katja's window, but before I can be sure, Twee grabs my arm and pulls me quickly to the end of the street, while saying, "Go home. It's an accident. We haven't been here. They forgot to lock the stable door; the horse got out on his own."

We separate and run. I think I hear the man's voice say, "One of them is the black man."

\*

I am unable to sleep. I think of the captain's offer to get me back to my homeland, and I wonder what life would be like for me now in the village of my birth. I begin to feel a new uneasiness in my stomach. It is the uneasiness of fear. I am afraid to resume my old life. My people would treat me as an outsider, as someone returned from the land of death. I would feel even less at home there now than I do in this flat land of deranged people. I realize I have become a little deranged, too. I wish Twee still owned me. It is a great comfort to be owned by someone who understands you.

I get out my drum and tap lightly on it.

I sing: "Ky-ri-e-e-le-i-son." I fit the newly learned words to a melody I learned as a child.

Soon, the tapping of my drum is joined by a tapping on my door. It is the captain.

"I woke you up," I say. "Forgive me."

"No. I was awake."

"First I must tell you about a thing that happened tonight . . . a bad thing. That is, it would have been bad if it had happened to a good person. But it happened to a bad person."

"What happened?"

"The bad person died."

"And who was the bad person?"

"The sheriff's man Vlieg."

"Most sheriff's men are good."

"But Vlieg was a twin."

"And that means he was bad?"

"In the village of my birth, it is believed of twins that one is good and the other is evil. We do not allow the evil one to survive."

"And who decides which twin is evil?"

"There is always a special person who has such knowledge."

"Well, the special people in *our* village — the clergymen, the magistrates — don't share your belief, Lenoir."

"And you don't find twins disturbing, Captain?"

"They're disturbing when you see them both together. But there's a difference between being disturbing and being evil. And even if a person *is* evil, it doesn't mean it's all right to kill him."

"Oh, I didn't kill Vlieg."

"Who did?"

"A horse killed him."

The captain smiles. "Oh, Lenoir," he says. "A horse?"

"Yes. The horse escaped from the stable and knocked Vlieg down."

"You were there?"

"Twee says we were not there."

"Did anyone see you being not there?"

"Someone said he saw the black man."

"That means he saw *you*. You're Amsterdam's main black man, Lenoir. But I think if you want to survive, you'd better become somebody else's black man."

I hear Anna's voice say, "How can he do that?" She has apparently been standing in the doorway, listening to us.

The captain says, "We would hide you here for a few days, Lenoir, and then try to get you to Haarlem and on that ship to western Africa."

"No," I say. "That would put you in danger. And besides, I have decided that there is no going home for me."

The captain says, "I suppose not." I am grateful that he does not try to argue with me, and his acceptance makes me think I have made the correct decision. He continues, with great energy: "Then you'll have to travel on your own. Walk. Travel south, over the border, to Flanders."

"But would I not be pursued? Would I not be seen?"

"Travel at night. Sleep during the day. Stay off the main roads."

"And how will I know the way?"

"There will be signposts."

Anna reminds her father: "He can't read."

The captain takes me by the arm and leads me out of the back door, into the night. He points up to the clear sky. He shows me the stars called the Big Dipper, and how they point to the North Star. "Walk away from the North Star."

"And what," I ask, "of the many nights when the stars will not be visible?"

"You'll usually be walking along straight canals. Keep the setting sun on your right and follow the canals. In fact, you could make much better time if you traveled by boat. But that would be more dangerous. You'd have to steal a boat. And there are people along waterways at all hours. So keep to back roads, but let the water guide you."

I realize that my trip will be difficult and that I will be lonely. I ask the captain, "Could you also show me the serpent in the sky?"

"Why the serpent?"

"For comfort."

He shows me.

Back in the house, Anna says to me, "In Flanders, go to see Rubens. Peter Paul Rubens. A great old man. A great painter who has been to many parts of the world. He'll be pleased by your talent for remembering colors. He'll want to paint your portrait. He'll protect you."

"Peter Paul Rubens?" I ask.

"Yes. Go to Antwerp and ask for him. He lives there."

I repeat: "Peter Paul Rubens, who lives in Antwerp . . . And how many nights must I walk?"

"Probably five or six, if you keep moving and don't get lost," the captain says.

Which means more than five or six, I think. Maybe more than nine. Then I remember the confusion of languages in these lands. I ask, "What language does Mr. Rubens speak?"

"Many, many languages. He's called the diplomat."

I stand for a moment and look at my two new friends. I wish

there had been time to know them better. I wish there were time to sit with them now over a bottle of wine and talk through the rest of the night. I say, "Maybe you can come and visit me and Mr. Rubens in Antwerp. And bring Katja and Twee."

It is apparently something she hasn't thought of. She thinks for a moment, then smiles and says, "Definitely. But now, pack a few clothes. I'll get you a sack of food and wine."

I pack my clothing, and then I take the painting that Mlle. Anna gave me, and I cut it from its frame so that I will be able to carry it with me. As I work, I think: Perhaps I, too, am deranged.

I am about to begin wandering alone through a land of clouds and rain, a land that offers no hills for shelter or concealment.

I am deranged by forgetfulness. I am forgetting the obvious truths about subjects as simple as death and magic.

And perhaps the people are also victims of forgetfulness. It is easy to forget when one has more than one language and only one god.

But the serpent is always here to remind us and to make us uneasy or to reassure us.

I leave quickly, embracing Anna and then the captain.

I do not say farewell to Nghana the parrot, but I remind Karin that if she doesn't want him to leave her, she must clip his wings after he completes each molt.

The night is cool, and a steady, gentle wind is blowing. I walk quietly through dark side streets, avoiding the boulevards in which I might encounter someone. I pass the brothel, where some of the windows show the light of flickering candles and others are dark. From behind the windows come sounds of laughter and pleasure.

I think of Uba, whose house I am near and whom I have not

treated well. I owe her something. In a minute I am knocking at her door. Luck is with us both. She opens the door. I say, "May I come in for a minute, Uba?"

She steps aside and closes the door behind me. She does not make her usual clever remarks. I think she realizes my visit is important. "I am leaving town tonight," I say.

"You're in trouble?"

"Nothing serious. But I have good news for you. Captain van Cott can arrange for you to go back to your homeland. See him tomorrow."

"Is that where you're going? Home?"

"I hope so."

Uba kisses me. "I hope so, too."

I leave her and begin walking quickly.

Soon, the city's night sounds are behind me and are replaced by the barking of the occasional dog that my footsteps have disturbed. Strangely, my greatest regret is that I am leaving the city where Sister Jeanne died.

At a crossroads at the edge of town, I stop and look at the sky, which is moonless but bright with stars. I find the North Star and turn to the road that leads away from it.

Before I take a step, I sing, again, the old song of my people:

> Don't think I won't come.
> The path before me
> is a crooked line.
> But I hope it will lead me to a safe end.
> The loss of my people
> has confused the route for me.
> Wish me well with neither hatred nor jealousy.

Then I take a hesitant first step upon the path.

But before I take the second step, I hear a hissing noise. I wonder if I have awakened a goose.

*Hssssss. Hsssss.*

I walk cautiously toward the sound.

A man steps from behind a hedge.

It is Twee, who grins delightedly and says, "I think you need a traveling companion."

# PART II

# IO

A PERSON DOESN'T LIKE to be interrupted after taking the first step on a path, even if the path is a crooked line.

I say, with obvious irritation, "I have made enough decisions for one day, Twee. Now it is time for me to walk. I have many miles to go tonight."

"Call me Dom."

"No. I call you Twee."

"I can help you. I can read signs and announcements. I can mingle with the people."

"Mingle in those clothes?" Under his gray cloak, Twee is wearing a suit the color of holly berries. Even in the darkness, it gets one's attention.

"I have other clothes," he says and pulls a large, heavy-looking sack from behind a hedge. I don't know how he, with his scrawny body, managed to drag the sack this far.

"This is the wrong time and place for a discussion," I say. And I realize that I am nagging my ex-owner. Free at last.

"I still feel a responsibility for you," Twee says. "I want to help you."

"And perhaps the sheriff is after us both."

Twee smiles, and says, "That, too."

I say, "I don't know why you must travel with me. I think we will be safer if we travel alone."

I begin walking south. The night is bright. My eyes feel as large as an owl's, and I move almost as quickly as I would in the daylight. I hear Twee struggling behind me, dragging his bundle of possessions. I know it would be helpful in some ways to have him accompany me on my journey, but it seems that when I took the first step away from the North Star, the responsibility for the journey became only mine.

I walk without stopping, and daylight arrives surprisingly soon. I am pleased to find that the sun is rising on my left. I move off the road, along a row of hedges and into a grove of trees.

In a few minutes, Twee joins me. He looks exhausted and unhappy.

I ask Twee, "Do you have food?"

He shakes his head. "No. Just clothes, documents, books, a painting or two."

I share some bread, cheese, and wine with him.

"The second Vlieg is definitely after us," Twee says.

I shrug. "I don't care. I am going invisibly to Antwerp, where I will see Peter Paul Rubens."

"Rubens will definitely find a use for you," Twee says. "He'll paint you. But I'm not sure he'll need me. But maybe he will. He may need an agent to travel for him. He's too old even to do much painting now. Stiff hands." Twee nudges me with his elbow and winks. "And that's not all that's stiff," he continues. "He has a young wife that he keeps making pregnant."

"How do you know all this?" I ask.

"Rubens is the king of painters. He's talked about. The only people who don't like him much are the Hollanders. They don't like him because he's a Catholic and he has painted and spied for the kings of Spain. But he's made more paintings and more money than any other painter who's alive — maybe more than any painter who's ever lived. He's what most people want to be: rich and famous."

"But he is old and has crippled hands," I say. "Most people don't want to be that."

"It's a hard choice, Lenoir: Do you want to be poor, mediocre, obscure, but young and healthy? Or would you rather be fabulously wealthy, world famous, a genius, but old and infirm, although not too infirm to paint a picture on your better days, or to give banquets, or to make a wife that's less than half your age happy and pregnant? It's a hard choice."

"There is no choice, Dom. Neither of us can be either young or a great painter."

"It's a theoretical question, Lenoir. I mean, which would you be if you *could* be those things? And remember, you're a free man now. You can make choices you couldn't make before."

"Theoretical questions will make you deranged," I say. "What is important now is to finish eating and to conceal ourselves and to sleep."

We finish our meal, then each goes off to make up a solitary bed.

But I find it difficult to sleep. The sky has become overcast, and a light rain is falling. Although I am beneath some dense shrubbery, which shelters me from the worst of the rain, I am splashed occasionally by large, accumulated drops of cold water. I find myself thinking not about the past or the present but about the future, and I realize once again that the people of these lands are driving me crazy. For in my homeland, it was thought that there is no point in thinking about the future, because whatever the future holds cannot be changed. And only the sorcerers can tell what the future holds. It is well known that sorcerers are always unhappy.

At the moment, I too am unhappy, not just because I am tired and wet but because Twee, who has moved closer to me, is sitting up, and I think he is probably inventing a senseless plan that he will soon want to discuss.

I wrap myself in my rain cloak and close my eyes. In my homeland, the weather would be warmer. There would be denser foliage to protect us. There would be drier high ground to lie on. But despite my discomfort, I soon feel sleep approaching.

Through my eyelids, I sense the sky becoming brighter. There will be at least a few breaks in the clouds today, and the spring sunshine will warm the air.

My mind brings me an image of Nghana, my parrot, and I am about to begin my sleep with a dream, as I often do. But I hear Twee say, "Our problem is the color of your skin."

Instantly, I no longer feel drowsy. "I don't see my color as a problem. I see it as a distinction."

"That's the problem. It's a distinction, and we can't hide it. If we could hide it, we could disguise ourselves and travel openly."

"If you wish to travel openly, go ahead. You're a free man, Twee."

"Very amusing."

"Perhaps. But I will let the night be my disguise. You may do as you will."

Twee says, "Don't be so gloomy, Lenoir. We need each other. The countryside is full of highwaymen who would kill us for a guilder."

"But I don't have a guilder."

"That's another part of the trouble. We need money. Everything is easier with money."

"Sleep is easier with silence," I say, and I lie down again and fold my cloak about me. But I am no longer so eager to dream. I wonder why Twee isn't traveling alone. I know he has many pieces of paper that give him different names and allow him to enter different countries. What is it he needs from me? It could be that one finds it difficult to be without a person who was once one's property.

The sun soon breaks through the clouds, and the mist that

covers the surrounding fields begins to rise and vanish into the warming air. The warmth relaxes me, but it seems to excite Twee. I hear his words occasionally as I am drawn once more to my dreams.

"What we *really* need is a plan. Market day, that's where there are some possibilities . . . money changing hands, bartering . . . people having a drink, looking for a good time, for something out of the ordinary . . . a black man singing and dancing. Can you dance, Lenoir?"

I don't answer Twee, but as I drift toward sleep, I think of the ceremony in my homeland in which the young men dance one by one, each hoping to attract his first wife. My dancing was not graceful, but it was highly energetic. Our saying was that an energetic dancer attracted women who would be good mothers. I hope that is true, for my children's sake. I seldom allow myself to think of my children, partly because such thoughts fill me with sadness and partly because children are not a man's concern.

I sleep uneasily, waking often and finding the warm, bright sunlight upon my face. I dream of a land in which one cannot walk without walking up or down a hill.

Then I am looking up at a terrifying being. I can only think he will take my life. I feel a fear I would not feel if confronted by some ordinary villain such as the second Vlieg or even the ghost of the first Vlieg. This person who looms above me is masked, which must be a sign of evil. The creature's half-mask is dark and horrible, yet his body is covered with a strangely festive costume made of many brightly colored patches.

The creature squats next to me and puts his mask close to my face. He says something that sounds like *"Bello. Un Zanni bello."*

The creature has been eating something that I hope tasted better than it smells. I scramble quickly to my feet and move toward Twee, who is sitting up and smiling. "Arlecchino?" he says.

*"Si, si,"* the creature says. He leans forward and sweeps his

arm from above his head to the ground. Then he begins to make a buzzing sound. He waves his hand in front of his face as though chasing away a fly, although I am certain there is no insect near him. Then he quickly reaches out with his hand as if to catch the fly. He slowly opens his hand and seems to take something from it with the fingers of his other hand. Making a buzzing sound, he puts the fingers into his mouth. He closes his mouth. The buzzing stops, and he seems to swallow.

Twee begins to laugh idiotically. He says something to the Arlecchino person in a new language. The Arlecchino keeps glancing and pointing at me. Finally I say to Twee, "That's enough. Who is this creature?"

"He's Arlecchino . . . Harlequin. From an Italian comedy troupe."

"What does Italian mean?"

"It's a language that's spoken in places like Rome and Florence."

Arlecchino points to the road, where there is a brightly painted little house on wheels. Two large, unpleasant-looking horses graze nearby. It is plain that the house will travel slowly and will attract the attention of even the least curious of people. It should be avoided by people who are trying to travel quickly and to go unnoticed. Naturally, Twee says, "It's a perfect situation for us. We're having great luck. We've only been on the road for a day and we're having great luck. They need a Zanni. Their Zanni left them to settle down with a widow."

"And what is a Zanni?"

"A Zanni is a type of actor."

"And you will find them a Zanni?"

"I've already found him . . . *you* are their new Zanni."

"I don't even speak their language, Twee. How can I be an actor?"

"Speak your own language."

"The language of my homeland?"

"Yes. That will be one of your *lazzi*."

"*Lazzi?*"

"One of the things you do. Like catching a fly and eating it."

"How do you know these things?"

"I used to represent people in the theater arts. They have a great zest for life, Lenoir." Twee's eyes are glittering with excitement. He puts his arm around the Harlequin's shoulder, and they walk away, saying more things I don't understand. Beyond them, one of the horses makes a screaming noise and digs in the damp earth with one of its front feet. I wish I were the other Zanni — the one who left and settled down with a widow. Then, from beyond the wheeled house, emerges another creature that is like a horse but is not frightening. In fact, it is attractive, small and gray, with large ears and white rings around its eyes. It trots quickly toward me, and I resist the urge to retreat. It stops in front of me and blinks its long-lashed, sad eyes several times. If I were to ride on its back, my feet would almost touch the ground. I think this must be an ass, the animal that was a friend to Sancho Panza. I put my hand carefully upon its head. It closes its eyes, and I run my hand up one then the other of its long ears. I believe I have found a friend.

Then, the door of the wheeled house opens, and four people emerge. The first is a woman wearing a red, gold-trimmed dress that is cut low in the front to reveal most of a spectacularly large bosom.

Next is a younger woman. She wears a white dress, also trimmed in gold and with a low-cut neckline, but there is less for the neckline to reveal. Not that she is slender, for although her breasts are small, her belly and hips are admirably ample. And the girl's eyes, unlike those of the older woman, promise passion and mischief.

Following the girl is a boy who might be her twin but who looks unwashed and wears raggedy clothes.

Finally, there appears a man wearing a large-nosed half-mask and a flowing brown robe.

*

Soon I am standing with Twee and these gaudy strangers in the middle of a field for any passerby to see. The strangers seem overwhelmed by my beauty. They chatter away in their singsong language, which is pleasant enough except that its words do not seem to end, all trailing off weakly as *oh, ay, ee,* or some such sound. As they speak, one or the other of them reaches out to touch me. Occasionally they say something complimentary to me or Twee in the language of France and the Walloons, and finally the girl makes a little speech to us in Walloon, which she seems to know better than the others do.

She introduces herself as Columbine. The older man is Pantalone, the younger man is known not only as Harlequin but also as the Captain. The boy is Adriano, and the older woman is Isabella. The little ass — a jackass, I am told — has the strangely long name of Baldassaro; the horses are Cavalla and Cavallo.

I am quickly overcome by the complexity of our situation. There are too many creatures, too many names, too many languages. I long to be walking alone in the night.

Columbine seems to sense my confusion. "Come, Lenoir," she says, "let me show you your costume." She leads me into the house on wheels — the caravan, as she calls it. She shuts the door behind us. I am comforted by the gloom and the sense of enclosure. She pours me some milk and gives me a piece of grayish blue bread that turns out to be fresh and delicious. As I eat, Columbine explains the activities of the comedy troupe.

After they arrive in a town, she tells me, the actors take down a platform that is stored on top of the caravan. They present their performances and then pass a hat among the people in the audience, asking for money. There was a time when this troupe presented their comedies in the homes of wealthy and important people or even in the castles of kings. But there have been misfortunes, and now they are working their way to their homeland as best they can.

I get the impression that these people live their lives in discomfort and confusion. Most of the actors, Columbine says, seem to believe they actually *are* the people in their comedies. And not even the comedies have a sense of order, with no two performances being exactly the same, even when they use the same actors and the same story.

When Columbine finishes her explanation, I ask her what the point of all this strange activity is.

"There has always been a comedy," she says, as though this explains anything. She looks around, as if to see if anyone else will hear her. She says, confidentially, "The comedy is older than our language."

"But what is the point?"

Columbine tightens her lips and tries to wrinkle her forehead. She says, "I don't think you will be a good Zanni, after all. We'll find someone else." She takes a mustachioed mask and a flowing red costume from a hook on the wall and starts to put them in a cabinet. I realize that the costume would look interesting on me — amusing yet handsome. And I have often envied long, silken mustaches, which I could never grow.

Columbine sees my interest. "Would you like to try it on?" she asks. She hands it to me. "This *salame* belt goes with it," she says. She gives me a belt that has a red, greatly exaggerated, stiff male organ attached to it. "We'll have to paint the *salame* black, of course," she says as she leaves the caravan.

After a little hesitation, I decide at least to try on the clothing. As I remove my robe, I notice that my own more modest *salame* is stiffening. As I put on the Zanni costume and its mask, my excitement increases. Finally, I decide to strap the belt around my waist. I find that when one is wearing a *salame*, one doesn't want to be alone. I open the door of the caravan and step out into the sunlight. I am greeted by applause and laughter. I turn my hips from side to side, making the *salame* swing. The laughter increases.

I catch an imaginary fly and eat it.

I hear the word *bravo* for the first time. I would like to hear it again.

Columbine comes to stand at my side. She points to the *salame*, then looks at our little audience. She puts her fingertips to her mouth and raises her eyebrows. She says something I don't understand. The little audience laughs. Suddenly, Baldassaro the ass trots over in a practiced way, turns his hindquarters to me, and begins to bray. The word *bravo* is said a few more times.

When the applause ends, Twee takes me aside and asks, "Do we join them?"

"What do they expect us to do?"

"I'm the advance man. I go ahead and make arrangements for the shows. You're the Zanni. They'll give you a little routine — the sort of thing you just did. We work our way south."

"Only to Antwerp. To Mr. Rubens. I think I like painters better than actors."

"Painters aren't as much fun as actors, Lenoir."

"Painters know that fun should only be for certain days."

"Actors supply the certain days. We arrive in town, and it's a special day. Time for fun."

"We could travel faster and more safely by ourselves."

"But what about the applause?"

"What about our dignity?" I ask, as I take off my belt and wave the *salame* in front of Twee.

"I think they'll let you perform without it. But you'll lose a few *bravi*."

"How many days would we be with the actors?"

"More than nine. Maybe nine and nine more. I can work it out. They have maps. We'll go to places like Leiden or Rotterdam, places with names like Oosterhout. Places where they speak Flemish, which is a kind of Dutch for people who like to be alone and angry."

"I would like to go faster."

"The actors want to go fast, too. They have a long way to go. They want to go to Rome."

"Are these people Roman Catholics?"

"I'm sure they are. Maybe not Columbine. She speaks Dutch very well."

I no longer feel like speaking. I don't understand what Twee has just said. I don't want to understand. Twee sees this situation — as he sees most situations — as a chance for adventure or pleasure or profit. When I belonged to Twee, I saw the world his way, but now I see dangers that he does not see. Life will not treat me the way it treats him.

Over Twee's shoulder, I see the woman Isabella. She is handsome, but her glance tells me she does not wish me well. Her hand, which rests at her side, is raised slightly, palm down, with the first finger and the smallest finger pointing at me. It is obvious that the man who shares her bed or the child who suckles at her splendid breasts will be cursed. I think she must be a friend of the Catholic Devil. I am not sure why this is obvious to me and not to Twee. I say to him, "Some of these people are evil."

"Well, we're not exactly saints either, Lenoir."

"But that woman Isabella does not wish me well."

"So return the favor. Get one of your nasty dolls after her."

"The power of the dolls is not endless. I will not waste any power on such a person."

My warning does not impress Twee. He says, "Then just stay out of her way."

"And besides," I say. "These clothes have an unnatural stink about them."

Twee says, probably with some truth, "You're just being difficult. I wouldn't be surprised if there's an old saying, 'If the clothes stink, it's better to wash them than to complain about them.' And I wouldn't be surprised if Columbine would be happy to wash the costume for you."

I shrug and go to the caravan to change back into my own

clothes. As I am about to leave, the door opens and Columbine enters. She asks, "Will you be joining us?"

"I don't think so."

She says, "Think again. We enjoy ourselves, Lenoir. So will you. Maybe it will help if I tell you the story we act in our comedy." She begins speaking in an odd, exaggerated way: "The Captain, who loves me, asks my father, Pantalone, for permission to marry me."

"Is this a sea captain?"

"No. An army captain."

"Too bad."

"Anyway, Pantalone refuses to let me marry and forbids me to see the Captain again. The Zanni — you, I hope — takes messages between me and the Captain. Isabella, my father's sister, falls wildly in love with you —"

I shudder.

"— Adriano, the boy, masquerades as me at home while I am out having meetings with the Captain. There are various complications in which the Captain sometimes takes the role of Harlequin. In the end, the Captain marries me, and you marry Isabella."

"I would not marry Isabella," I say.

"That would not be a problem. We often make changes in the events. In fact, *I* make the changes. I begin each performance by telling the audience what will happen. The actors listen to me, and they do what I say they will do."

"You are like a god."

"A god who can be disobeyed. They don't always remember what I say. But that just adds to the confusion and the laughter."

"Who gets the most *bravi*?"

"Baldassaro."

"Baldassaro the jackass?"

"Yes. He always manages to do something hilarious. But of course it is easier for an animal to get a laugh."

"And why is that?"

"I don't know. Maybe they are more innocent than we are."

I look at Columbine. I cannot tell whether she has yet become a woman. I ask her, "Are you not innocent?"

"According to Mr. Calvin, no one is innocent."

Him again. I have no desire to discuss him. But I am certain he is wrong. I put my hand upon Columbine's head. She smiles, and I see no guilt in her face. I am reminded that, in my homeland, it is thought that the ability to make another laugh is a misfortune that is visited on certain people by the gods. Thus, although such people are without dignity, they are protected by the gods.

Columbine puts her fingertips against my cheek and says, "I don't think you should use the mask. I think we should paint your face white."

"White for innocence?"

"White for laughs."

Later, I open my bag of possessions and take out Mlle. van Cott's painting of the laughing man. I think it must have come to me as an omen.

I think I will trade my dignity for the protection of the gods. I will travel to Mr. Rubens with the Italian comedy troupe. I stretch the painting out and attach the sides of it to two sticks. Then, holding the picture above my head like a banner, I walk uneasily toward the caravan.

# I I

PLEASURE CHANGES TWEE into a child. When I tell him that I have decided to become an actor, he makes a hooting noise and claps his hands. I wonder how he ever manages to gain the confidence of adults.

After he calms down, he says, "You'll be a great comedian, Lenoir — a great Zanni."

"I am being a Zanni only to get to Antwerp. I don't want to spend my life being foolish."

Twee's expression becomes less gleeful. "Ah," he says. "Surprise. Lenoir has been thinking about the future."

"No. Lenoir is thinking about the present. Lenoir doesn't want the present to continue as it is."

"It never does, my friend," Twee says. For a moment he looks at me without expression, like a person who has just removed a mask. I realize that he, too, is an actor. Then he is smiling once more. "Now I am going to negotiate salaries for us."

"They will pay us?"

"Of course. And if you knew our system of numbers, you could negotiate your own salary. If you want to make a success of being free, Lenoir, you should learn the numbers."

"I'm sure many great kings and queens did not know your numbers."

"But you're not a king, Lenoir. You're an ordinary man among people who like to count things. You might be respected if you can't read, but not if you can't count."

"I might be respected more if I had a clever agent negotiating for me." I decide that whatever offer Twee returns with, I will ask for more.

But Twee knows that I will probably not be able to tell more from less. He says, "Ten. Zero. That's all you really have to learn. Once you understand how ten and zero work, everything's easy."

I shrug, but as Twee goes off to negotiate, I wonder about ten. Ten would take a large piece of my soul, I am sure. It would be like having a lifetime of pictures made of me all at once. My soul might vanish. According to my people, a person without a soul can never feel pleasure of any kind. If I were to learn about ten, I would probably have to attend the church of Calvin.

Twee returns more quickly than I expected. "She won't pay us," he says. "Her offer is food and shelter for us both, plus a costume and acting lessons for you."

"Who is 'her'?"

"Isabella. She's the boss. And she doesn't like you."

"She doesn't know me."

"She knows your skin is dark."

"Her skin is also dark."

"What she really doesn't like is your hair. She calls you Savage Hair. She thinks you eat people."

"I will eat *her*."

"But she knows you will be good for the show. And the others don't mind you. In fact, Columbine seems to be fond of you already."

I can tell that Twee has decided to do whatever they ask of

him. He doesn't want to walk at night. I ask him, "So what do you think we should do?"

"We should go with them, have an adventure. It's better than stumbling around in the dark, not being sure where we are."

"But I am the one who must make a fool of himself and endure the hatred of that witch of a woman."

"And you're the one who gets the *bravi*."

These Europeans can always surprise me. They are devoted to making money and owning things, yet there is always someone who is less interested in money than in hearing *bravi* or in being a brother or sister of virtue.

I know there is no use protesting. Twee will eventually persuade me to go with the actors. But I say, "I must think about it tonight."

The setting sun is larger and redder than I have seen it since before the winter. The actors light a campfire and begin to roast a large bird that I am sure they have stolen. They sit in a circle around the fire to eat, and they pass a jar of wine from one person to another. I sit outside the circle and eat stale bread and hard cheese.

I watch as the wine jar is passed around and around the circle, while the actors become noisier. Harlequin goes to the caravan, and when he returns he is making music on a little violin of the type I have seen before but have not heard. As he plays, Harlequin does an odd dance. The violin makes a whiny, piercing sound, but the melody it plays is pleasantly simple. Soon, one by one, the other actors get unsteadily to their feet and begin to dance. Even Twee joins them, moving about awkwardly and with great concentration.

I cannot resist getting out my drum and playing along with the music. I begin to sing one of my own songs, which does not exactly fit the music but nevertheless sounds good to me:

> Woman, if you want a calm and gentle man,
> Pay a visit to Lenoir.

No trouble, no bad words from the chief.
Just true happiness.

As I sing, Isabella dances toward me with a squirming, snakish motion. She hooks her thumbs under her skirt and pulls it down in front, revealing a plump belly. A narrowing trail of black hair begins low down and ends at a deep lengthwise crease that stretches like a smile just below her navel. She twitches the fat-hidden muscles, making quivers move across her belly like circles of water where a stone has landed. Isabella looks into my eyes. She is trying to excite me, but not to please me. She realizes, as many of these people do not, that excitement can be frightening. She is less like the others and more like my people, who say that an excited enemy is more easily defeated. I suppose that Isabella does this same dance for the people who gather to see the comedy. Excited people are more likely to give away their money.

I look into Isabella's calm eyes and sing my song again, with new words:

Woman, if you want a fierce and cruel foe
make an enemy of mighty Lenoir.
Much trouble, no forgiveness from the chief.
Just true misery.

I twist around and turn my back on Isabella. She dances into my view again, her dark eyes glaring at me with evil pleasure. She raises both hands to her face, palms outward. Then she extends her outer fingers toward me like two pairs of horns. It is obvious that she is trying to cast a spell on me. I wonder if it is a Roman Catholic spell. I respond by making the gesture I saw people making when I went to the church ceremony with Katja: I touch my finger to my forehead and then to my chest in three places. Isabella lowers her hands and stops dancing. I make the gesture again. She looks puzzled. She pulls the waistband of her skirt up over her belly. I sing to her: "Ky-ri-e-e-le-i-son."

Isabella's head snaps back. "Sacrilege," she says. "Sacrilege. God will destroy you."

"Which God?" I ask. "This God?" (I make the sign of the horns.) "Or this God?" (I make the church sign.)

"This God," she says, reaching into the folds of her skirt and producing a thin-bladed knife.

I struggle to my feet and run toward Twee and the tipsy actors, who begin to laugh. Pantalone says, "Excellent. We must put it in the show."

When I reach the campfire, I stop and take a stand against Isabella, assuming that she will not have the courage to stab me while her laughing friends watch. My guess is right. The fury in Isabella's face does not vanish, but she lowers the dagger. She shouts to the others, "This witch-man has given me the evil eye."

Columbine says, "Now you have three evil eyes."

There is more laughter.

Pantalone says, "We must use this also in the show. We will have Zanni and Isabella enter with their faces turned away. When Isabella turns, there is a third eye in the middle of her forehead. When Zanni turns, there is a patch over one of his eyes."

"Marvelous," Harlequin says.

Isabella is not laughing, but she seems calmer.

Columbine, who is smiling unconvincingly, walks past me and touches my hand. She says, quietly, "Don't worry about Isabella. She's from the South."

Twee appears at my side. I ask him, "What is it they find so amusing in my fear and Isabella's anger? Is all of their comedy based on seeing people in distress?"

"There will be a happy ending. The distress will be overcome. The audience knows that."

Now I begin to see the purpose of the comedy troupe. They

tell pleasant lies to the people. Comedians are necessary when people are always thinking about tomorrow. Comedians tell the people that tomorrow can be happy. Just as Pope and Calvin tell them that the next life can be happy.

I think it is easier not to think about tomorrow — to have jokes rather than comedies.

And just to demonstrate that endings are seldom happy, somebody's god sends a sudden rainstorm to put an end to our little party. The flames of the campfire are quickly replaced by billows of smoke. Laughter and song are replaced by coughing.

The actors rush into the caravan. Twee follows them, but I think I will sleep under the caravan rather than in it. Twee appears at the door and says to me, "Come in. Shelter is part of our contract."

Columbine runs out of the caravan and takes my arm. "Come in," she says. "Be comfortable with me."

*Comfortable* is not the word I would use to describe what I find in the caravan. And even if I knew the right words, I am not sure I would use them. There is a tangle of bodies in the darkness. Clothing has been discarded, and the pattering sound of the rain on the roof is interrupted by nearby grunts and squeals. These people have become one large animal in the act of mating. I am excited, but my excitement does not overcome my embarrassment. I take a blanket and go outside to sleep under the caravan.

The ground is cold but dry. The rainwater runs in two streams on either side of me, in the tracks of the road. I feel as though I am on an island, separated from the rest of the world. There are thumpings on the caravan floor above my head. I am shivering and cannot sleep. Then I hear the caravan door open and close. A woman calls my name. It is Columbine, I think. I answer, "Under here."

I feel another blanket being placed over me, and then another body is next to mine — the slight, warm body of Columbine. "Drink some of this," she says, and hands me a bottle. It is brandywine, and it warms me immediately. A minute ago, I was alone and shivering, but now I am warm inside and outside. Columbine whispers, "You must learn to join the party, Lenoir."

"Life is not a party," I say.

"No. Life is shit. That's why we have parties . . . so have another drink."

The young woman pulls the blankets over our heads. She struggles to raise her sleeping gown. There is a rich aroma of brandywine and our bodies. She puts my hand on her secret place, where the hair is warm and sticky. But my thoughts will not let me join the party. I am thinking of Sister Jeanne, whose body was once warm and next to mine. I wonder where her body and the body of her unborn child are now.

Columbine moves closer to me and in a moment is asleep. I wonder if I will bring tragedy to her life as I did to Jeanne's.

In the morning, I push my head out from under the blanket and find that the rain has stopped. Columbine has gone.

After I relieve myself, I look into the open door of the caravan. The tangle of bodies in there makes me think of a picture I once saw that showed a crowd of people wearing bits of cloth and having either a battle or a mass rape. The picture was not made by a house-loving Hollander, and I think it is possible that it was made by Mr. Rubens. I suppose it is part of my corruption that the scene in the caravan reminds me not of a new-wives ceremony in my homeland — as it would have done last year — but of some colors daubed on a piece of cloth.

But soon I am conscious only of smells, which no picture can show. The rich odor of bodies is replaced by the moist springtime air, and then by the harshness of Pantalone's pipe smoke and the stimulating aroma of coffee beans being crushed in a stone mortar by Isabella, whose flesh quivers interestingly beneath her nightdress as she pounds the beans with the pestle.

Soon we are outside in the sunshine, washing our bodies in a stream as the coffee brews over a small fire. The actors are not yet my friends, but they are no longer strangers to me. And all of them — even Isabella — are admirers of my body. I hold out my arm and invite them to touch its strong darkness.

After breakfast, my lessons begin.

First, Pantalone has me catch the fly again, but in several ways. I let it escape from my mouth before I can swallow it; I chase it. I capture it again. "When you perform, listen to the laughter," Pantalone tells me. "Stop when the laughter is most great. Rub your belly. Say: 'delicious, *heerlijk, delizioso.*'"

Arlecchino shows me the *lazzi* of pretending to walk against the wind and of being stopped by an invisible wall, but I can't believe these actions would make people laugh.

Pantalone teaches me to fall down in an amusing way and without hurting myself. He tells me, quite seriously, "When you are not sure what you should do — and there will be many such times — fall down."

Adriano, the boy, has a special understanding of Baldassaro, the ass. I am to tell Baldassaro I am taking an important and urgent love letter from the Captain to Columbine. I hurriedly saddle the ass. I mount him, settle myself, and shout: "Forward!" He does not move. "*Avanti!*" He does not move. "*Laten we gaan!*" No movement. I dismount and turn away. He moves. I mount again. No movement. I read him the love letter. He brays. But he does not move.

Columbine, who is watching, says there is a good bond between me and Baldassaro. Adriano says I must not try to make the ass perform certain actions but must simply let the creature decide what should happen in each performance. I believe it is Baldassaro and not Isabella who is in charge of the troupe.

The *salame* is a source of trouble (as, says Twee, it often is). I have decided that I should not trade my dignity for a few laughs, or even for a few *bravi*. Isabella says I am not man enough to be a Zanni and that instead of a *salame* I should wear a dress and a split fig and be called *frutta*. Pantalone chases Isabella and slaps her with a stick that makes a loud noise when it strikes. Then he tells me that there are many jokes they would lose if there were no *salame*. He offers to let me use the stick if I will wear the sausage. It is a tempting offer. The stick is very amusing.

Then Twee makes a suggestion: "What about a big snake instead of a *salame?*"

Pantalone looks puzzled. "It is not the same thing at all," he says.

But I am interested. I say, "A male organ is often called a snake in my homeland. There are many quite funny jokes about it, but with godly overtones. A pregnant woman is said to have been bitten by the snake. We also speak of milking the snake, which is not so godly."

Now Pantalone is also interested. "Yes. I can see that there is more character, more dignity in a snake than in a mere sausage."

Columbine says, "I could change the *salame* into a snake easily enough."

"Then it is agreed," Pantalone says, and hands me the stick. I pretend to hit him with it. There is a loud, smacking noise. He squeals and runs. "I take your leave," he says. "I must ease the pain by milking the snake."

Adriano falls to the ground in a fit of laughter.

Twee giggles and winks at me.

Only I — and Baldassaro, who is solemnly nibbling some gray, dried plants — do not laugh.

Twee points at me, and his laughter grows louder. I begin to realize that one of the reasons Baldassaro makes people laugh is that he himself never laughs. I will imitate him. When I begin to play in the comedies, I will wear a look of dignified puzzlement at all times. My face will be painted white, but there will be dark circles around my eyes, to make my expression resemble Baldasarro's. I think the time will pass quickly enough.

There will be two scenarios for the comedies. The first is "The Young Lovers," in which the lovers are kept apart in various ways until the end, when they are married. The second, which is more interesting to me, is "The Stone Guest," in which the statue of a murdered man comes to life and sends his murderer to the Devil's underworld. Harlequin, in his Captain's costume, plays the Stone Guest, and when he appears as the statue, he is seated on a horse (played by Cavalla, who, once her belly is full, will stand motionless until it is time either to relieve herself or to eat again). Needless to say, the mention of a dead man and a horse makes me think of the late sheriff's man Vlieg, and I wonder if his twin is searching for me so that he can send me to the underworld.

# 12

I T IS BEST to think of the people in the comedy troupe as children. Their word for what they do is "play," and they are more interested in imaginary events and feelings than in real ones. And because the troupe also seems to have brought out the childish side of Twee, I find my only serious companionship with Columbine and with the jackass Baldassaro. At night, I sleep away from the caravan, looking up at the cold stars, in which Isabella says she can see the future. She sees pictures in the stars, as Captain van Cott did, but she sees them as "signs," which have to do with a person's birth. Apparently, the pictures in the sky do not have to do with the god Christ but with some other gods.

Tonight, as I lie under my blanket, I think of how I have "played" the role of Zanni in "The Young Lovers" and "The Stone Guest." I have been in two performances, which were watched only by a few farmers, who interrupted their work in the fields, and by some cows, who glanced up occasionally from their grazing to look admiringly at Baldassaro.

Adriano says my performances were "promising." This boy seldom speaks, but when he does, it is in a style that reminds me of strange Dr. Padmos. I wonder why the stars or the gods or the fates — or whatever it is that decides what happens to people in these lands — have decided that I must be associated with strange events that take place before large numbers of people.

Columbine joins me, as she sometimes does, and we lie on our sides, with her back to my front. Among the women of my homeland, this position means: Place your hand on my breast and stroke me until pleasing dreams overtake me. Apparently the position means the same to Columbine. She is soon asleep.

Today is market day in a town whose name is too mysterious for me to remember, and I will play in a comedy before an audience that Twee hopes will be made up of many generous people.

He and I are on our way to do the advance work. I am wearing my scarlet Zanni costume; my face is painted white except for a black ring around my right eye; and I am riding Baldassaro. Twee walks beside me. He is wearing a nobleman's outfit of a green fabric that shimmers and glints as he moves in the pale sunlight. He wears ruffed linen at his neck and wrists.

As we travel, I think of the ending of "The Stone Guest." I ask Twee, "Do you believe I can be sent to your Devil's underworld?"

"What I believe doesn't matter, Lenoir. Ask a priest. On second thought, *don't* ask a priest. He'll say you're a hell-bound heathen."

"Is that what *you* believe, Twee?"

"Twee believes whatever is called for. If I lived where you used to live, I'd be complimentary to snakes."

"But in my land there is only one thing to believe."

Twee smiles and says, "That's why things are more exciting in *my* land."

"Your land is not more exciting that mine, Twee."

"See? You're ready to fight me. That's where belief always gets you . . . into a fight."

It is true that I am becoming angry and confused, which is

not the proper condition for a comedian. And my anger should not be directed at Twee in any case. I say, "I should not have asked you these things."

Twee shrugs, and we continue our journey in silence for a while. I begin to realize that in my homeland, there is no such thing as belief: a person either knows about the world and about the gods or does not. Knowing is the same as believing.

Then Twee says, with some excitement, "I know the person to ask . . . Rubens. Yes, ask Rubens, if you ever get to see him. It's best not to trust anyone, but I'd trust an artist over a priest or a scholar — or an agent and advance man — any time."

"Of course," I say, and I begin to feel more cheerful. I can forget about belief and think about more important things, such as remembering what I must do in the comedies.

As I think about my *lazzi*, Twee puts his hand on Baldassaro's neck. I notice for the first time that he is wearing a peculiar ring. When I point at the ring, he says, *"Voilà,"* and turns his hand over, revealing a small, sharp blade that unfolds from the bottom of the ring.

But before he can explain the ring to me, some laughing children join us. I eat some imaginary flies for them. They are delighted.

The town is small but attractive, with a row of brick buildings built around a square that faces a canal. In the square is a crowd of people who are buying food at stalls and who seem to be in a happy mood. The scene reminds me of pictures I have seen, and I realize that I am sorry I no longer get to see the pictures or the people who paint them.

Twee begins shouting to the crowd in a peculiar tone of voice, explaining when the troupe will arrive. I hold up Mlle. van Cott's picture of the laughing man.

Twee says to me, quietly, "They are in a festive mood because Lent has ended."

"And what might Lent be?"

"A time when people stop doing pleasureful things."

"And why would they want to do that?"

"They don't *want* to do it. The priests say it's good for them. It has to do with the death of Christ. And most of these people don't have that much pleasure to give up anyway."

"Many things have to do with the death of Christ. Do you think these people would be as interested in their Christ if he had died in his bed?"

"The painters wouldn't be. They love the Crucifixion. Rubens has done some of the best."

The crowd is beginning to press closer to us. Twee resumes his shouting.

While I sit on Baldassaro, playing my drum and singing a few songs, Twee begins moving among the people. He puts his arm around a man who looks prosperous and who is drinking from a bottle of brandywine. It is probably not the first bottle he has drunk from today. Twee winks at me, and he runs his hand under the purse that hangs from the man's belt. A few coins drop from the bottom of the purse into Twee's hand. I am so astonished that I stop my song. Twee steps forward and puts his hand on my arm. He shouts to the crowd, "That's all for now. Just a small taste of the exotic entertainment that awaits you." He turns Baldassaro and me around and says quietly, "Go back to the caravan now. Quickly." He shows me the stolen coins, which appear to be gold. "I have to make a present of these to the magistrate and the sheriff."

When the caravan arrives in the square, we set up the platform with the help of some excited, eager children. Then, as Arlecchino plays his fiddle, Columbine tells the crowd (and the actors) what will happen in the comedy that is about to be presented. I think I have suddenly become hungry, but then I realize that my stomach is beginning to quiver unpleasantly with excitement and fear. I long for the times when I posed in the studio of Mr. Rembrandt or some other painter, with nothing to remember and no jackass to ride. In those times I might have been pictured riding upon the strange creature called a camel, but the camel was only in the imagination or the sketchbook of the painter, and not in the studio.

My first appearance as Zanni in the young lovers comedy seems to please everyone but me. Things do not happen as Columbine said they would. I am not always sure what language is being spoken, and I never know what I am expected to do. I fall down often. It does not help when I look out to see Twee, his new ring glinting on his finger, standing next to a well-dressed man who is looking expectantly at me. I know that if this man becomes more aware of Twee's movements than of mine, the whole troupe might end up huddled in a small prison or hanging from the gibbet that stands at a corner of the square.

It is not good for a comedian to think about gibbets when he is performing. But I am learning that people will laugh — for a time — at someone who merely stands before them looking confused. This is one of those times. And just as the audience is tiring of my confusion, I am saved by Baldassaro, who trots up and pushes my behind with his nose. I fall down. He brays. Isabella appears and begins to do her belly dance. I show her my snake.

And the comedy goes on. People laugh, and apparently no one suspects that when the show is over, when the hats are passed, some of them might discover that their purses have been cut.

When the show has ended, our caravan rumbles out of town as quickly as the horses can move it. I am certain not everyone is sorry to see us go. We travel as fast and as far as we can before total darkness stops us.

When we make camp, the actors are in the mood to celebrate. Using food that was given to us or that we bought before the performance, we prepare a meal that seems endless. As bottles of French wine are passed around, Pantalone roasts a young pig. Twee cooks fish and new peas with a sauce of scallions and Spanish wine, and I cook some potatoes and small cabbages with a sauce of cream and cheese. Columbine makes crepes with tiny strawberries, and Isabella boils many pots of dark coffee.

When we finally finish eating, Twee reads aloud drunkenly from *The Ingenious Gentleman Don Quixote of La Mancha*. The story he reads is one in which Sancho Panza is humiliated by being tossed in the air from a blanket held by jokesters in the yard of an inn. Don Quixote, who is outside the walled yard, sees Sancho rising and falling beyond the wall. I am lying on a blanket near the campfire, listening to Twee, who must hold the book close to the flames and close to his face to be able to read to us.

Arlecchino is delighted by the story. "We can use it in the comedy," he says. "We can toss the Zanni." Arlecchino, Pantalone, Isabella, and the boy Adriano take the corners of my blanket and try to lift me from the ground. I am too drunk and sad to protest, and they are too drunk to lift me.

Arlecchino collapses onto the blanket. "It will be easier to toss Adriano," he says. I roll off the blanket, and Adriano takes my place. I hold one corner of the blanket, and we lift the boy. Pantalone counts to three, and we toss Adriano into the air. We manage to catch him and to throw him into the air once more, but as we do, the boy screams, "No." Suddenly, no one is laughing, and when Adriano lands in the blanket, he rolls out and runs into the caravan.

Pantalone is frowning. "The boy is no trouper," he says. "He has no taste for heights. He should be a potato farmer." Pantalone wanders off and opens another bottle of wine.

I go to the caravan and find Adriano sitting on the floor. I expect I might see him weeping, but he smiles at me and says, "You can't let them get away with too much, Lenoir. They would cripple us for a laugh. That's what you and I are here for; we are victims."

"No, Adriano. I cannot believe they want to hurt us."

"They don't want to hurt us, exactly. What they *want* is to get laughs. And if we happen to get hurt in the process, so be it."

"But if we are hurt, we cannot get more laughs for them."

"There are always more youngsters. You've seen how they follow us around."

I say, with some pride, "But there are not many like me."

"Oh yes there are. There are plenty of freaks."

"Freaks? You think I am a freak?"

"That's what they call the Zanni. The last one was very, very fat."

"But I am not very, very fat."

"But you're very, very black."

"I am black, but I am beautiful."

"You may be beautiful, but you're a freak, Lenoir. Take my word for it."

"In my homeland, children do not speak disrespectfully to adults."

"I'm not disrespectful; I'm your friend, Lenoir. And I was raised by white Christians. I know how they see things. They see you as a freak."

"Some respected painters have painted my picture."

"They probably painted dogs and the Devil, too."

I turn away and leave the caravan. I will not be called a freak, a dog, and the Devil.

I drag my blanket off to a grove of trees, where I empty my bladder. As I look for the best place to make up my solitary bed, I see that Isabella is standing away from the others and is watching me carefully. I think she wants to say something to me — perhaps to put the curse of death on me or to do something sexual to me — or perhaps both. But at the moment, I am only interested in sleep, or perhaps in weeping. Fortunately, I fall asleep almost immediately.

In the middle of the night, I am awakened by something touching my head. I open my eyes and see a hand holding a burning candle. The hand has long, clawlike fingernails that could only belong to Isabella. She is kneeling next to me and running her hand lightly across my head. She says, "No Columbine, *si?*"

I don't answer, but watch her eyes glitter in the candlelight. She says, "Columbine whore, *si?*" She puts the candle holder down and raises her skirts, showing me her body from her knees to her flabby waist. She moves her belly, as she does when dancing.

I spit on her belly.

She gasps, and for a moment she does not move. Then she drops her skirt and produces her sharp little dagger. She moves the dagger toward my head, and I am afraid she will push its sharp point into my eye. I am so frightened that I cannot move. But she only pulls some of my hair with one hand, and cuts a tuft of it with the knife. "Savage hair," she says, and holds it over the candle flame. As the hair singes and releases its deathly odor, Isabella speaks rhythmically in the Italian language. I do not need to understand the words to know that she is placing a curse on me. She says the word *maledizione* many times, and she runs off to the caravan.

There was a time when her cursing would have frightened me more than her knife, but now I feel only relief that the dagger has not blinded me. I smile and remember the words that every child in my homeland learns for use in case of an encounter with the Evil One:

> Although you threaten me
> and speak words of evil
> I need not fear you,
> for I carry my innocence
> as a shield.

I begin to laugh at this silly, jealous woman. I will not curse her in return. I will find better uses for my powers.

Despite the partying of the night before, everyone is awake at first light. The actors seem to be avoiding me, and no one says anything to me as we eat and break camp quickly. I think the actors are all afraid that a sheriff's man may come riding up.

The only person who seems relaxed is Twee. "Business was good," he says.

I ask, "Is there a god of business?"

"I believe not."

Twee might want those three words written on his gravestone.

There will be no performance for a few days, and a great sadness has settled over me. I wonder if the evil thoughts of Isabella are affecting me. I think the actors are still avoiding me. Isabella talks to them while glancing at me.

On some nights I am visited by Twee, who tells me of one or another of the many plans he has to make us rich and famous or who reads to me about Sancho Panza and Don Quixote. But I am not interested in those things. Finally, Twee says, "Lenoir, you're losing your zest."

I say, "Isabella has cursed me."

"Well, curse her back. You're good at juju."

"I don't do bad juju anymore."

"Isabella just wants some attention. Give her some. It might be interesting. You've seen her do the belly dance?'

"Why should Isabella not like me?"

"Not liking is one of the things people do best. Forget about it. Do your job until we get to Antwerp or until there's another party."

On the next night, Columbine appears. She says, "Isabella told us that you tried to kill her. But I don't believe her." Despite what Columbine says, she stands farther away than she has to.

I sit down and pat the ground next to me. "Come here, my child," I say. Slowly, she approaches and sits facing me. We smile at each other. I tell her stories of the serpent-god until her eyes begin to close. Then I sing her a lullaby:

> What things are silent?
> Many good things are silent:
> the sun, the gliding serpent.
> But my child is not silent.
> Be good, my child.
> Be silent, my child,
> all through the night.

Columbine comes to me the next night, and we talk of *The Ingenious Gentleman Don Quixote of La Mancha*, for she has read the entire book. She tells me a story that Twee has not mentioned, which involves a ship called a galley, on which there are many slaves. Twee understands that I would be upset by such a story. But I cannot expect Columbine to know that I have had unpleasant experiences with ships. She is delighted by the story because one of the galley slaves is found to be a young woman — a Catholic Christian Moorish woman whose long-lost father suddenly appears after a confusing adventure involving Turks, buried treasure, and a man dressing as a woman. Columbine looks especially pleased as she tells of the father and daughter being reunited. I also feel tears forming in my eyes, but when someone called the boatswain whips the backs of the galley's oarsmen.

Columbine and I hold each other. She calls me her Moorish father. I wonder in what land my own father has found himself.

We make appearances in towns called Delft and Gouda, where people are much interested in things like pottery of a disturbing blue color and in tasteless cheese. These towns are too orderly to be much interested in comedies, and they give the troupe little money. Of course, it may be that my lack of zest has made the comedies less interesting to the audiences. I appear as Zanni, but I do not fall down, which puts me at a great disadvantage.

On the morning after our performance in Delft, the troupe sleeps later than usual because it is a Sunday. Not being a true member of the troupe, I do not have their habits, and also, ever since Isabella's threats to me, I sleep lightly and awaken early.

This morning, as I am shaving, I see Isabella leave the camp and walk quickly along the road back toward Delft. I like to know where this witch is at all times, so I follow her. She either does not expect to be followed or it does not matter to her, for she walks quickly and does not turn to look back. She wears a black shawl over her head.

I am disappointed at first to find that Isabella's errand is nothing more mysterious than a visit to a church. But, of course, it is not quite as simple as that. The building she enters looks as if someone has tried to destroy it. Most of its windows have been boarded over. Stone statues that stand upon the side of the church have had their faces smashed or their arms broken off. The edges of some windows are blackened with smoke.

The people who enter the church do not look at one another, and like Isabella they seem ashamed of what they are doing. There is no doubt that this church belongs to Pope and not to Calvin.

I am happy that Isabella has brought me here. Perhaps I will hear someone singing the Kyrie Eleison song. I listen, but I hear no singing, not even the music of the frightening organ. I hear the sound of bells, but from another part of the city.

I go from the grayness of the morning into the darkness of the church. Although a feeble light enters the building through a few windows that are not boarded, the church is lighted mostly by many candles, which give off a sour-smelling smoke. I stand at the back of the church and wait as Isabella sits on one of the hard benches. She bows her head for a moment and then looks at a small wooden house that stands against one of the walls. The house has two doors. I think it contains chamber pots. We sit for a few minutes, until a man wearing a long black dress enters one of the house's two doors. Then Isabella gets up and enters the second door.

What is happening? Is this some kind of odd sexual encounter? I must find out. No one seems to be looking at me or the little house, so I go quickly to stand beside it. I hear Isabella say, "Forgive me, Father, for I have sinned."

Is this her father? Yes, for he calls her his child. He says, "I think you were not born in this country, my child. You might be more comfortable speaking Italian."

Isabella says, "*Si, padre. Grazie.*" Then she and the man have a conversation, in which she does most of the talking. I would greatly like to know what Isabella considers sinful, but, unfortunately, I can understand only a few words.

A woman has entered the church and is looking at me angrily. I think it is time to leave. As I walk past the woman, she says to me, "Savage. It is not civilized to listen to a person's confession."

I must ask Twee or Columbine to tell me about "civilized" and "confession." I already know about "savage."

# 13

BY THE TIME we reach Rotterdam, some of my zest has returned, and I am ready to begin falling down again in my performances. Rotterdam is not small and orderly, and when Twee and I enter the city for our advance work, Twee cannot control his excitement.

"There's action here," he says. "Whatever you're looking for." Twee looks at me seriously. "Lenoir, I love cities."

I think this is true. Twee does not love a person or a picture or even money. He loves the way these things fit together; and they fit together best in big, crowded cities that have places for ships to rest in.

As we travel through the streets — me on Baldassaro and Twee on foot — I notice a person wearing a mask and dressed like our Arlecchino. I point the person out and ask Twee, "Is there another troupe here?"

"Oh, God," Twee says. "I hope not." He runs off to talk to the masked person. As they speak, I notice that the crowded streets contain a few more people with brightly colored clothes and strange masks. Twee is back soon. "Great good luck," he says. "There will be a masked ball tonight. Some sort of local after-Lent festival. Great good luck."

As we move through the city, announcing the approach of

the caravan, we see a sight that makes me greatly angry. A rope is stretched across the main street, just out of arm's reach, and hanging from the rope is what appears to be a large black snake, something like the snake I wear with my costume. Men jump up and grab the snake, trying to pull it from the rope, but no one can get a grip on it.

I ask Twee, "Why do they insult the snake in this way?"

"It's not a snake, Lenoir. It's an eel — a kind of fish. It's slippery. And as you might have noticed, it's something that would make any man envious. The man who finally brings it down will present it to his sweetheart. Very subtle."

"It is disrespectful to the eel."

"Nothing personal, Lenoir, but you have to be prepared for disrespect if you have an odd appearance."

When the caravan enters the city, the weather is clear and sunny. The crowds are large and excited, and I and the rest of the actors forget our problems and give excellent performances. Baldassaro and I receive many *bravi*, and I can see Twee moving happily through our audiences, offering to share his latest bottle of brandywine. His special ring flashes in the sunlight. When we pass a hat, it quickly becomes heavy with coins.

We perform many times during the day, and each performance is better than the one before. We present the last performance — a version of "The Stone Guest"— by the light of torches that the townspeople are holding around our platform. At the end, when the Captain goes to the Devil's underworld, Arlecchino lights a bonfire, which delights everyone but Baldassaro, who brays in fear. I can see also that there is some fear behind the laughter and delight of the spectators. They are wondering if one day they will join the Captain in the everlasting flames. I have no such fear.

I look out into the crowd and see the face of Twee. There is no fear there either. I think of what he has told me about the danger of belief. Can it be that there is no fear without belief? I don't know.

As the performance ends, the spectators — many of them masked and in costume — gather around, offering us food and drink. I am too tired for that kind of pleasure. I want to take Baldassaro to a quiet place where I can calm his fears and rest my body.

I can see Twee making his way toward me. A young masked person who could be either male or female is hanging on to Twee's arm. Twee shakes free from the person's grasp and is soon standing at my side. He opens my hand and places a heavy, bulging purse in it. "Bury this somewhere," he says. "There are dishonest people here. Bury it and then come to our party." He points to a house that has a lamp in every window. In one of the windows there is also a plump, golden-haired young woman who is raising her skirt with one hand and waving unsteadily to the crowd with the other.

I say to Twee, "Enjoy yourself," and I make my way toward Baldassaro. Although I am exhausted, I do not mount him, for I know he is also tired. I put Twee's purse in Baldassaro's saddlebag, take his reins, and lead him out of town.

As I walk, I turn frequently to see if anyone is following. A masked man is standing at the edge of the crowd, and although he does not move to follow me and is not looking directly at me, I know he is aware of me. He is dressed in a jacket, tights, and long leather boots — all of them black. His wide-brimmed hat is also black but has a large scarlet plume attached to it. I turn a corner, then wait and look back. The man in black does not appear, but another man does: it is Pantalone, who is carrying the leather bag in which he keeps the money collected at our performances. I have never seen the bag so full.

Pantalone waves to me, and I wait as he approaches. When he is close, he whispers, "I must hide this money carefully . . . bury it for the night. There are dishonest people here."

I smile and say, "I cannot believe that."

"No. Who can believe that?" he says, and removes his mask.

We look at each other knowingly. I have seldom seen this man without his mask. He is younger than he seems to be during our performances, but there are lines and creases of worry in his face. The night is mild, and Pantalone takes off the heavy jacket of his costume, which is the color of strongly brewed tea. I have never spoken to Pantalone of anything other than the comedies and the ordinary events of the day. Tonight is no different. I say, "I had the feeling as we traveled today that the ground was rising — that we had reached the beginning of hill country."

"You were wrong. We people who have lived among hills deceive ourselves — or our bodies deceive us. Our muscles want to feel the extra tug of a rising or falling road."

I don't answer. The sounds of the city fade. My companion says, "My name is Fiori. It means 'flowers.'" After more silence, he says, "In Tuscany, there are castles and large houses on hilltops."

Fiori's eyes are glistening. It is best not to remember one's homeland.

Fiori says, "Isabella is not a bad person. She doesn't wish you ill."

"She has *made* me ill, I think."

"She is jealous of your witch-power. She thinks your power is stronger than hers. But I have lain next to her at night when she touched herself and said your name."

"When a witch does that, it does not have the meaning it has when a young bride to be does it. And in any case, pleasures of the body have nothing to do with trust. Isabella would give me — not even *sell* me — to any devil at any time. I know this is true."

"But even if she wanted to give you to a devil, that doesn't mean she is able to do it."

"Has she never used her powers on you, Fiori?"

"She tried, but she wasn't successful. She couldn't affect me, because I don't believe in witchcraft. And witches can only hurt you if you believe they can hurt you. Disbelief is the best protection. I trust in disbelief and comedy. What do you believe in, Lenoir?"

"I believe in everything. Twee believes in nothing."

We look at each other for a time. Fiori is too trusting, I think. But he is still not trusting enough to let me know where he is going to bury his money. We are at a crossroads. We go in different directions.

As I bury Twee's money I stop digging often, because I think I hear the sound of someone moving in the darkness. The actors have told me that even though they travel in a group, they worry about being attacked by highwaymen, who may also travel in groups and who would not hesitate to kill someone just for amusement.

When I have finished, I stand in the darkness with Baldassaro. He is so still that I think he may be asleep. Clouds drift across a small, slender moon. A few of the brightest stars appear occasionally, but I cannot see the pictures they form.

I awaken Baldassaro and lead him back to the city and the caravan, which is on a side street near the square in which we performed the comedies. I lead the animal to a water trough, and I get him some of the horses' feed. In the caravan, I find only Columbine and Adriano, who are asleep in each other's arms.

I remove my costume and put on my robe. I go back to the street and walk until I find a fountain. I can hear the sound of laughter and singing coming from nearby houses, and I smell roasted meat and boiled cabbage. I wash my costume and then remove my robe and wash my body. A few people walk past and look at me with the surprise and admiring curiosity that I am used to. Without my makeup and costume, I still attract attention, but no one smiles at me.

When my body is clean, I go back to the caravan and hang my costume out to dry. I am less tired now, and I am hungry. I decide to join Twee at the ball. I put on an old red, beak-nosed half-mask that is hanging on the wall.

When I reach the house where the party is being held, I am pulled through the door and embraced by a woman whose face is hidden but whose body is well displayed. She says she remembers Zanni's eel from the comedy. I say the comedy has ended.

Members of the troupe are scattered throughout the crowd. In the center of the room is a large table on which, amid platters of food, stand two musicians playing instruments I have never seen before — one that is blown into and the other scraped upon. Some of the foods are also new to me. I think some of them are eels, which are ever present in this city. There are also pieces of large animals, which for all I know might be horses or jackasses — or even a person left over from an anatomical theater.

The eating of meat is most important in this part of the world. I think it is their way of telling themselves they are more important than other animals. In my homeland, although we eat certain creatures, we allow them the respect of the hunt, and we give them the chance to elude us. A meal of meat is dedicated to the animal's spirit. I prefer the things these people grow to the things they kill.

I satisfy my hunger with many types of cooked green plants, an excellent bread that is almost the color of my skin, and a cheese that is too soft to stay in a chunk.

Pantalone makes his way through the crowd and gives me a bottle of bluish red wine from his homeland. He says it reminds him of the sun rising over the fragrant hills of his village. Although I do not tell him so, its aroma reminds me of bodies after sex.

I look around the room to see if there are any women who are not obviously the property of an attentive man. I don't see any, except the woman who greeted me at the door. But to my surprise, Twee seems to be enjoying the attention of a woman — a woman whose long face and moving nostrils give her a horsey look, which I do not find attractive. She is wearing what I believe is a costume of some sort, but she might just have an odd taste in clothing. Her full-skirted dress is pinched unnaturally at the waist, and she wears a large pleated ruff at her neck. Her hands are gloved. She is the tallest woman I have ever seen.

As I reach Twee and his friend, the musicians begin a new melody. The woman starts to hop about. She says something in a language I don't understand. Twee answers her in the same odd language. Then he says to me, "This is an Englishwoman, Lenoir. Miss Hart." He pronounces her name with an escape of breath at the beginning. The woman continues to hop. Twee says, "The music is English . . . 'Cuckolds All in a Row.'"

"Cuckolds?"

Twee explains: "A man whose wife is unfaithful to him."

"They have many cuckolds in this woman's homeland?"

Miss Hart answers me awkwardly in Walloon: "We have many, and we are proud of them. We write songs and comedies about them. It is our national game." She bounces away. Twee says, "She has been asking to meet you, Lenoir."

"She is not for me."

"No. Probably not."

I look further about the room. There are not many pleasant costumes being worn. I think there are not many pleasant people here. My gaze is stopped by the man in black whom I had seen on the street earlier. I think that behind his mask, he is watching me and Twee. I take several swallows of wine, and I make my way casually toward the man, not looking directly at him. I stop near him and turn away just enough so that I can still see him with a sidelong glance. He moves away from me, and as he moves, I hear quite distinctly the clinking sound of a chain. I can hear it despite the noise of the room, because it is a sound that has special meaning for me — a sound I will never forget.

Why does this man have a chain? I turn to look at him directly. I can see a few links of the chain, which he is wearing around his waist, beneath his jacket. But he is not wearing it as a belt; it is too heavy for that, and it is secured by a lock. And I can see part of a wrist shackle.

I approach the man, trying to imagine the face behind his mask. Then suddenly I know exactly what his face looks like. I know, because I can see through the openings in his mask that one of his eyes is brown and the other is green. He is the second Vlieg.

Does he know that I have recognized him? It isn't likely. My own mask will have hidden my look of alarm. I smile at a young woman who is moving past him. "Good evening, mademoiselle," I say. She smiles but does not stop. I follow her for a few steps and then veer away toward Twee. I say to him, trying to smile, "Don't look around, but the man in black is the second Vlieg. And he has prisoner's shackles with him. We must flee."

Twee smiles. Then he surprises me by producing a knife — the pretty little knife that Isabella threatened me with. He says, "I think we can handle the weasel ourselves."

Miss Hart, who leaped back to us as Twee was speaking, says, "Give the knife to me. I'll kill the bastard, whoever he is."

Twee says to Miss Hart, "I love the way you say 'bastard,' my dear. Now tell me more about the Puritans."

I ask myself what I am to do with these silly people — and what I am to do with myself.

"Excuse us," I say to Miss Hart, and I pull Twee aside. "This is serious," I say to him.

"Of course it's serious. That's why we have to kill the weasel."

"Then there will just be someone else chasing us."

"Not if we're subtle about his death. You can help by using your juju. It worked with the first Vlieg."

"I told you, I no longer make bad juju. But we have money. Maybe we can bribe him to let us go."

Wrinkles appear in Twee's forehead. "Where *is* the money?" he asks.

"It is safe. It is in the ground."

"And you're the only one who knows where?"

"The only one."

"Maybe you could draw a map for me."

"I don't think so."

Twee smiles. "Then we'll have to take good care of you, won't we?"

"We must leave this city, Twee. Now. There are probably people who think you have robbed them. I think there are bad people at this party. They might be waiting for the best time to kill you. If we flee, there will be no need for death."

Twee looks annoyed. "Lenoir, you have no breadth of vision. Relax. Leave things to me. Everything will be fine."

Miss Hart comes leaping back again. "Oh, God," she says, in her odd, rough voice. "Can it be that I'm too old for this?" Midway through the sentence, her voice becomes much lower, and she takes one of her gloves off. When I see her hands, I realize that Miss Hart is actually a mister.

Twee says to him, "Nonsense, Miss Hart. You're just out of practice. Too many months at sea."

So Miss Hart is an English sailor. And Twee is more interested in flirting with this person than in saving my life — or in saving his own life. He puts one of his arms around my waist and the other around the sailor's and says, "Let's get some air." We push our way through the crowd, out to the street. It is raining lightly, and we take shelter in the covered entrance of a building across the street. The night air is chilling instead of refreshing. It is no night for fleeing. If the second Vlieg were not at the ball, I would gladly go back there. I would like to discover a new wine and find a woman to admire me.

By the time we cross the street, my suspicions about Vlieg are confirmed. The man in black appears at the doorway we have just left, and he stares across at us.

Twee shouts, "Fuck you, Vlieg."

The sailor shouts, in a man's voice: "Bloody right. Fuck you, Vlieg." Then he says, quietly to us, "Who's Vlieg?"

"A sheriff's man."

"Can't stomach a sheriff's man," the sailor says. "He's after you, is he?"

Twee says, "He's after us both — me and Lenoir."

The sailor shakes my hand. "I'm Will Hart, Lenoir." His handshake is strong, and his hands are callused.

Twee says to me, "Will is a seaman."

"A captain?" I ask.

"Sort of," Will says to me. Then he shouts again across the street: "Fuck you, and fuck the sheriff, Vlieg." Then he walks toward Vlieg, who goes back into the house. Hart also goes into the house.

Twee says, "A good man. The best Englishmen go to sea."

In a moment Hart reappears, pushing Vlieg ahead of him. They stop a few feet in front of us, and Hart takes Vlieg's mask off. "Is this the villain?"

"That's him," Twee says.

Hart says to Vlieg, "Let's take a walk. A walk in a soft rain clears the head."

Twee and I follow along. Vlieg has said nothing, but he is obviously very frightened, and probably confused to be treated so unpleasantly by someone wearing women's clothes. And he stinks.

Hart says, "Beshit himself, I believe. Might have been something I said."

We enter a narrow alley. Hart stops in front of a hitching post. He removes the chain from around Vlieg's waist, chains Vlieg to the post, locks the chain, throws away the key, and ties a cloth around Vlieg's mouth. "Get yourself a wash when you can," Hart says to Vlieg. Then he says to us, "Now then, for another dance or two."

Back at the ball, Twee looks quickly and intently around the room. "We missed the grand moment. Every good party has a grand moment, just before people begin yawning or vomiting or passing out."

People are indeed doing all the things he has mentioned. But I am not displeased. I believe I have always preferred moments that are not quite grand. Even so, I have had enough of this particular party. I wish I were in a quiet room with Sister Jeanne.

Twee and Hart find two abandoned but not empty wine-glasses and begin prancing about to the rhythms of the music. The rhythms are not as fast as they were earlier.

As I look around the room I see not the partygoers but a re-membered image of the second Vlieg. Soon someone will find him chained and wet and will remove the gag from his mouth. It is only a matter of time before angry men come looking for us. We will not be safe; we will never again be able to appear before a crowd with the Italian comedy troupe. I sit down and sip some wine.

A woman who has been dancing by herself stops in front of me and says, "Smile, Lenoir."

"You know my name?"

"Everyone knows your name, Lenoir. You're the talk of Rotterdam . . . you and the jackass."

Oh, good, I think. The two jackasses.

The woman lowers herself onto my lap and places my hand in her bodice. "Will you show me the snake?" she asks. I auto-matically begin to pinch the large, firm nipple that my hand has encountered, but I do not smile.

The woman rolls her eyes. "They're making a Calvinist of you, are they? A Calvinist among the comedians? What next?"

She stands up and dances away and whispers something to another woman. They look at me and laugh. I wish they were chained in the drizzle with Vlieg.

The music stops, and Will Hart and Twee come and sit next to me. They are breathing hard and sweating. I say to Twee, "We must leave soon."

"The party will go until dawn," he answers.

"Not just leave the party, Twee . . . leave the city."

Twee frowns. Will Hart says to him, "Lenoir is probably right, Twee. A little retreat might be in order. Ship out with me. I'm sailing at first light."

I suddenly feel more cheerful. "Could you go to the city of Antwerp?" I ask.

"I could put in there," Hart says. "Or near there. I'm not popular around the docks there. And I'd need a few florins for me and my captain to make it worth our while."

Twee still looks displeased. "What kind of vessel is this we'd be on?" he asks.

I had not thought about the ship. Now I think of my past unpleasant voyages, and I remember the story of the galley slaves in *Don Quixote*. I ask Hart, "Is this by any chance a galley?"

"Relax," he says. "It's what they call a *jacht* around here. A pleasure craft."

Twee asks, "Would we have a cabin? A cabin in the fo'c'sle?"

I doubt if Twee knows what a fo'c'sle is any more than I do.

Hart says, "You'd not exactly have a cabin. But you'd have shelter. It'll be a pleasure cruise, my friends."

Soon, Twee and I are digging up the money and collecting our belongings. Twee writes our farewells on a piece of paper for the sleeping actors. My most important farewell, however, has to be said in person, for it would have no meaning in writing. That, of course, is my farewell to Baldassaro. I find him standing quietly in the rain near the caravan. I rub his nose and say, *"Bravo."* He looks at me. There is no sign that he recognizes me. Once more, I say, *"Bravo."* Then, as I begin to walk away, he suddenly swings his rear against my legs. I fall down. When I get up, some of the drops of water that run down my cheeks are warm and taste of salt.

At first light, Twee and I stand at the river where we are to meet Will Hart. We are away from the main docks, where the large ships stand. In fact, there are no ships at all here.

I say, "We must be in the wrong place."

"No. This is right. We'll wait."

It is our good luck that the morning is foggy, and if a search party comes looking for us, we will hear them before they see us.

After a few minutes, we hear from out of the river's mist, the voice of Will Hart: "Ahoy, passengers."

Twee answers, "Ahoy."

Gradually a ship becomes visible. But as Twee points out, it is not exactly a ship. "It's a skiff," he says. "The ship must be out in the main channel. He'll take us to it in the skiff."

There are two people in the skiff. One is Hart, who is, to my relief, wearing a jacket and trousers rather than a dress. The other person is a man who has a black beard and has a piece of red cloth tied tightly around his head.

When the skiff is tied up, Hart says to the other man, "Captain Rodriguez, these are our passengers, Twee and Lenoir."

Captain Rodriguez nods at us and says, "Where's the money?"

Twee takes out his purse, and he and the captain talk about money. While they talk, I look at the skiff. It has places for three pairs of oars, and at the front stands a pole with a piece of cloth on it. Twee and the captain finally reach an agreement, and we load our belongings into the boat and step carefully aboard.

"You'll have to give us a hand at the oars," the captain says.

Twee and I look at each other unhappily. Twee says, "How far to the ship?"

"What ship?" Captain Rodriguez says.

"The ship we're sailing on."

"This *is* the ship you're sailing on, you fool."

Twee says, "This is just a rowboat with a toy sail."

"Shut up and row," the captain says. "Or maybe you want me to call for the sheriff." He speaks Walloon, but in a way I have not heard before.

Twee jumps up, and the boat begins to rock. Will Hart stands up and puts his hands on Twee's shoulders. "Steady," he says. "There's no need for commotion."

Twee is doing a sort of belly dance trying to keep his balance. He finally sits down and says to Hart, "A pleasure cruise. You said this would be a pleasure cruise."

"It *will* be," Hart says. "Relax. We'll catch the breeze. It'll be a fine day once the morning mist burns off . . . fresh air . . . away from the cares of the land."

Twee says, "We're nothing more than galley slaves." But he is calming down. I think he realizes we are better off than we would be on land with the unhappy second Vlieg pursuing us.

"We'll be in Antwerp in no time. Or near Antwerp, so you don't have to deal with the customs officers. Well rested. Everything nice and easy."

I ask Hart, "Just how long is the 'no time' that our cruise will take?"

"With a fair wind, we'll have you there tomorrow."

Twee asks, "Where do we sleep?"

"We'll put in somewhere overnight. A pleasant cruise. You'll see."

Hart, Twee, and I settle ourselves at the oars, and Captain Rodriguez sits facing us, steering. Hart, who is at the oars in front of us, says, over his shoulder, "Simply do what I do."

As I pull at the oars, my tired back begins to hurt. I decide it is not a good idea for me to exert myself. I hear Twee grunting and breathing heavily. He says, "Miss Hart, how can a self-respecting English sailor take orders from a Spaniard?"

Hart says, "I don't have any self-respect, Twee. I'm surprised you haven't noticed."

"Shut up and row," the captain says. "Mr. Hart has not self-respect, but I have much. And I demand respect. All men of Spain demand respect. Here in the North, there is little respect. There is no ruler. There is respect only for Calvin and gold. But soon, if you shut up and row, we are in King Philip's Antwerpen. God save King Philip. God preserve the Supreme Pontiff."

Hart says, "The mighty armada has come to this."

Captain Rodriguez spits into the water. "I am captain, you are mate. I steer, I talk. You shut up and row."

We shut up and row, although I do not do my share of the rowing. The captain tells us about the glories of the country of Spain and its empire. I cannot follow his talk, which sometimes — like the talk of Pantalone the actor — drifts into another language. There are so many languages, so many captains.

After many minutes of rowing while the captain talks, we reach a sharp turn in the river. A strong, steady wind suddenly grows up, and our sail begins flapping and fattening. Magically, we move forward faster than we can row. The mist vanishes, and we find that we are out of sight of land.

The sail pushes us forward, bending the pole it is tied to. Hart, Twee, and I stop rowing. The captain pulls a rope with one hand and holds the steering handle with the other. He talks continually, but I do not pay much attention to him until he says, ". . . the birthplace of Miguel de Cervantes, the world-famous author of the adventures of Don Quixote de la Mancha and Sancho Panza."

I know there is no use trying to tell Captain Rodriguez of my respect for this Cervantes. I will only be told to shut up and row. I relax and enjoy my cruise. I wonder what the land of Mr. Rubens will be like — a strange land that is ruled by a king and a pope who prefer to live elsewhere — a country in which Twee has told me many languages are spoken, all of them borrowed.

All clouds vanish, and though the strong wind is cold, the sun warms our little boat. The captain finally stops talking, and we sail quickly along in silence. I have some fear that the wind and rough water might sink our boat, which is overloaded with people and belongings, but my fear is soon replaced by the feeling of pleasure that Will Hart promised we would have.

I hope I am headed for a more dignified life than I have lived so far among these people. I think it is time, now that I have gained my freedom, that I make a friend other than Twee. For although Twee will not cut your throat, he *will* cut your purse. And he will never settle anywhere. He is like the Italian comedy troupe, passing through life, trading imaginings for the money of the other people, who make children, bread, or pictures.

I realize I will never be one of them, and I do not want to be one of them. But I have had enough departures. I may never own a house, but I at least want to have a friend who owns one. In my homeland, it is sung:

> She may not be a godlike person,
> but she is your mother.
> You may not be brave and handsome,
> but you can keep her house in repair.

I think it is time for me to help repair the house.

# 14

"ONE OF THE THINGS that is good about this pleasure craft," says Captain Rodriguez, "is that it goes easily past the enemy."

It is not yet dawn. The sky remains cloudless, but the wind no longer blows. We have slept on the sandy shore for a slight time, and now we are rowing quietly toward the mouth of a large river called the Scheldt. Ahead are the sparkling lanterns and the black silhouette of a large ship the captain calls the enemy and Twee calls a Hollander. We hear the sound of laughter coming from the ship.

"Women aboard," the captain says. "Partying. They won't hear us. But anyway, we should make no noise."

Twee has explained to me that ships from the North will not allow other ships to go along the river to Antwerp, where Mr. Rubens has his house. This, he said, is the kind of thing that happens when there is too much belief. But I suspect that what he is thinking now is that he has never been to a party on a large ship.

Soon, Captain Rodriguez steers us alongside a dock of old, moss-covered wood. Mr. Hart hands our belongings to us and pushes the boat away. He begins rowing, and without a word, he and the captain vanish into the darkness, which is changing from black to purple-gray.

Twee and I walk along the river toward the center of the city. There are many docks but few boats. The waterfront is uncared for, and we pass only a few workers, who fortunately do not seem interested in us.

Twee quickly finds an inn. The innkeeper seems more than a little interested in us, and is not very welcoming. Twee produces a piece of paper and a bag of florins. The innkeeper seems to relax a bit. Twee asks him, in Walloon, "Can you read the Spanish on the paper?" The innkeeper shakes his head. Twee smiles and says, "This seal is the seal of King Philip IV. The king asserts that I am free, with my Moorish companion, Señor Lenoir, to have safe conduct in all the lands of His Majesty's empire."

The innkeeper nods. "So you say. But what does the purse say?"

"The purse," says Twee, "speaks Flemish."

"That is my language," the innkeeper responds, and he and Twee begin speaking what sounds to me like the language of the taverns of Amsterdam.

Soon, Twee puts some florins in the innkeeper's hand, and a boy leads us up a flight of stairs to a spacious room that contains a large bed and a wood-filled fireplace. The boy fetches a burning stick, and before long there is warmth in the room — a type of warmth I have not felt since we left Amsterdam. The boy brings us food, and although it is only fatty sausage, dry bread, and watery ale, it is satisfying.

I eat, wash in warm water, and fall asleep.

When I awaken, I see Twee sitting at a table, putting words on a piece of paper. When he sees that I am awake, he says, "Let me read you a letter: 'To my honorable acquaintance, Mr. Peter Paul Rubens.'"

"I didn't know you were an acquaintance of Mr. Rubens."

"I'm not. This letter isn't from me. It's from Rembrandt."

"But didn't you just write the letter?"

"I'm putting the words down, but they're the words that Rembrandt would have used if there had been time for us to ask him. It's only a letter of introduction."

"Can we not introduce ourselves?"

"Not a chance, Lenoir. Rubens is a very important man. Royalty come to see him. Hundreds of painters want to work and study in his studio. You can't just knock on his door."

"Then why have we come here if he will not see us?"

"He *will* see us. He'll see us because he's curious about Rembrandt, and he likes to collect old coins."

"Do we have any old coins?"

"Dr. Padmos gave me some when he bought you. Remember? I still have them. Rubens will want to see them. Listen to the rest of the letter: 'This is to introduce my good friends Mr. Dom Twee and Mr. Francis Lenoir.'"

"Francis?"

"You need a Christian name. Francis is a saint's name. Rubens is a devout Roman Catholic. He'll be pleased if you're a Christian."

"But I'm not a Christian."

"He'll be pleased if you have a Christian *name*. Listen to the rest: 'Mr. Twee, who is a dealer in art and antiquities, owns some remarkably pagan coins from ancient Rome.'"

"What does 'remarkably pagan' signify?"

"They're naughty, Francis. Very naughty."

"Please call me Lenoir. And why would a devout Catholic be interested in naughty things?"

"It's art. Roman Catholics don't mind a little naughtiness in art. Let me finish: 'Mr. Lenoir is a Moorish artist's model, whose striking features and ability to hold a pose make him an ideal subject for portraits, historical representations, and religious depictions.'"

"These don't sound like the words of Mr. Rembrandt."

"It's a letter, Lenoir. People sound different in letters. Here's the rest: 'It would please your inferior but devoted fellow painter Rembrandt van Rijn if you could allow my friends the honor of visiting your studio. On a personal note, I congratulate you on your remarriage after the regrettable death of the first Mrs. Rubens. I have heard that you continue to produce offspring and masterful paintings. I fear I cannot begin to rival you in the production of either. I am merely your admiring and humble . . . and so forth.' So what do you think?"

"What does the Moorish Francis think? He thinks we should tell the truth."

"If we do that, we'll never get to see Rubens, Lenoir. Successful people don't tell the truth. And since when has the truth been that important to you?"

"I think the letter should not be from Mr. Rembrandt. It can say the same things, but it should be from us."

Twee looks into my eyes for a long time. Finally he blinks and says, "All right. Actually, I'm not sure they are friends, anyway."

While he rewrites the letter, I wonder whether truth has become important to me. After a moment, I decide it is ridiculous to be trying to find the truth about truth.

While we wait for a reply to our letter, Twee and I stroll through the streets of Antwerp, or Antwerpen. The city is large, but I am disappointed because the buildings and people look much the same as those in the cities I have seen to the north. Twee tells me that these people have fought a long war with the people we have just left, but whatever they dislike about each other must be something that cannot be seen.

There are tall church buildings everywhere, as if to make up for the lack of hills or mountains. The largest church is called Our Lady, which Twee says contains a very big picture by Mr. Rubens showing some people taking the dead man-god down from his death-post. Twee says Mr. Rubens thinks large is good.

In the main square, there is also, as there seems to be everywhere in these countries, the wooden pillory, with the three holes, which are often encircling the neck and wrists of bad people.

There is a building for girls who have no parents. On the front of the building is a strange, big-mouthed stone bird. Twee says it's a pelican and it symbolizes charity. To symbolize is to mean something else. Good art always means something else, Twee says. Mr. Rubens always means something else.

We see Mr. Rubens's house, which is big — too big for one family, even a large one, which I assume Mr. Rubens would have. It has white stone people on it. I am sure it means something else.

We stop at an outdoor café and drink a strong wine from the land of Portugal, while Twee tells me how Mr. Rubens has made pictures of many kings and queens and has talked to them of ending or starting wars. This makes Mr. Rubens a diplomat, which is a person whose words mean something else.

Perhaps the reason the people here seem so worried is that they are not sure of what anything means.

As I have these thoughts, I am watching the people who pass us. I am hoping ridiculously that one of them will be Jeanne. Once in a while, a woman passes whose body or face or hair might be Jeanne's, but I see no one who moves as she did or whose eyes have the distant, gentle look that hers had.

Twee says, "What are you looking for, Lenoir? The second Vlieg? He won't follow us here. This isn't his country."

"I am looking for what doesn't exist."

"I think you might have spent too much time with Rembrandt."

Two days after Twee writes his letter to Mr. Rubens, we receive a reply — not from the great man himself but from his secretary. Twee reads it to me:

Mr. Twee and Mr. Lenoir:

Sir Peter Paul Rubens would be pleased to have you attend the visitors' gallery of his studio. Unfortunately, because of infirm health, the master cannot specify which days he will be able to spend in the studio. I suggest that you appear any day except Sunday, and if it is convenient, you will be admitted.

Respectfully,
Erasmus Quellyn III

Twee is delighted. "We won," he says.

"What is it we have won?"

"We get to meet Peter Paul Rubens."

"The letter doesn't say we will meet him."

"Of course we'll meet him. He'll want to hear what's new in Amsterdam."

"We don't *know* what's new is Amsterdam."

"You worry too much, Francis."

"Lenoir, please. And you don't worry *enough*, Twee."

"When we're introduced, call him Sir Peter."

"We use his Christian name?"

"I know you don't like those, but it's the custom when addressing a knight."

"A knight? He's a knight? Aren't knights called Don?"

"Actually, you could call him Don Pedro. He's been knighted in both Spain and England."

"I thought there were no longer knights."

"There aren't. Forget I said it. It's not important. What's important is that we look good."

We spend the rest of the day grooming ourselves. Twee even persuades me to visit a barber, who calls me unpleasant names but cuts my hair evenly.

It has been many days since we have had our shirts properly

washed, and we ask the innkeeper to find someone to launder some things for us. In a few minutes, there is a knock on the door, and when I open it, I discover the most beautiful light-skinned woman I have ever seen. Not that she is as pale as a flatlander; her skin is the color of dark-golden wood. I have seen no one like her either in my homeland or in any other land. She is short and slender enough to be a child, but she has the dignity and calm that only an adult can have. And there are delicate lines of age around her eyes, which are brown-black and folded at the corners. Her hair is long, black, and glossy. She wears a black jacket and a narrow black skirt.

"Come in," I say. "May I sing for you?"

"I am the chambermaid. There is some clothing you would like to have cleaned?"

She speaks Walloon almost as clearly as I do, but without any pride. Her magnificent eyes are lowered, as so many women's eyes are in these lands. "Please sit down," I say. She shakes her head, but she raises her eyes to look at me serenely and steadily. I believe she finds me intriguing, if not attractive. I say to her, "In the North it is said that cleanliness is next to godliness, but I prefer a clean shirt, myself."

The woman does not smile, as I had hoped she would, but merely nods and asks, "Where are the garments?"

I get them for her.

"And when would you like them returned?"

I look at Twee, who smiles and winks at me. He says to the woman, "Could you return them in the morning? Nine o'clock?" The woman nods. Twee continues, "And could we know your name?"

"My name is Amboina."

I am certain Amboina is her only name.

After she has left, I say to Twee, "She has excellent teeth."

"You miss Katja, don't you?"

\*

On the day of our visit to the Rubens studio, Twee and I look our dazzling best. The sky is cloudless when we leave the inn, and the sun glints on the lilac silk of Twee's suit. I am wearing a large black velvet hat that drapes onto the left shoulder of my red-and-gold robe. We have spent much of our money on clothing, but Twee says it is extremely important that we make a good appearance for Sir Peter, because painters are obviously impressed by the way things look. I wonder if the better painters might be used to looking beyond the surface of things.

But I am happy. My happiness would be complete except that our clean shirts were not delivered by Amboina but by an older, unattractive woman.

Twee and I find the gate to Sir Peter's house open, and after chasing away several admiring children who have followed us, we enter the courtyard. There are buildings on both our left and right. Ahead are open arches of stone leading to flower beds and neatly trimmed hedges. In the garden and on the arches there are more of the mysterious, ghostly people carved of stone.

Twee believes that the building with the most windows must be the studio. We knock on the door, and after a time a young man appears and asks our names. He seems especially interested in me, and he glances at me often as he leads us into a large, high-ceilinged room, bright with sun captured by the windows. Scattered around the room are pictures, some of them not yet finished.

The young man, who wears a gray, paint-stained gown, shows us up a flight of stairs to a landing overlooking the large room. "I am Erasmus Quellyn the Third, the master's assistant. The master is at work now. He will speak with you when he can. Do you prefer to speak French?" We nod, and he leaves us.

While I wonder why there were not just one but three fathers who called their sons Erasmus, Mr. Quellyn joins another man at one end of the studio, before a large, unfinished picture of a naked woman. The second man is seated. He wears a black cape and a large black hat that is similar to mine. He is old, and he looks ill — or rather, he looks as if he is fighting illness — but his chin-beard and mustache are full and only slightly white. This is obviously Sir Peter Paul Rubens, and he looks like some pictures I have seen of the Christian God-in-the-sky.

The master and the younger man seem to be discussing the unfinished picture, although I cannot hear what they are saying. The younger man steps to the picture occasionally and daubs colors on it.

Twee says, "It's probably Venus. I've heard he does more Venuses than Virgins these days."

I remember seeing a Venus that Mr. Rembrandt painted. She is a god who is supposedly no longer worshiped, but there is still much interest in her. I think I can see why.

As the two men continue their work, I look at some of the other pictures in the studio. They are not like the small pictures I have seen in the North — pictures of seated merchants in black clothes or young women reading letters in a kitchen. Instead, these pictures tell stories of soldiers, kings, queens, and gods — people doing things that are very good or very bad. There are many colors I have never seen before, either in or out of a picture.

The master and Mr. Quellyn seem to be trying to decide which colors to use in the picture they are making. I have noticed that painters often make their pictures first in odd, dull colors and then add better colors later. If I were doing it, I would start with good colors. I say to Twee, "Is it possible to have a picture that is only colors?"

"Who would want that?"

"I would. I would rather look at the color-mixing board than at most pictures."

"The palette, you mean. Well, you have special ways, Lenoir."

Before long, the master stands, and his assistant looks up at us and says, "Come down, please, gentlemen."

Mr. Quellyn introduces us to the master. Twee takes off his hat with a sweeping motion, and he bows. I do the same. The breeze made by our motion stirs up the pleasing smell of the paints.

Twee says, "It is an honor to meet you, Sir Peter . . . and to watch you at your work."

Sir Peter nods and looks at me, then at Twee, and then back to me. I think he expects me to say something. I say, "In my homeland, old men do not work . . . especially if they are *great* old men."

Twee bumps my arm with his elbow.

Sir Peter smiles.

I continue: "Of course, among my people, young men do not work, either."

Sir Peter's smile becomes questioning. He says, "And if a man doesn't work, how does a man become great?"

"A man is born great. And in battles, he may become a great warrior, but warriors are never as great as those who are born great."

"Of course not," Sir Peter says. His smile becomes broader. "And what does an old man do if he does not work?"

"Old men tell stories."

Sir Peter points to the picture he and Mr. Quellyn have been painting. "I, too, tell stories. This is a story about Venus."

I nod. "Yes. The Venus you used to worship but now just make naked pictures of. Mr. Rembrandt also made a picture of her, with that same red color in it."

Sir Peter looks puzzled. "Which red color is that?"

"The one I have seen in these two pictures and nowhere else . . . this red." I point to the cloak of a man who is standing behind Venus in the picture.

"Remarkable," Sir Peter says. "When I visited Rembrandt a

few years ago, I made him a gift of an unusual cinnabar . . . the one I've used here. I call it my erotic cinnabar. I can't exactly see how it differs from my other cinnabars, but I *feel* a difference."

Twee, who has been looking unhappy — as he usually does when he is not doing the talking — says, "Lenoir would *see* the difference. And remember it."

"Indeed?" Sir Peter points to two large pictures that are leaning against the wall. They show people — some with wings, some with jeweled clothes — who seem to be on a platform in the sky. "Quellyn," he says to his assistant, "I think you supervised the grinding and mixing of the paints for these?" Quellyn nods. "And we used the erotic cinnabar in just one?" Quellyn nods.

I also nod. "In this one," I say, pointing to the one in which a woman is bowing before a crowned man.

Quellyn nods again. "Mr. Lenoir is correct."

"Here," I say. I walk up to the picture and point to a red in the kneeling woman's gown.

Sir Peter turns to me. "A remarkable talent, Mr. Lenoir. You could be a great help in our studio. Have you ever wanted to be a painter?"

"To make pictures? No. Never. We did not have pictures in my homeland. Pictures can injure the soul, as I'm sure you know."

Sir Peter laughs. "I've sometimes suspected it. Fortunately, I attend mass every morning."

"Ah yes. I know about Kyrie Eleison. But I need someone to explain penance to me."

"That's easily arranged . . . more easily arranged than finding a good color blender. You would be perfect, Mr. Lenoir: excellent color perception and no artistic ambitions. Generally my good color blenders leave to become bad painters. If you are ever interested, I think I could find a position for you in my studio."

I tell myself that although I know little about this city, and although Twee and I have not talked about how long we might stay here, I might be happy staying in one place and making colors for a great old man in a large house. But before I can say anything, Twee says, in his doing-business tone of voice: "It is good of you to make such an offer to my client, Sir Peter, but I'm not sure how long we will be staying in Antwerp."

Sir Peter says, "Your *client?*"

Twee nods.

Sir Peter raises his eyebrows.

No one seems to know what to say next. As we wait in silence, a familiar-looking young woman appears. "Excuse me, Paolo," she says to Sir Peter. "It is time to rest."

Sir Peter introduces us to his wife. And then I realize why Mrs. Rubens looks familiar: she is the woman who posed for the picture of Venus. As I look at this woman standing next to the painting, I have many feelings. I am embarrassed that she knows that I know how she looks without her clothes. But I also realize that what I see in the picture is not her naked body but something different . . . like a ghost. Where, I wonder, is her soul? Is it in the picture, or does she still have it? Or is it somewhere else? Perhaps some of it has entered me.

I am ready to leave the studio. I am ready to be on the street, where there are no ghosts.

But Sir Peter, although he is looking at me, says to his wife: "I think I would rather work than rest today, Hélène . . . that is, if Mr. Lenoir wouldn't mind posing for me."

I look to Twee for permission but then remember that I can make my own decisions now. "It would be an honor, Sir Peter."

Mrs. Rubens says, "You're sure, Paolo?"

"I'm sure," he answers.

She shrugs and says softly, "Well, then." She nods to me and Twee and leaves the room. I think she wishes we were not here to distract her husband.

Mr. Quellyn asks Sir Peter, "Am I needed?"

"Can you find a small panel somewhere?"

Twee looks displeased. "Am *I* needed?"

The master says, "Not at this time, thank you, Mr. Twee. But we must talk business another time."

Twee takes his leave, and Mr. Quellyn returns with a small panel of wood.

"Fine," Sir Peter says. "Just for some studies. That's all for now, Erasmus."

And I am alone with the master. He says, "We'll chat a bit. I may have a few questions . . . but you needn't answer them."

I look up at one of the room's high windows. The sky is still cloudless.

"What do you think of us Europeans, Lenoir?"

"I don't know what to think of you. Just as I don't know what I believe. I once knew what to believe, but no longer."

Sir Peter says, "Perhaps that is our gift to you."

I look again at the picture of Venus. "Sir Peter, how is it that a person can be a god?"

"It's not that a person can be God. It's that God can be a person."

"Could your God be a serpent?"

"If God wanted to be a serpent."

"In my land, God wants to be many things, but especially a serpent. And never a person."

Birds fly past the window, some of them carrying bits of dried grass. I think of the pelican carved in stone. "Sir Peter, have you ever made a picture with a pelican in it?"

"I'm not certain. My assistants often add birds to a picture."

"If you had one, I believe it would have meant charity."

"Yes."

"And what would a serpent mean?"

"Wisdom."

"Excellent."

*

The master says, "You speak French well."

"It has an odd music to it, but it has more than enough words."

"You must forgive me if my French is lacking. I think of it as my sixth language. I have preferred Italian since my youth."

"With the Italian comedians, I heard the word *maledizione* many times . . . but also *bravo.*"

Sir Peter says, "It's good for the character to have not just one but both those words directed at one. I think I have heard more *bravi* than are good for a person."

"Do you enjoy making pictures of people, Sir Peter?"

"I'm beginning to enjoy it now that I have passed my sixtieth year. I'm beginning to get the knack, I think. But I still think the creature I do best is the horse." He pauses, then says, "I once kept a lion."

Sir Peter steps back from the picture and puts his brush and palette down. "I think that's enough," he says. "Come see."

There are four of me. Smiling, not smiling. Looking one way and another. The picture makes me uneasy, as though juju has been performed on me. I ask, "How can there be four of one person in the same picture?"

"It's just a study, Lenoir. Four of your moods at four places in time. Think of it as four pictures, not one."

We look at the picture together. I say, "It is more like the Northerners' little pictures than the big ones here."

The master smiles a little but also looks unhappy. "Someday someone will look at this and say I cannot have done it."

"And why is that?"

"It is a painting. I stopped being a painter many years ago and became a designer. My students filled in my designs; I corrected what they did. It wasn't their work, it wasn't mine." He picks up the new picture. "This is mine," he says. "Now come with me."

The master leads me to a room in which there are many white stone heads — like the heads of large dolls. I don't know how anyone could be comfortable in such a room. Certainly no one could sleep here. "A room full of ghosts," I say.

"In a sense, yes. These are people who lived long ago."

"Long ago is important to you."

"Yes. But someday our time will be long ago. Someone may look at the picture we have just made and know something about what we think and feel."

Although I don't say so, I wonder if what the master says is true. He thinks people in the future will be like his people. But maybe they will be like my people.

The master goes to a large cabinet and opens its two doors. Within the cabinet are many trays containing finger rings and coins of silver and gold. He picks out a gold ring and holds it out to me. "Here," he says. "Keep this as payment for posing for me."

I take the ring. Set into the gold is a flat stone. Carved in the stone is a stick with wings at its top and two snakes entwined about it. I am delighted. "Great beauty," I say. "And great power."

"It is from long ago," the master says. "It is the sign of medicine and healing."

"I cannot thank you enough, Sir Peter." Kneeling, I take his right hand and kiss it. The fingers are stiff and twisted. Why has no one healed them?

The master smiles. I think he likes to see people kneel before him. He reaches into his elaborate clothing and finds a heavy coin purse, which he gives me. He says, "Return at any time, Lenoir."

# 15

WHEN I GET BACK to the inn, Twee is waiting for me. I show him my ring. "For posing," I say. "No money?"

I don't tell him about the coin purse. "This is better than money," I say. "It has the ancient power of healing."

Twee is unhappy. He says, in a high-pitched voice, "But what about me? What about my share?"

"You no longer own me. You no longer get a share."

"But you get a share of mine. I paid the Spanish captain for two. I'm paying the innkeeper for two."

Twee is right. I must no longer take his money. I say, "Yes. I must pay my way. I will pay you soon."

"With what?"

"I will make colors for Sir Peter. He will give me guilders." I still do not mention the purse Sir Peter gave me. Before I tell Twee I have money, I want to know how much money I have.

Twee looks at me as if he is trying to keep from saying something unpleasant. I think he is not as fond of me as he was before I could earn my own guilders. Finally, he says, "When do you see him again?"

"He says I may return at any time."

"And what about me?"

"I will ask him when I see him again. Tomorrow, I hope."

Twee says angrily, "Well, in the meantime, I'd better see what other business I can do." He puts on a cloak and hat, then asks me: "And who will read to you? Who will count your money for you?" He leaves, knowing that I cannot answer those questions.

I look through the window of our room. The sky is still clear. Standing against the sky are the tops of many churches. I must visit one of them soon. But now I am thinking of Amboina. I must learn where she lives. I go downstairs to find the inn-keeper, who gives me an unfriendly look. He asks, "Will you be supplying me with a passport, Mr. Lenoir?"

I wonder if Twee has a passport for me among his many papers. I say, "I think Mr. Twee will give it to you."

"He has given me a passport for himself but not for you. If you don't have the correct papers, I must report you to the magistrate. It's the law."

Twee has told me that every law has its price. I ask the inn-keeper, "What is the price of that law?"

He looks at me in puzzlement for a moment, and then he laughs. "Let me think about that," he says.

"Let us both think about that. In the meantime, I wonder where I might find the woman Amboina."

"She doesn't make friends easily. We've all tried."

"That is no problem for me."

"She's running an errand. She'll be back soon."

The weather is fine, so while I'm waiting, I decide to have a little stroll. Before I have taken many steps, a raggedy young boy holds out his hand to me for money. Because I do not yet know the value of the coins I have with me, I wave him away. He says words that I think mean "black shit." They are among the first words I get a chance to learn in a new language. But I do not get angry with the boy. In my homeland it is said that if you become angry with a child, you are yourself a child.

I return quickly to the inn, but Amboina still has not come

back. It occurs to me that if I want a chance to talk to her, I should see her before she returns and starts to work again. I move down the street to a spot where I can see anyone who approaches the inn from either direction. I find a space between two buildings, and I squat down to wait for Amboina to appear.

After I have waited a few minutes, I begin to feel hungry. There is a square nearby with a café that has two outdoor tables. If Twee were with me, he would take me there and order me something I have never eaten or drunk before. Maybe Amboina will do that for me. I'm sure I have enough money. I take out the purse that Sir Peter gave me. I pour the coins into my hand. They are made of different types of metal, and no two of them are the same shape or have the same pictures or writing on them. These people seem to have as many different coins as they have languages. If I am lucky, after Amboina explains the coins to me, she will let me buy a meal for her.

I smile and wish people a good day as they pass. For reasons I don't begin to understand, a few people throw coins in front of me.

Just as I am growing impatient, the sky becomes filled with the sound of bells. But these are not like the sensible bells of the North — these are bells that play complicated music. The music is simpler than what is played by the machines in churches, but it is music of more than five tones, and it is coming from the top of a church. Although I cannot say I enjoy it, I do not find it upsetting, and it makes me forget my hunger. I notice that some of the people who pass me smile and sing along with the bells. They sing — and most of them speak to one another — in a language much like the language the Northerners call Dutch.

I can see, as one can see from most places in this city, the stone tower of a church. This is a city of stone, but the stone is made into unnatural, regular shapes. Stone makes me think of a song that is sung in my homeland, and I find that I sing the song; it fits quite well with the bell song:

The gods of the stone
make little caves
so that the serpent-gods
may have a home.
Can I do less than the gods?
Welcome to my house, stranger.

As I sing, I admire my serpent ring.

When Amboina finally appears, she looks at me immediately, as if she knew I would be here. Her eyebrows are flattened, and I think she is displeased. She walks across the street and places a coin on the ground in front of me. "Poor unfortunate fellow," she says. "You haven't chosen such a good location for begging."

Does she really think I am begging? No. There is a trace of a smile around her lips. I say, "This place is where I will find the only thing I would beg for."

"And what is that?"

"Your friendship, Miss Amboina." I stand up, pleased with the cleverness of my reply. Amboina seems tinier than ever, and I think she liked me better when I was squatting on the ground.

She asks, "And what would this friendship consist of?"

"I would buy you a meal and sing you songs. You would explain some coins for me."

"I have work to do. I have no time to listen to songs, and I take my meals with my father. Also, I don't think you realize that I am a serious person."

"Then you are a follower of Calvin?"

Amboina smiles and shakes her head. "I am a follower of no man and no god," she says.

I am amazed. This must be a person who, like Twee, has no beliefs. I say, "My friend Twee says we would all be happier if we had no beliefs."

Amboina shakes her head again. "Your friend is wrong. We

would suffer as we suffer now. There must be belief in the Eight-Step Path."

Then this woman, too, is deranged. But in a new way. I say, "That is a very short path indeed."

"Yet few reach its end."

"And what would they find at the end?"

"Nothing."

"I see." But, of course, I don't see.

Amboina smiles again, and this time I find her smile a little irritating. She says, " 'Nothing' in the sense that the absence of desire is nothing." Her smile broadens. She continues. "I think you would not want to be without desire."

"No," I say. "That is something I cannot imagine. In my birthplace, we have a song about a path. But there is something at the end of the path . . . home."

Amboina says, "Well, I think you are not home now, are you?" I look into her eyes for a moment. Is there really no desire in this person? At least there seems to be no desire for me. She says, "I must work now," and she enters the inn.

What a pity, I think, to have great beauty but no desire. As I have this thought, I am walking, and I find myself in front of the big church — the biggest I have seen anywhere. I go inside, and I feel as if I am in a great dark forest of stone tree trunks. Little of the late-day light gets through the colored pictures in the windows, and there are few candles burning. Unlike the Calvin church in Amsterdam, where there are not many places to sit, this building has many rows of benches. Scattered among the benches are a few people with bowed heads. I wander through the dark forest, looking at the high ceilings and the statues and pictures. I pass the little houses for confession and I remember that I still have not found out what confession is.

Eventually, I find two large pictures, twice as tall as I am, that show the man-god Our Lord and Savior Jesus Christ. They both show the scene of torture that everyone seems to like so much. In one picture, he is being raised on his post, and in the other he is being taken down. For some reason, everything changes from one picture to the other. One has a tree, the other doesn't, the posts are different, the people are different. Even the man-god's little beard changes, but his very muscular body stays the same in shape, although its skin is paler and bluer in one.

As I look at the colors, it surprises me to see, in the taking-down picture, the erotic cinnabar in the robe of one of the women who reaches out to the dead god. So these pictures were made by Sir Peter. Perhaps it was naughty of him to have used this color in this picture.

There are smaller pictures at the sides of the big pictures, including one of an excited horse. This makes me wonder, as I have wondered before, whether the people of these lands worship horses. The huge creatures are everywhere, fouling the streets with their droppings. The people build shelters for them and decorate them with beautiful leather and silver. Even Don Quixote sometimes seemed to have more respect for his horse Rocinante than for his devoted friend Sancho Panza. Even though — as the first Vlieg learned — these are dangerous animals. I must ask Sir Peter why he put the horse in the picture — whether the horse has another meaning, as things do in pictures, or whether he simply enjoyed painting it.

When I return to the inn, Twee is in a happy mood. "I'm going to see Rubens tomorrow," he says. "He sent me an invitation."

"And what will you talk to him about?"

"Business. Rubens is one of the great businessmen. He could teach me a lot."

"And what do you bring to him in return?"

"Good health. Energy. He used to be his own agent, but now he needs someone to help him."

"Someone he can trust. Why would he trust you?"

"He trusts *you*, Lenoir."

"Why do you think that?"

"He painted your picture. And the note he sent me says he'd also like to see you again tomorrow."

"If I'm the one he trusts, why shouldn't *I* be his agent?"

"Because — to put it bluntly — I'm the one with the pale skin and who pretends to believe in Jesus Christ; I know how to read; and I can count to ten. I've got those things; you've got some other things. We're a team."

"But you're the boss of the team. Why can't *I* be the boss?"

"I just explained that, Lenoir. It's because I'm the one who's pale and can read."

"What if I learn to read . . . and become a Christian?"

"Well, the truth is, it wouldn't really help, Lenoir. You know that, don't you?"

We look at each other. I know what he has just said is the truth, but I cannot say so. I wonder what Twee is thinking. I know he is fond of me, but I wonder for the first time if his fondness is based on the fact that he is the boss.

Then Twee smiles and says, too loudly, "Enough of that. Let's get something to eat. I think the food will be better here than it was in the North."

I say, "I need sleep more than food."

Twee shrugs and stops smiling. I lie on the hard bed until he goes out to look for a meal — and whatever else he might have in mind. A few minutes later, I go downstairs and find the innkeeper. I ask him, "Where can I find someone who will change money for me?"

"I can do that," he says.

I doubt that I should trust this man, but I don't have much choice. We sit at a table, and I produce my purse and pour out the money that Sir Peter gave me. The innkeeper looks at the coins intently and begins sorting through them, putting them in different piles and turning them over. He says, "You're a traveling man, I see." I nod. "Well," he continues, "what is useful here is Spanish money — reales, escudos, crowns, doubloons. But the sovereign is good, the esclin, the sol. You've got

English here, you've got Northern ducats and florins. You've got new and old Roman. You've got *very* old Roman. But whatever is silver or gold is good. Copper, we're not much interested in. I'll weigh the silver and gold for you. I can give you some nice Isabella ducatons."

"Isabella of Rome?"

"Isabella of Flanders," the innkeeper says as he produces a little device that has an arm that goes up and down. I watch him carefully as he puts coins on the device and writes numbers down on a piece of paper. He glances up at me once. I return his glance sternly and continue watching the coins carefully to be sure he does not try to steal any of them.

At the end, he hands me the paper. "This is the total," he says. I look at it for a time, pretending it means something to me. "Is this correct?" I say, and point to some marks he was making when he glanced up at me before.

The innkeeper's face reddens. "Ah," he says. "Perhaps a little error. Forgive me." He changes the writing. He talks about ounces and grains, and he shows me how some of the old silver he is taking has the same weight as the new ducatons he is giving me. He takes one of the very old Roman coins "for his trouble." Then he asks, "Have you thought about how much the passport law is worth?"

I had forgotten, of course. I say, "I'm sure we have both thought about it."

He nods and says, "I think it is worth about *this* much." He pulls some of the coins toward him.

"I had thought this," I say, and I pull most of the coins back toward me.

He pulls some of them back again. We play this game a few more times, and he says, "Done, my friend. You're my honored guest."

I go upstairs. I am exhausted by this process of money changing, but I feel safe and more important now. I fall asleep immediately, seeing in my mind the heads, birds, and animals that decorate my new ducatons. And I wonder how badly I have been cheated.

The next morning, Twee is saying, "Classy. Or, rather classical."

We are standing outside Sir Peter's house, and Twee is looking at some words carved in the stone of a wall. "It's Latin," he says. "Something like 'Pray for a healthy mind . . . a healthy body . . . no fear of death . . . no anger . . . no desire'."

"No desire?"

"I think so. Something like that."

"I talked to a woman yesterday who wanted to escape from desire."

"I think there are a lot of women like that. But I'm not exactly an expert."

Mr. Quellyn meets us at the door. He asks me to wait while he takes Twee to see Sir Peter, then he returns and takes me to a room that contains the things that are used to make pictures. Placed along the top of a table are many jars holding colored powders. Mr. Quellyn takes a jar of blue and a jar of yellow. He puts some of each powder on a piece of smooth white stone. He asks me, "Have you ever mixed dry colors?" I shake my head. With a little knife, he mixes the blue and yellow. They magically become green. It is one of the most exciting things I have seen. I feel as if I am behind bed drapes with a woman.

Mr. Quellyn opens a well-worn book. "In here," he says, "are the formulas; the amounts of each color that will produce the colors the master likes us to use."

I shake my head. "I do not need the book," I say. "Show me what green you want." Mr. Quellyn brings me a small jar and says, "Here is some that is mixed with oil."

"And what color is the oil?" I ask.

He shows me a bottle with a liquid in it. "The oil is clear," he says. "We don't consider that."

"It should be considered."

I look at the green again, then I quickly change the amounts of yellow and blue powders and mix them with the oil.

Mr. Quellyn smiles. "Perfect," he says.

"Almost," I say, and add a little more yellow.

He shows me many more jars of oil-mixed paints. "These," he says, "are the colors the master may like to have on his palette."

I say, "These are not like the colors Mr. Rembrandt uses. They are more like the colors in my homeland."

"The master calls them Flemish Italian."

I think about the colors in the master's Venus painting — the colors in these paints and the colors of his wife. I say, "I think, Mr. Quellyn, that the master makes pictures with the colors he wants to see, not the colors he sees."

He laughs. "Call me Erasmus," he says.

Erasmus tells me the names of many colors, and I mix them for him. My pleasure remains great, but it becomes the pleasure of a child playing rather than an adult making love. There are many good names for colors — names such as viridian, alizarin, cerulean, and umber.

Soon, Twee enters the room, also looking as happy as a playing child. "Sir Peter would like a word," he says. "I'll see you at the inn." He makes a thumb-up sign with his hand, which I think he learned from the Italians. A thumb-up is apparently different from a finger up.

Erasmus leads me along some corridors, through the round room that has stone people in the wall, and up a cozy stone winding stairway. "We are fortunate to know the master," he says. "He is a man of many talents and has a flawless personality. Unfortunately, his body is developing some flaws." We enter a room where Sir Peter is sitting up in the largest bed I have ever seen. The cloth of the bed curtains is covered with golden three-petal flowers. Sir Peter asks: "Did it go well?"

Erasmus says, "Mr. Lenoir has a talent. He also says that you paint with the colors you *want* to see, not the colors you see."

The master laughs. "Sit down, Lenoir. Thank you, Erasmus." Now that he is no longer laughing, I can see pain in Sir Peter's face, but not unhappiness. "So, would you like to join our studio, Lenoir? Become controller of the colors? Live in a little house? I own some cottages near the city."

It is my turn to smile. I remember little houses I passed in the countryside when I traveled with the Italian actors — houses with warm lamplight showing through the windows at dusk. I nod. Sir Peter continues, "So you have a talent for color, my friend. Do you have other talents?"

"I do some medicine."

"At my age, medicine becomes almost as important as color. But unfortunately our artists are much more skillful than our doctors. I have been treated by the doctors of kings and queens. It doesn't matter where they come from or whom they treat, the doctors are obsessed with the giving of enemas and the taking of blood."

"In my homeland we say only the warrior, the woman, and the fool part with their blood. With us, a medicine person helps people *keep* their blood."

"And how does a medicine person do that?"

"With medicine, as you might expect. And with dolls and serpents and songs."

Sir Peter throws aside the bedclothes that have covered his legs. He is wearing a sleeping robe that goes to his ankles. The skin of his swollen, bare feet looks like skin being shed by a snake. He says, "They call this the gout."

"We call it the old chief's foot."

"Can you make it better?"

"I think I can make it so that you can walk while waiting for death."

"And when will I die?"

"Soon, Sir Peter."

Sir Peter smiles. "You're not a diplomat, Lenoir."

"No. Twee has told me you are such a person, but I don't understand. There are many things I don't understand."

"Such as?"

"I don't know why a person would want to escape from desire. I met a woman yesterday who wants to do that down the eight-step path."

"She would be from the East Indies, I think. A follower of the Buddha."

"And you also follow the Buddha?"

"Why would you think that?"

"Twee said it is written on your wall."

"Ah. There's a difference. What is on my wall means one should not be *ruled* by one's desires. What is on your friend's mind is that one should not *have* desires — not the same things at all."

Sir Peter looks tired, and our talk is beginning to make me uncomfortable. I stand up and say, "I think your desire now is that I should leave you alone."

"I've seldom wanted to be alone in my life — maybe never— until recently. Now I retire like a wounded dog."

"Oh, at least a lion."

"Maybe you *are* a diplomat, Lenoir."

"Can I be what I don't understand?"

"That's what we all are."

I no longer know what we are talking about. I bow slightly and back away. Sir Peter says, "Mr. Quellyn will see to it that you may enter the workroom at any time. I will have a cottage prepared for you."

"I will leave medicine with Mr. Quellyn. And may I walk in your garden as I leave?"

"Of course. I hope I will soon be able to do the same."

The garden is large and strange. I can see no plants that would be good for food or medicine — only flowers and hedges made to grow in unnatural rows. This is a garden made to look at, like a picture. I think it is more interesting to look at flowers and shrubs that have planted themselves.

But I am not here for idle looking. I find a certain arrangement of gray-green rocks near a low hedge where mice might run. I quickly lift one of the rocks, revealing a small, homelike cave. In the cave is a startled serpent the color of the moist underside of the rocks. Before the handsome creature can move, my hand darts out and captures it. I pop it into my pocket. Although the serpent struggles now, it will soon feel the warmth of my body and will be lulled into sleep.

When I return to the inn, I find Twee sitting at a table next to our little window, looking at a book. He speaks to me in a language that is definitely not Walloon and is not quite Dutch. Then he explains, in Walloon: "I'm practicing my English. I'm saying, 'I am most pleased to make your acquaintance, sir.'"

"Are you expecting to make a journey?"

"Exactly. To England. With a letter of introduction from Rubens to Lord Cottington as a possible purchasing agent of art objects for the sovereign."

"Sir Peter trusts you with such work when he doesn't know you?"

"No one trusts anyone in royal courts, Lenoir. Rubens's important friend Balthasar Gerbier got thrown out of England for spying. I might be able to fill part of the gap. Just a small corner . . . a small, small corner. But it's many steps up from the Italian comedians."

We have a busy night, Twee practicing his *th*'s, and I searching my medicine bags and making a doll with large feet. I also make a home for my serpent. Judging from skittering sounds I hear in the walls of our room, it will not be difficult to find little gray meals for the snake.

Twee does not ask me if I might want to go with him to England. A few times, we glance at each other uneasily. I think we both know that when we next part it might be forever.

Later, lying in the dark, I say to Twee, "I will live in a cottage."

"Alone?"

"It is time for me to be alone, I think."

"Yes." He begins to sniffle. I put my fingers on his cheek; it is wet. He says, "You don't think I've wished you any harm?"

"Your wishes are always good, Twee. But they are always only for yourself."

"You don't blame me for that?"

"No blame, Twee. In my homeland, we have a song:

> Neighbor, are you angry
> when I think first of myself?
> Neighbor, in whose self lives the anger?
> If you were thinking of me, you would smile.
> Look at me and smile.
> Look at me and smile, friend.

Twee sniffles. I smile. And we sleep.

The next morning I finish making the doll of Sir Peter, and I stand it in a bowl of medicine. I hold the snake and chant, "Illness be gone." Twee frowns and quickly leaves to seek out people who can make him some glorious new clothing.

When I have chanted the correct amount of time, I take medicines to Erasmus Quellyn at Sir Peter's house. One medicine is to drink, and the other I mix with painter's oil to be rubbed on the master's feet. I memorize some colors, then I find a café in which I eat cheese and cold meat. The young woman who serves me does not seem to want to escape desire. She tells me I should eat some oysters, but I will never have the courage for that. She splits the shell of one of the disgusting creatures. "Wet and delicious," she says, and waggles her tongue against the glistening meat. She apparently knows, as I do, that an oyster is one of those things that, in a picture, means something else.

I wander through the city and find that the people look

much the same as those in the North. I wonder what unseen difference has caused them to fight each other. I suppose it is as Twee has said: they are different in their invisible beliefs. If these people will kill over an invisible difference, what will they do over a difference as obvious as black and white? I suppose I will find out eventually.

One thing that is the same in both the North and the South is a fondness for flowers. Here, however, the blossoms have colors and shapes that are new to me. The people seem to be less interested in the strange tulip plant.

The noise made by wagons and the hoofs of horses against the stones of the street is replaced often by the pleasant sound of the song bells, and I have feelings of great joy. I think about having an important new friend and about the possibility of having my own house to live in. I also have moments of sadness when I remember that Twee will be going away, but I know it is time for me to begin to rely on myself. I wonder if self-reliance must mean being the only person in the house.

Within three days, as I had expected, Sir Peter is able to walk without feeling pain. When I go to the studio workroom, I find the great man waiting for me. "No work today," he says. "I have something to show you. Do you ride a horse?"

"I don't ride horses, and I stay as far from them as I can, Sir Peter."

"Then we'll walk. It might be good for both of us."

We walk out of the courtyard and along a sour-smelling canal, then turn away from the center of the city. Sir Peter is wearing boots of a color I now call burnt sienna. He could not have gotten his feet into them three days ago. As we proceed, people smile, bow, remove their hats, and without exception look surprised. I think they are surprised both to see Sir Peter walking and to see him walking with me. Several times, we stop to speak to people, and Sir Peter introduces me as his associate. He says I have at least two important talents.

Soon the houses are no longer joined together in the strange way the flatlanders prefer. The clouds rise in great, changing mountains of shapes, making the land look even more featureless than it is. The wind is growing stronger. I say to Sir Peter, "The wind is important to your people."

"Yes, although I hadn't thought about it."

"It turns the arms of your mills. It pushes your boats. Maybe the reason you do not think of it is that you cannot make a picture of it."

"I have pictured it moving the hair of a woman or the mane of a horse or the leaves of a tree."

"Just as I have pretended to walk against it with the Italian comedians."

"The *dell'arte?*"

"I think so, yes."

"Yes. That's where you heard *bravo*. When was this?"

"Only days ago, in the North. They cannot be far from here now. Twee should know the road they are taking."

"I would like to see them. I saw such troupes in Rome when I was a young man."

"Twee says they are not as in Rome."

"They have an Arlecchino? A Pantalone?"

"Yes."

"Then I would like to see them."

We walk in silence. Sir Peter seems to be thinking of the past: thinking of himself as a young man. Although I do not approve of remembering the past, I do not interrupt him. We are passing fields in which there are many straight rows of young green plants, but soon the rows stop and trees begin — not the neat rows of trees with flowers but a forest of trees that could give a dark shelter to animals, including, I am sure, many serpents. Farther down the road, past the trees, is a crossroads, and where the roads meet, there is the familiar outline of a gibbet against the sky — another reminder that this new country is not very different from the old one.

Sir Peter leads me off the main road, along a path between the little forest and the fields. The path leads to a clearing in the trees, and we stand before a house. Sir Peter says, "Your new home, Lenoir."

I am overjoyed. The house is small, with brick walls and a baked clay roof. I saw clay this color in my childhood. There is also a chimney, which no one in my homeland ever had.

"I must sit," Sir Peter says.

We enter the house, and we both sit at a table in front of a fireplace. Sir Peter tells me, "It's only a one-room gamekeeper's cottage, but it is comfortable. It's dark, I'm afraid."

There are two windows that face the sun, but this morning the sun is hidden. I say, "I will not be making pictures in here, Sir Peter. But I will be saying many thanks."

The master hands me a piece of paper. "This states that you are the tenant of this cottage until I decree otherwise or until I die . . . and I wonder if I have tempted death with this morning's walk."

"I am sure you are joking, sir. But I can go back to the city and have Erasmus send a horse or carriage if you'd like."

"I *would* like to ride. But there's a simpler way. Go out of the cottage. Straight ahead there is a footpath through the field. It leads to a house. Go there, please, and ask Mrs. Normand if she would put reins and a blanket on Jenny for me."

"What language would I ask her in?"

"She would prefer Flemish."

"That is the one like Dutch?"

"Yes. But speak slowly in Walloon French and she will understand."

I nod and head across the field, not pleased that I will probably have trouble with language and even more that I might have to lead a horse back to Sir Peter. Mrs. Normand's house is not as handsome or sturdy as mine; its walls are clay and wood, and its roof is made of dried grass. Just as I reach the house, Jenny steps from behind a hedge. But Jenny is not exactly a horse. And she is not exactly a donkey — just as Mrs. Normand turns out to be not exactly the milkmaid I have seen in pictures. She is as tall as I am, and she is not frail. She wears trousers, a rough shirt, a cap, and heavy wooden-soled shoes. Most of her red-brown hair is pushed up beneath her cap. But her face is smooth and the colors of a certain pink-and-white flower I have seen recently.

"*Aangenaam kennis te maken,*" I say, which I hope she will understand as "How do you do?" Then, slowly, in Walloon: "You are Mrs. Normand?"

She nods and answers, slowly but clearly, "Normand is enough. A widow."

"I am Lenoir."

"So you are."

"I am your new neighbor." I point to the cottage. "I will live in that house with the permission of Sir Peter Paul Rubens."

The widow looks into my eyes firmly but blankly. I have no idea what she is thinking.

"Sir Peter is there now. He asks if you will put reins and a blanket on Jenny for him."

Mrs. Normand nods. I follow her as she goes to a shed and gets some complicated leather straps and begins to put them on Jenny. I ask, "And what kind of creature is Jenny?"

"She is the kind of creature I am. Her father was a jackass and her mother was a horse. She works hard and she's stubborn. She's a mule."

I lead Jenny to Sir Peter. He mounts her, and I lead them both through the streets of Antwerp, to the smiles and pleasure of the people.

I say, "I think we look like Don Quixote and Sancho Panza. Do you know of them, Sir Peter?"

"I've been in their land. They are greatly loved by the people there."

"I think *you* are greatly loved by the people here."

"I have a great deal of money. I'm friendly with rulers. People want to please me. That's not exactly love."

"I, too, want to please you, Sir Peter."

"Don't try too hard, Lenoir. I've spent too much time trying to please, I think. I've pleased people and neglected my primary talent. You should honor your talents, Lenoir. Other people will honor them, too. Will you remember that?"

"Yes." And I wonder why this great man should make a confession of an error in his life to a simple new acquaintance like myself.

"Soon you will be without my protection, Lenoir. Your talents will have to protect you."

I don't ask Sir Peter what I am to be protected from, or what is to become of me if my talents are small or wrong or nonexistent.

Twee moves into the cottage with me but says he will leave for England as soon as his new clothes are ready and he can arrange passage on a ship.

During our first day in the cottage, we see Mrs. Normand working in the field. Twee says, "I've heard she's a witch. But she's Rubens's tenant farmer, so people leave her alone."

"She's not a witch. Come and see."

We walk out to see her. I say, "This is my friend Twee."

She asks, "Friend?"

Twee says, "Friends in the sense that Lenoir could make either of us happy, but he'd prefer to make *you* happy — something I couldn't begin to do."

Mrs. Normand looks calmly and unblinkingly at Twee. "I've got the feeling that neither of you could make me happy." She speaks quietly and without emotion — a manner that always irritates Twee. He says, "And *I've* got the feeling that *no one* could make Mrs. Normand happy."

"Only God," Mrs. Normand says, again calmly.

Before Twee can make an unpleasant remark about this woman's god, I say, "We wanted you to know that we will be glad to help you in any way we can, Mrs. Normand. Just shout." As soon as I say it, I realize that Mrs. Normand has probably never shouted in her life. I bow and take Twee's arm, turning away and starting him along the path to our new home.

"She's a peasant," Twee says.

"I'm not sure what a peasant is."

"She's dirty, dim, and unsophisticated."

"Her face was clean. And I think she understands our words. Also, I think all my ancestors were peasants."

"But *you* aren't a peasant, Lenoir — not anymore. And you're not in the land of your ancestors. Take my advice and stay away from this woman. Peasants don't like strangers — especially dark strangers."

I don't reply. I wonder if Twee is afraid Mrs. Normand will take his place in the cottage when he leaves. But I am sure neither Mrs. Normand nor I would want that to happen.

Now that I have a home, I believe I need more and better belongings. I try to remember what I have seen in homes and in pictures of homes. Using ducaton coins I got from the innkeeper, I buy some pottery and glassware, as well as a basket that will serve as a home for my new serpent. The merchants have great respect for my ducatons, which will apparently keep me supplied with food, clothing, and other needs for a long time.

The only decoration I have for my walls is the picture that Mlle. van Cott gave me. But the paint on the picture is cracked and damaged. I roll it up and take it to the studio, where I show it to Erasmus. He smiles and asks, "Who did this?"

"A Mlle. van Cott of Amsterdam made the original picture, Mr. Flinck, her teacher — himself a student of Mr. Rembrandt — made some changes, and I made the cracks and holes."

"A picture painted by a woman? We don't see many of those. I think the master would enjoy looking at it."

When Sir Peter appears, he is walking quickly and without hesitation, although there is something in his eyes that makes me think his steps are causing him some pain. But he is delighted when we show him the picture and explain how it came to be. "An entertaining picture," he says. "But I can see why the student would be disturbed by what her teacher has done to it. He was probably in a hurry. It is quicker to make changes than to tell the student how to make them, but it can result in a muddled style. However, it's worth repairing."

I say, "I think the mademoiselle would be honored to meet you, Sir Peter."

"You know her well?"

"I was her protector for a short time. Her father is a sea captain, often away from their home."

Sir Peter looks back at Mlle. van Cott's painting. "It would be interesting to watch the woman paint. I've heard unkind painters of this city say that the men of our northern provinces paint like women — like either housewives or harlots. Perhaps they would be happy to find a woman from those provinces who can paint like a man."

Erasmus says, "Do you think it is possible for a woman to paint like a man?"

"One paints the way one sees. If one sees like a man, one paints like a man."

Erasmus looks troubled. He asks, "But can a woman be like a man?"

I think I would not like to be Mrs. Quellyn.

The master says, "Women have ruled like men."

I say, "In my land, it is said that a woman can do well everything a man can do except pee neatly into the narrow-necked gourd."

Sir Peter smiles. "In my land it is said that a woman's three interests should be children, cooking, and church."

From behind us comes the voice of Mrs. Rubens: "I've heard it said that any activity that is worthy of a man's interest is also a fit and decent activity for a Christian woman."

Thinking of Amboina, I say, "Or perhaps even a non-Christian woman."

Sir Peter holds up his hands in surrender. He says to me, "Please let Hélène see Mlle. van Cott's painting, Lenoir."

I watch Mrs. Rubens as she looks at the painting. She is young enough to be Sir Peter's daughter, I think. And although she is splendidly dressed and seems to be an intelligent person, I think there is also something of the peasant in her. She asks, "A woman did this?"

"A woman in Amsterdam," Sir Peter replies. "Lenoir knows her."

Mrs. Rubens is excited, I think. She speaks quickly: "Amsterdam is not far from here, Paolo. Could we send a carriage? I would like to meet this painter. What's her name?"

"Mlle. van Cott," I say. "Anna van Cott."

"It isn't a simple matter," Sir Peter says to Hélène. "Our countries are not friendly. There would have to be papers."

"But you are known in the North," Mrs. Rubens says. "You've been there working for peace."

Sir Peter still looks troubled. He asks me, "Is Mlle. van Cott a member of the painters' guild?"

"Yes, I'm sure she is."

"Then we might arrange it," he says to his wife. "She's also known to Rembrandt van Rijn. He might be able to escort her. It might be arranged as a painters' project. I'll write him today and ask."

Hélène smiles at her husband, then at Erasmus and me. She says, "But it won't be entirely business. We can have a party." She looks at me. "Is there anyone else you would like to invite, Lenoir? A woman friend, perhaps?"

"There is Katja," I say. "She is in some of Mr. Rembrandt's pictures. She is like Venus."

Mrs. Rubens looks at her husband and says, "One cannot have too many Venuses, can one, Paolo?"

The master's face becomes a color like erotic cinnabar.

Mrs. Rubens puts her hand on her husband's arm and says to me, "We will invite your friend, Lenoir."

When I tell Twee that there may be a party at the Rubenses' house, he makes a childish *woooeee* cry and moves his shoulders from side to side. "The best," he says. "This could be the best party of my life. Who will be there?"

"Some old friends."

"Nobility?"

"Not exactly. Some of *our* old friends: Mr. Rembrandt, Mlle. van Cott, maybe even Katja."

"What about the *master's* old friends? You and I both need some *new* friends, Lenoir. You shouldn't waste your time, the way you've been doing here, with peasants. Remember that it's traditional for royal courts to have a Moor or two in the retinue."

"Yes. You told me — Moors and fools."

"There are two kinds of fools, Lenoir — the kind who please important people and the kind who are stupid. Don't be one of the stupid kind."

"I think it is time for me to please myself rather than others."

"Lenoir, the only people who don't have to please others are the king and the pope — and even that is changing."

"Sir Peter says one should first please oneself."

"He *says* that, but has he *done* that?"

"I think he's doing it now."

"Maybe we can do it, too, when we're old and rich."

Twee knows as well as I do that neither of us will ever be rich. And I think that, like me, he doesn't really care. The difference is that he wants to try.

It rains at least an hour or two almost every day now. The water in the canal outside Mr. Rubens's house seems higher and faster running. I often go to the studio to help Erasmus Quellyn, who is polite to me but who has given me no idea of what he thinks of me or of anyone else except Sir Peter, whom he has only praise for. I have watched Erasmus make many pictures, some of which he and the master do together to send to the Spanish king, who will put them in a building he uses when hunting. The master makes little uncolored pictures of events from the time of Venus, and Erasmus makes them large and in color. I like the small ones better.

Erasmus and I work quietly together. He teaches me about paints, brushes, canvases, and frames. He wants only to please Sir Peter. Twee, of course thinks Erasmus is mistaken to do that. Twee says there is a Mr. Jordaens in this city who seeks out nobility, and because of that, it is he, rather than Erasmus, who will take the master's place.

I think there might be another reason: I have seen the eyes of both Sir Peter and Erasmus as they work, and I can see in their eyes even more than in their pictures why one is the master.

I have seen a few pictures by Mr. Jordaens, but not his eyes. I hope he will be at the party.

When I am not in the studio, I sometimes sit in my home and place a chair so that I can look out my window toward the house of my neighbor, Mrs. Normand. Even on the wettest days, she is out in her fields, scraping the muddy soil. There are times when she stops for a moment and looks toward my house. It may be that she sees the smoke rising from my chimney and that she thinks of me. I sometimes tap my drum and sing — but quietly, so that she does not think I am trying to attract her attention. I am sure she does not want attention from me or anyone else. I am beginning to admire her proud and simple way of living. I think I can learn from her.

In less time than I expected, Erasmus tells me that Mr. Rembrandt, Mlle. van Cott and her father, and Katja have agreed to visit the Rubenses for a few days. Sir Peter has also sent a rider along a road recommended by Twee, and he has located the Italian comedy troupe and asked them to entertain at the party being planned by Mrs. Rubens.

The master, however, has asked me for fever medicine, and his visits to the studio are not as frequent as they have been.

I spend more of each day in my home. I make a new doll for Sir Peter's fever, and I collect small creatures that I think will satisfy the hunger of my serpent, who seems happy in his new home — as I am in mine. At night, Twee reads to me and tells me of his plans to become rich and famous in England. He thinks I should come with him. He says if I stay in Antwerp I may die of the plague, which is becoming worse, although the people pretend it is not.

Then I notice that it has been some days since I have seen Mrs. Normand working in her fields. Nor have I seen smoke rising from her chimney as I usually do in the evenings.

I walk to her door and knock. There is no answer. I call her name, and I hear a faint voice. I open the door and see my neighbor lying on a bed in a corner of her cottage. She is covered by a pile of blankets and clothing, and the room stinks of sickness.

"Please get a priest," Mrs. Normand gasps.

"Lenoir will be your priest," I say. She looks at me blankly. There is no understanding in her gaze, only pain. I touch her forehead, which is hot and dry. She is whispering something. I lean close and hear her say, "Plague." I pull back the blankets and put my ear against her chest, which is bare. Her breathing is clear. "No plague," I say. "I have seen people with the plague in the North. Their breathing was not clear as yours is. I will bring medicine."

I go to my cottage and get a mugful of boiling water from the pot that hangs in my fireplace. I find some of the leaves I had used to make Sir Peter's medicine, and I place them in the mug. I put the serpent in my pocket.

Back in Mrs. Normand's cottage, I lift her hard, unmoving body so that she sits up. Her body has fouled her bed in several ways, but I soon adjust to the odor. She drinks the medicine slowly but steadily, and I can see that she is grateful to me. When the medicine is gone, I ask, "Are you afraid of serpents?" She shakes her head. I take the snake from my pocket and hold it before her. She smiles at the serpent and whispers, "Beautiful." I wonder how many people in this country would say that. I hold the serpent to Mrs. Normand's forehead, and I sing, in the language of my homeland:

> When we look at you, little god,
> we sense that your power is great,
> and our skin tingles.
> We wonder how, with your great beauty,
> you can permit fever
> to live in this head,
> which, in its human way,
> is beautiful, too.
> I ask you to banish the fever.
> I pray to you.

The serpent encircles Mrs. Normand's slender neck. I cover the woman's chest with the blanket. Soon, she goes to sleep and begins to sweat. I return to my cottage, where I find Twee. I say, "I have been healing Mrs. Normand."

"Oh?"

"She has a fever."

"Hot, is she?"

I ignore Twee's jealous remark. I take the serpent from my pocket and put it in its basket home. To reward it for its work with Mrs. Normand, I feed it a fat grasshopper. Twee makes a face. "Do you have to feed that thing when I'm here?"

I say, "I will make some soup for Mrs. Normand." I begin

searching in the vegetable box, where I find potatoes, onions, and tiny cabbages.

Twee says, "You're becoming quite the housewife, Lenoir."

"I have a home now."

"You have a mucky little building. It's hardly worth trading your freedom for."

"I am employed by a great man."

"And what happens when the great man dies — which, despite your efforts, probably won't be long from now? Try to keep in mind that Rubens's friendship is what keeps you off the gibbet."

"Have I done anything to deserve the gibbet?"

"You're a dark man practicing the dark arts. When you're those things, it's best to keep moving."

"I will stay here. People will like me when they know me. Just as you like me."

"I'm not a farmer or a constable, Lenoir. I'm not normal."

"You think normal people can't be my friends?"

"I think they'll put you on the gibbet."

"I think you are joking," I say. Twee shrugs. He is not smiling, but his eyes are not entirely serious. I think he would like me to go with him to England and be his servant. I do not want to talk about these things. I say, "Will you want some soup?"

"I'm going back to town. A business dinner. Lots of walking these days. Maybe we should buy a horse. We've got room for horses in the woods. Horse trading is a good business. We could rent them out. The people here can't afford to buy them."

I stir the soup. "Soon you can tell the English people about your business ideas."

"Theater. That's the thing over there."

"Anatomical theater? Italian theater?"

"All those things. As long as the Puritans don't take over. But Charles won't let that happen. He likes a good time. That's why he'll like me."

"Charles?"

"The king who made Rubens into Sir Peter."

I stir the soup again. Could a real king actually like and trust Twee? Does Twee think he will become a sir? Sir Dom? I ask, "And do they have gibbets in England?"

Twee puts on a new hat and looks into the mirror — the mirror that is one of the two new furnishings he has brought into our home. The second, which is hidden away, is the picture that Mr. Rembrandt made of Uba — Uba, who may now be in her homeland once again.

When I return to Mrs. Normand with soup, bread, and a jug of hot water, she is awake. Her forehead is cooler, but she is weak. When I have fed the soup to her, she says, "I am not clean."

"If you notice such things, you are no longer so sick. I have brought you hot water. I will leave you alone now, Mrs. Normand."

"Rachel."

"Rachel, then."

Rachel says, "Wash me, Lenoir."

After I wash her, I ask her the question that is beginning to seem most important: "Whose god do you believe in?"

"I believe in the one true Christian God," she says.

"My friend Twee says it is better not to believe."

"Your friend has not had a husband who became a soldier and died. He hasn't had children who began coughing and died."

"You believe in the Christian God, but I have heard it said that you are a witch."

"That is said of any woman living alone."

I look carefully at Rachel Normand as she lies on the bed that I have freshened for her. She is not a witch. Her body, when I washed it, had the innocence of a muscular boy's body.

And now her expression also tells me that she is innocent — and that she is grateful to me but would not want to be my friend.

The next evening, I take Rachel more soup. As I leave her cottage, she is strong enough to walk to the doorway with me and, to my surprise, embrace me. I put my arms around her in embarrassment and wonder what I should say.

Then I notice, standing nearby, on the path, a young man I have never seen before. He shouts: "Whore . . . nigger." And he runs away.

When I tell Twee what happened, he says, "Time for England, Lenoir."

But I know that they have words like that in England, too.

# 16

O N THE MORNING of the party, the sun shines brilliantly — which I think means this will be a day of great importance in my life.

When I reach Sir Peter's house, I find a familiar sight in the center of his gardens: it is the caravan of the Italian comedians. My friends from the troupe (and my enemy, Isabella) are setting up the platform for a performance. Baldassaro the jackass is the first to see me. He brays. I walk toward him, as if against the wind. The actors see me, and there are cries of "Zanni" and "Lenoir." When I reach Baldassaro, I fall down. I hear laughter from Sir Peter's house. He and his wife are standing at an open window. I get up and greet the members of the troupe. They are all as I remember, except that there is a new man dressed as the Zanni.

Columbine says, "We can do a two-Zanni story tonight."

"No," I say. "Tonight I will watch. I will shout the *bravi*."

Columbine takes me aside. "It has not been good for us," she says. "We thought the Flemish would like us more — give us more money — than the Hollanders."

"The people here do not have money."

"Mr. Rubens seems to have some."

"Oh, yes. And he is generous."

"He loves to speak Italian. He and Pantalone have had a talk about Venezia and about pictures by the dead man Tiziano."

I nod and think to myself that Sir Peter will soon be dead also. And I realize that, many years from now, people will meet and speak of *his* pictures. They may even speak of the picture he made of me. I don't know why it has not occurred to me before that Sir Peter Paul Rubens will live on in his pictures the way the ancient chiefs and gods of my homeland live on in the stories that fathers and mothers tell their sons and daughters — the way Señor Cervantes lives as the man who told the story of Don Quixote and Sancho Panza.

I turn to look at the window where Hélène Rubens stands with her husband, who is Paolo to her. He has an arm about her shoulder. I believe they are in their bedchamber. And I know that Sir Peter would have awakened many hours ago. I know also that he never sleeps during the day. He has the look of a happy man. I think I will never know the happiness of spending a leisurely morning in a large, bright bedroom with a young, adoring wife who is also the mother of my child.

At midday I sit in the courtyard awaiting the arrival of the carriage with my friends from Amsterdam. Sir Peter joins me. Although he still looks happy, he does not look healthy. His beard, in the sunlight, seems whiter than it has in the past. I say, "You will never die, will you, Sir Peter?"

"I hope not, Lenoir. I hope my soul will live on in Heaven."

"I meant that you will live in your pictures."

"The pictures will not last forever. Heaven and Hell will. It is one of the reasons I attend mass every morning that I can walk."

"And is Heaven a place for pleasure?"

"It is a place where the soul has the pleasure of being with God."

"I am not sure I would want my soul to live forever, even in great pleasure."

"And I don't suppose you would want to live forever in the flames of Hell."

"No one would want that, Sir Peter."

"But mere wanting may not prevent it."

Sir Peter and I sit in silence. I don't know what he is thinking, but he looks frightened.

I remember that Twee has told me there are many pictures of the flaming Hell. I suppose Sir Peter has made some of them, but I have not noticed any in his studio or on the walls of his house. Twee has told me that God on the cross, Venus, and Hell are what the good pictures are about. I understand about the Venus pictures, but I wonder why people make pictures of Hell or of the death of God — things they have never seen. When I stop wondering, the master is no longer with me. I hope I have not upset him with talk of death.

But soon there is a feeling of new life as Sir Peter's covered carriage comes bumping along the street and through the gates to the house. Captain van Cott is sitting with the driver, outside the compartment, from which I hear excited voices.

The captain shouts, "Ahoy."

Mr. Rembrandt's head appears through a carriage window. He is smiling more broadly than I thought he was able to. Sir Peter goes immediately to the carriage, but I wait until the driver quiets the sweating, snorting horses.

I shake hands with Mlle. van Cott, her father, and Mr. Rembrandt, and I embrace Katja, who is the last to leave the carriage. Sir Peter and Mr. Rembrandt embrace, and I introduce Sir Peter to the others.

The visitors seem glad to be out of the carriage. I notice a bottle in the driver's pocket, and I suspect he has given his passengers a frightening ride. They all tell Sir Peter how much they admire the outside of his grand house and his gardens — all except Mr. Rembrandt, who asks to see the studio.

Mrs. Rubens joins us, and she shows the guests to their

rooms while I go to the studio, where they will join me. Erasmus Quellyn is there, standing on a box, painting the top of a large story-picture, filling in around horses that the master has just painted. Erasmus says, "I see that your friends have arrived." He pauses, then says, "Mlle. van Cott is attractive." Erasmus has an expression in his eyes that I have not seen before. I think I have heard that he is married, but until now he had not given me a reason to think that his wife or any other woman was important to him.

I think maybe I should encourage Erasmus to think of Mlle. van Cott not as a woman but as someone who makes pictures. I say, "Her pictures are not like the ones you have been making. They are of people who are doing nothing or doing something in a house — things she actually sees, not things she has only heard about."

I look up at the picture Erasmus is finishing. There are storm clouds, windblown trees, many horses, and two half-naked men.

"This one is about Hercules — a pursuit," Erasmus says. "Maybe we can teach Mlle. van Cott to paint things she has only heard about. And I'm sure she has heard about pursuit."

I hope Mlle. van Cott does not have bad hours ahead of her.

The studio begins to fill with people, including some of the master's children — young children by Hélène and grown ones by Sir Peter's first wife. The picture maker named Mr. Jordaens arrives.

Mr. Rembrandt stands in a corner of the studio, gazing intently at everything and everyone. I think he feels a great emotion, but I do not know what the emotion is.

A servant enters, pushing a little-wheeled platform on which stands a bottle of wine as tall as a small person. Sir Peter says that the wine is a gift from Richelieu, whose name I have heard before — a man who is not a friend of Mr. Rubens but who wants to own a certain picture of an unclothed woman.

Some toasts are drunk, but I think most of the visitors will not become silly or sick from drinking. There are many people here who don't look happy.

But my spirits lift when Katja appears. She is wearing a dress I have never seen before, a modest gown that is the color of a rainy-day sky and that shows her pleasing arms but covers the rest of her body from her chin to her feet. There is white lace at her neck, and she wears one red flower at her shoulder. Her beauty is quieter than I have seen it before. I take her to meet the master and his wife.

"This is my friend Katja," I say.

"Katja Groene," Katja says. It is the first time I have heard her use a second name. "It's an honor to be in your house and your city."

Sir Peter says, "Our city is not as prosperous as yours, I'm afraid."

"But the spirit is allowed to prosper here, I think."

Hélène says, "Then you are devout, Katja?"

"After my fashion."

"I believe there is only one fashion." Sir Peter looks admiringly at Katja, then walks across the studio, pausing once to look quizzically at her. He stops in front of a large, confusing, unfinished picture and says to his guests, "While we wait for dusk, I hope you will not mind if some of our visitors help me finish a picture: Hercules and the Diomedan horses."

And then Sir Peter, Mlle. van Cott, Mr. Rembrandt, Mr. Quellyn, and Mr. Jordaens take palettes and brushes and begin finishing the picture, some of them standing on boxes, others crouching.

Several singers appear and start making a kind of music called the madrigal and written by a Mr. Josquin. At first I think the wine must be confusing me: every person seems to be singing something different. I don't understand how they always finish at the same time. And I don't enjoy hearing them get to the end. It is old-fashioned music, someone tells me. Then things improve greatly when some men arrive with many strange noisemakers and play dance music by a Mr. Praetorius. Katja takes me by the arm, leads me to the center of the floor, and starts dancing. I do not know what she expects of me, but I begin a little dance that I learned as a young man. Katja and I try to talk with each other, but the noise is too great.

Soon I see Mlle. van Cott dancing with Erasmus Quellyn. Her dance has much less jumping than Katja's. The way Erasmus dances is by tapping his toe and nodding his head. He looks unusually happy.

Meat, bread, and cheese are brought in and heaped on tables. I am pleased that there is no food that looks like eel.

As the picture making and dancing proceed and more people arrive, the sky we see through the tall windows becomes the colors of one flower after another. I go outside to see the Italian actors, who are having their own party. When I get back to the studio, the Hercules picture is almost filled in, but it doesn't exactly look finished. The group of people who have been working on the picture have been doing a little dance of their own, some moving their brushes in time to the music. Their smiles soon turn to laughter as they step back one by one to see the results of their work. Sir Peter puts down his palette and brush and walks to a chair. Because he is laughing, I don't think he realizes that he is limping more than he did earlier.

The music stops, and Katja comes to me and says, "How kind of Lenoir to remember his old friends."

"How kind of Sir Peter to *invite* Lenoir's old friends."

Coming toward us from different directions are Mlle. van Cott and Mrs. Rubens. They and Katja immediately begin talking to one another as if they were old friends. As people often do in the flatlands, they use words from two or three languages. They don't notice as I walk away from them toward Sir Peter, who is beckoning to me.

Sir Peter says, "It is dusk now. I have had the torches lighted. Maybe your actor friends are ready to perform."

"Yes," I say. "They are happy now. Soon, some of them may be so happy they will not be able to perform."

I go outside again and ask Columbine to prepare the troupe for the performance.

When I return to Sir Peter, he is looking intently toward his wife, who is still talking with Katja and Mlle. van Cott. The three women stand close to one another in a circle. Hélène says something that seems to startle the other two women. Katja raises her hand and grips Hélène's bare upper arm. Mlle. van Cott watches intently with an expression I do not understand. Katja says something that makes them all laugh. And then for a moment they look more serious and are touching one another's arms as if they are about to dance.

I look back to Sir Peter. He says, "The three Graces." There seem to be tears in his eyes. I wonder what it is that he finds so moving. Does he find these women beautiful? I think he probably finds all women beautiful. But he does not desire all women, for Twee has told me that Sir Peter has never been known to be unfaithful, either to Hélène or to his late first wife. For him, it is apparently possible to find a woman beautiful but not to desire her.

I still do not understand why so many people think desire is bad, or why people without desire think themselves better than those who have desire.

Erasmus Quellyn suddenly appears beside Mlle. van Cott and leads her away from the other two women. He stops her in front of the Hercules picture. He hands her a palette and brush. Then he stands behind her and takes the hand in which she holds the brush and guides it, first to the palette and then to the picture. His mouth is close to her ear. I think that, at least for the moment, he does not feel superior to people who have desires.

Columbine appears in the doorway and hits the floor three times with a staff. Sir Peter stands up and says to everyone,

"Let us proceed to the garden." He goes to his wife and takes her arm, holding it as Katja had held it. Hélène smiles at her husband.

I grasp Katja's arm as she had grasped Mrs. Rubens's arm. She winks at me.

The actors, although they look tired and shabby, present a comedy that is better than any they presented when I was with them. The new Zanni is not as good as I in appearance and actions, but he has many funny things to say about his wife, who never appears.

In honor of Sir Peter, the story the actors present is about a man who makes a picture of a woman. Baldassaro takes bites out of the picture. The actress who is portrayed in the picture is watching Baldassaro, and with each bite he takes, the woman screams in pain. I am the only person who does not seem to find this amusing. I am perhaps the only one who believes that such a thing could actually happen. I am more interested in the picture that is being used in the comedy. I think it has been painted by Mr. Rembrandt, very quickly, on a sheet of paper. Baldassaro had always enjoyed chewing on paper. What pleases me the most is that the woman shown in the picture is the unpleasant Isabella. I remember the words of a curse that the children of my homeland would chant as they threw stones in a pond:

> Your face is reflected on the water.
> I throw this stone in the water.
> What hurts?
> Water — no.
> Face, yes.

I change the words and whisper them as I watch Baldassaro eat the picture:

Your face is reflected in the picture.
Donkey takes bites from the picture.
What hurts?
Picture — no.
Face, yes.

Either Isabella is a better performer than she used to be, or she is actually in pain. Now I join the others in the laughter.

After the comedy, the people of the audience return to the studio for more eating, drinking, and dancing. I stay behind for a moment to be with Baldassaro. I run my hand through the coarse hairs of his coat. In the center of the garden, fires have been lighted, and the carcasses of animals are being roasted. I feel uneasy as I think that Baldassaro could have been born a sheep or a pig.

Back in the studio, I join Twee, who is speaking to Captain van Cott. Twee is excitedly slapping himself on the side of the head as he talks. "In three days?" he asks the captain, who is smiling calmly and nodding.

Twee says to me, "The captain is sailing for the West Indies in three days. He stops over in England first, and he can take us there."

I shake my head. "Just you, Twee. I told you I am staying here."

The captain says, "You've found a home here in Antwerp, have you, Lenoir?"

"Exactly. I have a cottage. I have the friendship of a great man."

"Well," the captain says, "all you need now is a wife."

Twee says, "I think there will be candidates."

I say, "I think there is also a candidate here for the captain's daughter."

"Mr. Quellyn?" the captain asks. "I've noticed that he's been attentive. But he's a candidate for something other than marriage. He already has a wife, according to Mrs. Rubens."

My feelings are strong and confused. I am troubled by the thought that, in a day or two, Twee may vanish from my life forever. And I think about the strength of human attractions. At the moment I sense many such attractions: the captain to Mrs. Rubens, Mr. Quellyn to Mlle. van Cott, Sir Peter to Katja, myself to every woman in the room.

I ask, "And is there no marriage candidate for a widower-captain?"

The captain says, "Ships are called 'she.' They are enough for this captain now."

"But would you not like to have a real *she* on your ship?"

The captain does not answer my question. I think he glances at Katja. Then he says, "I have news of your friend Uba. She has sailed for Africa. Comfortably, I think."

Later, I find Katja sitting in a shadowy corner, away from the music. I say, "Every man is attracted to you."

"It's strange, isn't it? It's as if I cast spells."

"Am I not right that one can be punished for casting spells?"

"Yes. You'll find me in the pillory one day."

"But isn't the pillory only for bad people?"

"That's what I am, Lenoir. I'm a bad person."

I am embarrassed by what I have made Katja say. I excuse myself and go out to the garden, where I find Mlle. van Cott rising from behind a hedge. Settling her skirts and smiling guiltily, she says, "Nghana, your parrot, can now say 'Life is good' in six languages."

I ask, "And is your life good, mademoiselle?"

"Oh, yes. I will become a mother this year."

"Have you become a bride?"

"Not yet, but soon."

"With Mr. Jean Guelfe?"

"Yes."

"You will be able to make pictures together."

"I think Jean will make the pictures. I will make the babies."

"Babies are more important than pictures, I believe."

"*I* believe that *some* babies are more important than *some* pictures."

"Is that what Mr. Calvin said?"

"Lenoir, you're becoming a theologian."

"I don't know what that is, but I do not think I am that."

"We must remember that Mr. Calvin did not make either pictures or babies."

"But some men, like Sir Peter, make pictures and also help make babies."

"Yes. And according to Mrs. Rubens, he is not only still making pictures but still helping to make babies."

"Mrs. Rubens will have another baby?"

"About the same time I have mine."

I say, "I think Mr. Quellyn would like to make a baby with you."

"No. I think he would like to make a picture with me."

I remember the moment that Sir Peter called the three Graces — when his wife, Katja, and Mlle. van Cott were talking together. They must have been speaking of becoming mothers. Could Katja also be expecting a child? Before I can seek her out and ask her, Twee introduces me to an English lord, who is dressed in even brighter colors than Twee is and who is holding a small, sad-looking black-and-white dog. I tell the lord I am enchanted to meet him. He says something I think only another English lord would understand, and he turns away. Twee turns with him.

Mr. Rembrandt and I are standing together as Sir Peter's four youngest children say good night to their father. There are two girls and two boys, and I must admit that they are quite beautiful. Pale skin is less disturbing in children — one feels that it is something they might grow out of.

Mr. Rembrandt says, "His second family. Maybe it's not too late for us, Lenoir."

"It is too late for me."

"You're no more than half Rubens's age. And I've seen some women looking at you with interest."

"It is not too late for me to *make* children. But it is too late for me to *want* children."

Mr. Rembrandt shrugs. "I think I will keep trying," he says.

Later, Sir Peter takes Mr. Rembrandt aside and shows him some of the smaller pictures that are leaning against the wall in a corner. As they look at the portraits Sir Peter has done of me, they beckon to me to join them.

Mr. Rembrandt is smiling with excitement. He says to me, "They're better than the ones I did of you, aren't they, Lenoir?"

"I cannot tell better from worse in these matters."

"I'll destroy mine," Mr. Rembrandt says.

I am frightened. "That would not be good for me," I say.

"I suppose not. I'll just paint over them. Cancel them."

Sir Peter says, "I hope you leave them alone." Then he turns to me and asks, "Have you seen Rembrandt's etching *Death of the Virgin?*"

He shows me a sheet of paper with a black-line picture of a woman in bed, surrounded by many people and with a winged person above the bed. Light seems to be coming from some of the people in the picture. I wonder if it was wise of Mr. Rembrandt to give Sir Peter a picture about death.

Sir Peter smiles at Mr. Rembrandt. "You're more concerned with the earth than with Heaven, my friend."

Mr. Rembrandt blushes and nods. "What I'm really concerned with is light and with myself, I'm afraid. I could not do Christ as you have done Him."

"You have not been to Rome, that is all. I watched you as we played with the Hercules canvas. There is great strength and no frivolity in you."

"Maybe there should be frivolity."

"There is no 'should.' There is only ability. You have that. You may waste it, as I often have done with mine. But at least once in a while our circumstances will permit us to do something memorable. It doesn't matter greatly."

"Does anything matter greatly?" Mr. Rembrandt asks.

"Only God."

Mr. Rembrandt looks calmly at Sir Peter and says, "Yes. Of course." Then he begins to look about the room. I do not think he is looking for God.

By the time people start to leave the party, Sir Peter is looking not only tired but ill. I wonder if he will live to see his new child. But whenever he dies, he will be a happy person, I think. I join him and Erasmus Quellyn as they stand before the strange Hercules painting. Sir Peter is grinning.

Erasmus says, "We will have much repairing to do."

"No, no," Sir Peter says. "I will keep this as it is. We can do another for the king's collection. This is my souvenir of this happy night." Sir Peter turns to me and says, "I must thank you for this night, Lenoir. You are the person who brought us all together here."

Erasmus excuses himself and walks toward Mlle. van Cott, who is sitting alone and seems to be almost asleep. Sir Peter seems to be looking at Katja. I wonder what he is thinking. I say, "Sir Peter, I think some of the people I have brought here may not be as good as the people you have brought here."

"Don't be sure. And if some of them have made mistakes — as I have — they can be forgiven."

"Is this to do with the penance that you were going to explain to me?"

"It is not complicated. Roman Catholics go in remorse to a

priest and confess their sins. The priest gives them a punishment and forgives the sins."

"Is there no bad act that cannot be forgiven?"

"No."

"But my bad acts cannot be forgiven?"

"You could become a Roman Catholic."

"What if your priests are wrong about all this?"

"The proper question is, what if they are *not* wrong? And the answer is, everlasting agony."

Twee arrives as Sir Peter finishes speaking. "Everlasting agony?" Twee says. "I guess the party's over."

"Not yet," Sir Peter says, "but soon."

Twee, who believes he will live forever, does not understand that Sir Peter is talking about more than the party.

We say good night to our friends in the studio and to the actors outside, and we arrange to return in the morning.

Although I think Twee would be safer on foot, he accepts Sir Peter's offer of a saddled horse to use for our short journey back to the cottage. I borrow little Baldassaro, who is gentle and whose back is close to the ground.

It is a starless night, and the horse and jackass — who seem friendly to each other — walk slowly. My head is confused, and my eyes keep closing. I realize that if Twee and I were walking, we would be doing much stumbling and might easily end up in a canal. Twee's chin is on his chest, and he has dropped the reins of his horse. I think he is asleep. It will be my job to stay awake and lead the animals to our cottage. I take the horse's reins, and it follows along quietly, although I can sense its great strength.

As we turn onto the road that leads to our cottage, I see an orange glow in the darkness. As we move closer to it, I have no doubt it is fire, and it is close to our cottage. I reach over and prod Twee. "Wake up," I say. "The cottage might be burning."

Twee takes a little time to understand where he is and what is happening. Eventually, he says, "Farmers are always burning things. They are elemental people. Earth, water, air, fire."

But after looking for another minute, he grabs the reins away from me, slaps his horse with them, and shouts, *"Avanti."* The horse raises both its front legs slightly, and begins to run. Baldassaro and I follow at a trot.

Soon I can see that there are two fires, one much bigger than the other. The bigger one is Rachel Normand's cottage; the smaller one is mine.

When I catch up to Twee, he is still on his horse, but he is holding the saddle with one hand and leaning off to the side and trying to pull a torch away from a man who is on foot. "Monster," Twee shouts. "Monster, my clothes are in there." Twee jumps off the horse. The man drops the torch and begins to struggle with Twee.

I slip off Baldassaro's back and run toward Twee. "Don't hurt him," I shout. "Remember the first Vlieg." The stranger turns toward me. He is young and looks stupid and frightened. He runs into the woods.

Twee runs toward my cottage. He takes a bucketful of water from the rain barrel and stands at the smoke-filled doorway, saying: "My clothes." He coughs violently and then stumbles into the cottage, where there already seem to be fewer flames than before.

I turn away and look at Rachel's cottage, where the fire also seems to be dying — but it is dying because there is little left to burn. Rachel is standing quietly outside the cottage and looking into the flames. The last of the building's dried-grass roof collapses in a beautiful spray of sparks.

I go to Rachel's side. "Are you hurt?" I ask. She shakes her head. I take her by the shoulders and turn her to face me, and we embrace. She whispers, "They called me a nigger's whore and a witch."

Twee reappears, shouting, "Help me." He is carrying clothes with one hand and the empty bucket with the other.

But I do not want to leave this unfortunate woman, whose

body has begun to shake. I am certain now that the fire in my cottage is not serious. I yell to Twee: "My serpent. Save my serpent from the smoke."

"Save your own serpent." Twee drops the clothes and refills the bucket.

But I must stay with Rachel, whose situation is much worse than mine. She is strong, and I think she will not be defeated by these terrible events, but I want to be sure.

And in a moment, she shows me that I am right. She suddenly pulls away from me and says, "We must help your friend save your house. Mine is beyond saving." She takes my hand and leads me quickly to the doorway of my cottage, where there is hardly any flame now, but still much smoke.

Twee staggers out of the cottage again. He is coughing harshly, and his reddened eyes keep closing. He hands me my serpent basket. I open it and watch the snake raise its head and move its coiled body. It is safe.

As Twee doubles over coughing, I take a deep breath and rush into the cottage. Avoiding the many glowing and smoldering embers, and working more by touch than by sight, I find the chest in which Twee keeps his documents and the one in which I keep my medicines. I take the chests out into the fresh air and drop them. I move toward the cottage again, but I find my arms being held by Rachel and Twee.

We stand and watch the thickening smoke billow out of the cottage door. Twee holds his newest cloak, I hold my serpent basket, and Rachel holds some beads from which dangle a little cross.

Twee begins to cough again, and he grasps my arm to steady himself. His face has a look of great surprise. His weight increases on my arm, and I realize that his legs can no longer support him. I lower him slowly to the ground, and he lies awkwardly and does not move. I put my hands under his arms and move him into a more comfortable position. He is remarkably heavy, and I think of the words "dead weight." Then I see that my hands are wet and glistening. Twee's yellow vest has turned dark red.

Rachel is watching carefully. "He's been stabbed," she cries. "I thought I saw a knife."

I say to my old friend, "I will cure you, Mr. Twee."

He says, quietly, "Mister again?" His words are not clear. I think there is liquid in his throat. He speaks again, even less distinctly: "No cure."

"He's dying," Rachel says.

"What can we do? We must do something." Then I remember the Roman absolution. I ask her, "Can you give him absolution?"

I lean closer to Mr. Twee and say, "Would you like to have absolution?"

He smiles slightly and says, faintly, "For what?"

He is taking shorter breaths now. He says something I cannot understand. He says it again: "So much."

I ask, "So much pain?"

"So much . . . to lose." He tries to take a deep breath. I wait. Eventually he says, "So good."

He takes another deep breath. His face shows pain for a moment, then he smiles. His left eye twitches as if he were trying to wink. Then his eyes are open wide and he is no longer breathing.

Our friendship is gone.

Rachel and I spend the night lying side by side on our backs, staring up into the darkness at the silhouettes of the trees' young leaves.

I say, "Mr. Twee was a brave man."

"A foolish man," Rachel replies. "There's not much difference."

The bitter smell of dead fire drifts over us. Through the branches I can see the clouds moving across the full moon. Occasionally the stars are revealed. I think I see the serpent in the stars.

At daylight, Rachel gives me a spade from her toolshed, and I dig a grave in the woods. I dress Mr. Twee in one of the new suits he had made for his trip to England. We carry the body to the grave. I touch my friend's forehead with the serpent ring Sir Peter gave me, and we slide Mr. Twee into the grave.

As I cover the body with earth, I wonder what Mr. Twee thought of me. I believe he was fond of me, but only as he would have been fond of a child who was left in his care. I was expected to be useful to him and to obey him. He taught me to speak. He gave me food, shelter, and some pleasures. I was a child, but I was not his child. I was something other.

Later in the morning I go to the city and make the announcement of Mr. Twee's death to those who knew him. In the afternoon, some of us gather at his graveside. It is most sad and most odd. A few people and many trees.

Columbine asks if she might read words from the Christian Bible. I say no. That was not Mr. Twee's book. After a time of silence, I say, "Serpent of death, in the dark earth, Dom Twee joins you, as we all must. He did you no harm. We ask you to bring none to his spirit." Then, for the others who stand with me, I sing the two words "Kyrie eleison." We stand in silence for a while longer.

When we walk away, I see Columbine put crossed sticks into the soil of the grave, but the sticks will fall over when the next heavy rain comes.

Sir Peter has not attended the burial, as he is not able to stand up this morning.

# 17

RACHEL NORMAND AND I spend the day cleaning out my cottage. I find pieces from the frame of Mr. Rembrandt's picture of Uba. The picture has gone, as she has. My drum has been damaged but can be repaired. All the words are still readable in the book of Don Quixote.

In the evening, I give my neighbor shelter. We sit in the dusk at a charred table. The windows and door are open to ease the stench of dead fire. Rachel, who is facing the doorway, says, "There is a man coming toward us."

I jump up and take hold of the clublike tree branch I have found in the woods. The man is moving toward us slowly and openly. He calls, "Hello."

"I know him," Rachel says. "He's a constable." She answers his call.

As the constable approaches, I hear the clinking sounds of chains. I hold my club more tightly.

"Mrs. Normand?" he asks. I can see his features now. I think he is a man who is trying to look friendly but has not had much practice at it. He talks to Rachel in the almost-Dutch language. She says my name to him. He nods to me. I hear the word for "trouble." Rachel and the constable stand facing each other and talk through the open doorway. I give up trying to follow the conversation, but I hear the name "Rubens." I wait for the man to move toward me or to walk away. After a short time, he walks away from the cottage.

Rachel smiles at me and says, "We are disturbing the well-being of the community. I think that, if you were not a friend of Sir Peter, you would be in jail."

"What of the man who burned our homes and killed Mr. Twee?"

"Apparently he is not disturbing the community."

I throw my stick into the corner in anger. "In what way is it that we are disturbing the community?"

"By being here."

I turn away. The sun is gone now, and the air seems cold enough to make ice. I think it is becoming plain to Rachel as well as to me that it would not be wise for us to be together. She says, "It will take a few days for me to make arrangements elsewhere."

"And where will you go then, Rachel?"

She smiles and says, "I've heard that there are caves in the South."

The next day, I find Sir Peter in his studio. He is sitting with Katja, who is wearing a thin dressing gown and probably nothing else. They are before a large canvas, Sir Peter seated and Katja standing. When Katja sees me, she embraces me. Sir Peter stands and asks, "You are not hurt, Lenoir?" I shake my head. He continues, "But you must be disturbed and angry . . . and you have lost a close friend."

"In my homeland, it is said that a departing friend has two destinations, the first being the memories of others."

Sir Peter nods. "I have sent a carpenter to repair the cottage." Then he holds his hand toward the canvas. On it is an uncolored picture of three naked women. "The three Graces," Sir Peter says.

"A Grace is like a Venus?"

"Yes. Three sisters who controlled beauty and charm."

Katja says, "And I am to be all three."

It is plain to me that the picture shows the moment at the party last night when Katja, Mrs. Rubens, and Mlle. van Cott were talking together.

Sir Peter points to the picture's middle Grace, whose back is shown. He says to Katja, "We'll do this one first." The Grace he is pointing to has her arms raised. Her left hand grasps the arm of one, and her right hand rests on the shoulder of the other. The two Graces on the left are looking at each other in a strange way. Katja studies the picture carefully. Then she takes off her gown and walks, naked, to a small platform and turns away from us. "Like this?" she asks. Sir Peter stands up, walks stiffly to her, and moves her body and arms slightly. Then he returns to the canvas, picks up his palette and brush, and begins to put color on the picture. He works quickly, without stopping, and like a magician, he makes the Graces appear.

As Sir Peter works, his wife comes to stand next to me, behind the master. She gestures to me not to speak to her. But Katja's expression changes and her arms begin to shake. I think she has seen Mrs. Rubens out of the side of her eye. Sir Peter turns to see what has distracted his model. "Ah," he says. "My dear." I think he is blushing slightly. He says to Katja, "You may rest now." She puts on her gown and comes to look at the picture. She says, "I was hoping you would be less honest, Sir Peter."

Hélène says, "Honesty is a failing of Paolo's." She tells me she is sorry to hear about the fire and then asks if Katja and I will excuse her while she talks to her husband about household matters for a minute. Katja and I go to a corner of the studio. She says, "I will stay here for a time, but the others have returned to Amsterdam. They asked me to say good-bye for them. I am to give you a big kiss."

"Not now."

"No. Not now."

Next, Katja poses for the Grace whose arm is being held. Sir Peter asks his wife to hold Katja's arm for a few minutes so that he can make the correct picture of the grasping hand and the gripped arm. There is great confusion in my mind as I look from the picture to the women who are posing for it — one woman clothed in reality but not in the picture. I wonder what Sir Peter thinks as he works. Does he see his wife as clothed? What is the meaning of the women's expressions in the picture? Why are the expressions different from the ones on the models? I am sure that something remarkable will be seen in the final picture.

Sir Peter continues to make the picture, stopping only when Katja and Hélène must rest. The daylight becomes brighter in the studio's windows, and Sir Peter seems more and more excited about the picture he is making. Hélène poses again with Katja for a short time, and then Katja poses alone. The master continues to work long after it seems to me that the three women in the picture are finished. I think he does not want to stop, but Katja's raised arms are trembling again, and he finally says, "Enough," and lowers himself heavily into a chair. Katja puts her robe on and joins us before the picture. She and Hélène look at each other and smile, but there are tears in Katja's eyes.

I remember that Dom Twee once told me that a woman can only really be understood by another woman. He would have liked this picture.

Yet the person who saw the understanding and love among the three women at the party and who preserved it in the picture was Sir Peter.

When I return home, there is a man sitting on a box where the path to the cottage begins. Even though the man looks friendly, I stop and look for a fallen tree branch to use in case I have to defend myself. He waves to me and says something I cannot understand in the near-Dutch language.

I walk toward him until we are at talking distance. In Dutch, I tell him I do not understand him.

He says, "Rubens." He gets up and opens the box he has been sitting on. It contains tools.

"Carpenter?" I ask.

He nods and points back to the cottage. He says a word like the Dutch word for "witch."

I point back to the city. "Go," I say.

He goes.

Rachel is waiting for me at the cottage door. She says, "He's heard that I'm a witch. He says he saw a black cat sitting on the path. He's afraid to work here. But never mind. I have tools. We can do our own work." Pointing to the ceiling, she says, "It is the weak beam there that we must worry about."

I don't know what she is talking about, but I say, "Just tell me what we need and what to do."

As we eat our soup, Rachel says, "I am not a witch."

I smile. "No. But *I* am."

Erasmus Quellyn fills in the painting of the three Graces. He puts in trees and bushes. In one of the trees is a long piece of cloth so delicate that it can be seen through. Some of the same cloth is covering parts of the Graces, but not the parts that are usually covered. I wonder what the hidden meanings of this picture are. I have many feelings as I look at it. The strongest feelings are naughty ones.

In the next days, Sir Peter does not leave his room. Erasmus is going about the house with sheets of paper, writing the names of the pictures that are on the walls.

I bring some medicinal powder for Sir Peter and take it to his bedroom. When I see him, I know I will not be able to lengthen his life but only ease his pain.

I have never seen him look happier.

He says, "I hear you have a witch in your house, Lenoir."

"Mrs. Normand is not a witch."

"No. But I think your life would be easier — and less dangerous — without Mrs. Normand."

"This woman has no house."

"You are a kind man, Lenoir."

"Perhaps. But she makes good soup and works hard."

Sir Peter smiles.

In the little woods behind the cottage, I find valuable plants growing. Rachel shows me how I can make more of them grow in the fields where she plants her many vegetables — which seem smaller and stranger than those the people grow to the north.

In the coming weeks, I begin taking my plants to the butchers' hall, where farmers bring their foods to sell. I stand in a shadowy corner of the market square. I sing the words "Medicines of the earth . . . leaves that cure your ills . . . roots that make you strong." But no one seems interested except the children who taunt me.

Each day there seem to be fewer people on the streets and more bodies on the plague carts.

When I go to the studio now, I find Erasmus Quellyn working unsmilingly on a picture for the Spanish king. I do not see Sir Peter at all. There are always doctors and lawyers in his house now.

One night, Rachel Normand surprises me by joining me under my blanket. Because I do not know what to say to her, I pretend not to awaken as she kneels above me and makes us both happy enough to gasp. The next morning, Rachel and her few belongings are gone. Nailed to the inside of the door is a piece of paper with a few words of writing on it. I put the paper away in a drawer. I do not want to know what these words are — words that could not be spoken.

Then, at the studio, Erasmus leads me to Sir Peter's bedroom. Outside the room are seated some of the lawyers and doctors. They do not seem pleased to see me.

When we enter the room, the master is sitting up in his big bed. At the far side of the bed stands the picture of the three

Graces. On the bed is a palette, some brushes, and two long sticks. As Erasmus and I watch, Sir Peter puts paint on a brush and attaches it to the end of one of the sticks. Using the second stick to steady the first, he touches the brush to the picture. Then I notice that on the shoulder of the middle Grace there rests a hand that was not in the picture the last time I saw it. I am not sure whose hand it is. It could be a ghost's hand. Sir Peter says, "We can see five hands now. The most interesting one is the unseen sixth."

I say, "A man in Calvin's church once said to me that what we do not see is more important than what we do see."

Sir Peter says, "I am sure that the man who said that was not a blind man." He looks back at the picture. "I may soon be a blind man myself. I want to borrow your eyes for a minute. Lenoir, is the color correct on the hand — is it like the color here?" He points to another hand.

"It is enough like it. The same color in a slight shadow. It is very good, I think."

"And Erasmus," the master says, "does the hand rest correctly? Does it have a certain tension?"

Erasmus nods.

We three men look at the three women, who look only at one another.

After a few moments, Sir Peter says, "So be it." Then, after another moment, he waves us away and sighs.

Erasmus and I carefully move the picture out of the room, and as we reach the doorway, I look back at Sir Peter. He glances at me and at the picture and smiles. I think it is a smile of farewell.

In the studio, we put the three Graces into a dark corner. In the center of the room, catching the morning light, is a picture of a woman holding a baby. Around her are many people who have the expression of children who have been caught doing something naughty and are pretending to be good. I do not recognize any of them.

"This will be in the master's chapel, above his tomb," Erasmus says.

I look back at the Graces. They will never be in anyone's chapel. Perhaps, someday, they will be in someone's bedroom.

The next day, as I stand near the butchers' hall, a priest of the pope crosses the square, followed by many of the people of the city. Someone nearby says, "Rubens is to receive the last rites."

And the day after that, I am awakened by a mysterious sound. Eventually, I realize it is the sound of many distant bells. All the bells of the city ring throughout the day without stopping.

In town, I find the gates to Sir Peter's house locked and draped with black cloth.

I look beyond the gates at the wall on which are carved the words that say one should not be ruled by desire. I think of the last words I heard Sir Peter speak:

*So be it.*

And so I begin to live as a stranger in a place of sickness and sadness. But it has become my place. A lawyer has come to tell me that it is Sir Peter's will that I live in the cottage as long as I choose to.

Erasmus Quellyn has finished the pictures for the king of Spain and no longer goes to the master's studio.

Hélène Rubens has had a new baby, and it is said that she has sold many of her husband's pictures. I wonder what has become of the three Graces and of the pictures the master made of me. It is odd to think that some part of my soul and Katja's soul are captured on a stranger's wall or have been destroyed.

Katja has decided not to return to Amsterdam. She has many important customers and acquaintances here now, and although I visit her, I no longer think that I am her special friend. She has received a letter with greetings to me from Mlle. van

Cott, who is now Mrs. Guelfe and whose father is sailing toward the Indies.

When I visit Katja, she reads to me from the book about Don Quixote, which makes us both think about Dom Twee. We are nearing the end of the book.

I am still occasionally asked to pose for pictures. Mr. Jordaens has put me into a picture of a saint called Martin.

The days have more light than darkness now. I often stand in the market square with my medicines. The children have stopped taunting me.

Jenny, the mule, carries me to and from the city, and in the night she brays if some creature approaches us. She comes to me so that I may rub her large, sensitive ears.

The people no longer seem deranged to me. They are small and weak, and there is much they do not understand, but they persist, as I do. I try to be patient and courageous, as they are. I remember that Sir Peter told me to obey my talent and not to try too hard to please. The serpent-god has told me that my talent is for healing. I try to believe that someday soon a weeping mother and father will come to see me with their sick child. They will say, "We think our child is dying, Mr. Lenoir. Our doctors cannot help us. Will you help us?"

Sometimes I visit the church of Our Lady, where despite the enormous size of the building, I feel less small than when I am standing at the edge of the square.

I look at the many candle flames and think of Mr. Twee.

I look at the picture of the dead man-god and think of Mr. Rubens, who made the picture.

I watch the colored light from the church's windows move across the many white stone pillars and remember the way the light once moved across the slender body of Sister Jeanne. I remember how she wanted to love the church and how she made love to me, like a serious child at play.

# EPILOGUE

I T IS A WARM NIGHT. Katja is wearing a loosely tied negligee. The lamp in her bedroom casts a soft, yellowish light that falls gently across her plump face and body and across the final pages of *The Ingenious Gentleman Don Quixote of La Mancha*. She reads more slowly than usual. I think that she, like I, does not want the story to end.

Katja tells me how Sancho Panza says to his dying friend, "Don't die, master, but take my advice and live for many years; for the most foolish thing a man can do in this life is to let himself die without rhyme or reason, killed not by human hands but simply by the hands of melancholy."

I say to Katja, "Then maybe it was not so bad after all that our friend Mr. Twee was killed by human hands."

"Well, there was never much chance that Dom was going to be killed by the hands of melancholy." She kisses me on the forehead. "But I can't say as much for *you* lately, my dear."

"There has been so much death."

"And you don't understand what Sancho and Twee and Rubens understood: Nothing is as ordinary as death. But if you try, you can make it extraordinary."

I say, "Our friend Sister Jeanne had an extraordinary death."

"As did the man-god she loved."

"And Jeanne also had an uncommon *life*, I believe."

"Like *your* life, Lenoir."

"And like yours, Katja. You are Sir Peter's three Graces." I touch her as I have not touched her since I left Amsterdam, and I say, "At the party, I thought you might be pregnant."

"No such luck. Not yet, my sweet."

She closes the book and opens her negligee.

When I leave her, I say not good night, but farewell.

In the morning, I am up early. I pack a few belongings, load them onto my mule's back, pull myself up into the saddle, and guide the beast out of the woods.

Katja's words echo in my mind. Ordinary death can be overcome by extraordinary life, and life can be made extraordinary in many ways: Jeanne's way, Twee's way, Sir Peter's way, Katja's way.

And now, perhaps, Lenoir's way.

The sun is warm, and I am singing:

> The path before me
> is a crooked line.
> But it may lead me to a safe end.
> The loss of my people
> once confused the route for me,
> but now I see more clearly.
> Wish me well with neither hatred nor jealousy.

# AUTHOR'S NOTE

ALTHOUGH LENOIR is an imagined character, I have tried to put him in a real setting. The following sources were of particular help:

*The Embarrassment of Riches: An Interpretation of Dutch Culture in the Golden Age* by Simon Schama (New York: Alfred A. Knopf, 1987); *The Netherlands of the Seventeenth Century* by Pieter Geyl (New York: Barnes and Noble, 1961); *Rubens and His Circle* by Julius S. Held (Princeton, NJ: Princeton University Press, 1982); *Rembrandt and His World* by Christopher White (New York: Viking/Studio, 1964); *The Italian Comedy* by Pierre-Louis Duchartre (New York: Dover, 1966); *Stand the Storm: A History of the Atlantic Slave Trade* by Edward Reynolds (London: Allison & Busby, 1985); *Sins of the Fathers* by James Pope-Hennessy (London: Weidenfeld & Nicolson, 1967); and "The Music of West Africa: Togo" (Rounder CD 5004, 1992).